Hail to the Chief

Archer Swift

Hail to the Chief
First American Edition

Published in 2020 by Archer Swift
Copyright © Archer Swift 2020
All Rights Reserved

ISBN-13: 987-1-7337695-0-1
ISBN- 13: 987-1-7337695-1-8
Library of Congress Control Number: 2019907349

Publisher's Note

Hail to the Chief

Archer Swift

Other Titles by Archer Swift

Bigpox (2004)
The Joy of Frustratia (2013)
Tiny Tom's Talks with Dear Old God (2017)

Acknowledgments

The inspiration behind this story lies in the compelling and tragic tale of looting and theft by Hungarian Nazis of personal property owned by Budapest's Jewish community in 1944.

The Gold Train by Ronald W. Zweig (2002) details how the stolen valuables of five hundred thousand Jews dispatched to concentration camps were packed into more than fifty railcars for onward transmission to the German or Swiss Alps.

The train itself was eventually found hidden in a train tunnel in Austria. But to this day, the whereabouts of most of its contents remain a mystery. Few of the residual valuables were ever returned to their original owners.

The story that follows attempts to unravel this mystery. It does so in a current context where political instability around the world may possibly give rise to old and new forces of extremism and nationalism.

As always, I thank my wife for her consummate patience and for giving me the time, space and feedback needed to reach completion with a better end product. Support from Bookhelpline.com was most helpful for editorial content. Two other parties, a lawyer and an avid reader, provided valuable insights but chose (wisely perhaps) to remain anonymous.

The Mohammedan religion would have been much more compatible to us than Christianity. Why did it have to be Christianity with its meekness and flabbiness?

Adolf Hitler

There is no doubt this is the most horrible crime ever committed in the whole history of the world, and it has been done by scientific machinery by nominally civilized men in the name of a great State and one of the leading races of Europe. It is quite clear that all concerned in this crime who may fall into our hands, including the people who only obeyed orders by carrying out the butcheries, should be put to death after their association with the murders has been proved.

Winston Churchill, upon reading the first detailed account of the Auschwitz concentration camp in July 1944

Hail to the Chief we have chosen for the nation,
Hail to the Chief! We salute him, one and all.
Hail to the Chief, as we pledge cooperation
In proud fulfillment of a great, noble call.

Yours is the aim to make this grand country grander,
This you will do, that is our strong, firm belief.
Hail to the one we selected as commander,
Hail to the President! Hail to the Chief!

Lyrics by Albert Gamse (1901–1974)

Islanders

Y ou might say it all began with Jillian and Frederick Tinker. Had it not been for their marriage, their son Adam may not have been here in the first place, and so this tale might never have been told.

Jill and Fred were happily semiretired and entering their umpteenth year as summer residents of Montego Island. This was a crescent-shaped paradise set many miles off the United States mainland. In fact, this island was so far away from the mainland that any number of foreign countries might lay claim to it…and, in a manner of speaking, they already had.

Endowed with a year-round population of some ten thousand to seventeen thousand souls, depending on whom you asked, the island also served as a summer refuge for driven, overworked, tired, and largely retired captains of industry and commerce and their extended families. Their presence helped to swell the summer population to a peak of some sixty thousand souls.

To support them, contingents of young people from places as far away as Ireland, Bulgaria, Romania, Russia, and several Latin American countries provided the infrastructure, as restaurant servers, housekeepers, retail store staff, and so much more—to the point that anyone's competence in speaking any Eastern European language, or simple Spanish, was a helpful asset for any resident or visitor.

Which brings us to young Adam Tinker, all of twenty-two and freshly graduated from Columbia with a degree in International Relations. The island provided his first real, direct taste of 'foreigners', who could invariably be found staffing the many bars and restaurants.

Adam had a younger sister, improbably named Eve, whose parents evidently felt that her forename was the natural companion to that of their only son.

Adam's father, Fred Tinker, was God personified. A tyrant by any other name, Fred had failed dismally to forge a close and healthy bond between father and daughter. He had little time for babies and small children as a species, and even less time for small females. However, he rested his hopes on young Adam, the son who would surely follow faithfully in his father's footsteps and, as and when his father fully retired, would take the helm of the Tinker Hedge Funds.

Fred's greatest social gift for which he was renowned was as raconteur of amusing stories at social gatherings. The Tinkers were always in demand at summer dinner parties, whether in New York City or here on the island. But when at home, or at work, Fred ruled like an autocrat.

Jill, his wife of twenty-four-years, hid quietly in the shadow of his persona, rarely uttering a word. As if to compensate, she always dressed immaculately and, of course, most

2

tastefully.

Her mane of blond hair contrasted sharply with Fred's balding pate, which, as the years progressed, became ever shinier as all but a residue of graying hair above his ears remained. His build, like hers, was short and squat. Both clung religiously to a healthy diet of raw vegetables, gluten free and just a little dairy, interspersed with occasional fatty delights. And, as if a mostly healthy diet were not enough, a little Botox here and there would help the married couple maintain their public aura of endless youth and vigor.

Like many other lonesome wives or widows on the island, Jill was a self-taught painter—not of house interiors, of course, because that just wouldn't do, but of assorted canvases, sometimes landscapes, sometimes portraits, and even the occasional odd (very odd) abstract. Nothing soothed her soul more than getting oil paint all over her delicate white hands. As time went on, she discovered that paint brushes were quite useless; and that painting with one's fingers and with the heels of one's hands was *sooo* much more satisfying.

But we digress and now return to her spouse, Fred, to share how he came to be the man he was, and his influence on his son, Adam, the male hero of our story.

Fred was his anglicized his name, for he had been born in Germany as Friedrich, that is, Friedrich Basteln. He had started from nothing, the son of a refugee from Nazi Germany. His father had miraculously escaped with his son from the city of Leipzig in the summer of 1943, just months before Allied bombers firebombed that city for the first time.

Fred's father, a widower named Heinz Basteln, was a prominent violinist in the Gewandhaus Orchestra of Leipzig. Heinz had declined to join the Nazi Party. As a result, it soon became clear that his future in the Orchestra was tenuous, at best. Just as well, for in February 1944, the Allies followed up their December attack of 1943 with a devastating bombing. It destroyed not only the Gewandhaus concert hall but also most of the nearby Erla Maschinenwerk aircraft factory which produced the Messerschmidt Bf 109 fighter planes for the Third Reich's war effort.

Fortunately, Heinz had somehow secured a temporary pass in the late summer of 1943 to take his son with him to Switzerland where he had been invited to perform as a soloist, in Basel.

At the time, relations between father and son were tense. Fred, barely ten years old at the time, had expressed a strong interest in joining the Hitler Youth, after hearing a speech at a Hitler rally where the führer had declared in a fiery speech that, among other things, "The weak must be chiseled away. I want young men and women who can suffer pain. A young German must be as swift as a greyhound, as tough as leather, and as hard as Krupp's steel." Fred, like many other youngsters, took this to heart as a personal summons to duty.

Father and son argued frequently and violently about whether Hitler was truly good or bad for Germany. He had turned on his father to the point that, when they had left on the eight-hour drive to Basel, Heinz felt obliged to pretend they would return to Leipzig in a just a day or two. He knew

4

all too well that if he revealed his plans to escape from Germany while still in Leipzig, Fred might possibly denounce him to the authorities. That was not an option.

Fred never forgave his father until years later for fleeing from the Third Reich. He despised him for his profession as a "mere musician" and did all he could to rile him up. Heinz nonetheless became not only a successful American immigrant but also went on to become a distinguished member of a world-renowned East Coast orchestra. His musical prowess over time even earned him the nickname "Heinz 57" to reflect the wide scope of his musical repertoire.

There also came a point when it occurred to Heinz that his family name of Basteln, the German word for "tinker," might hinder their integration into the dominant white Anglo-Saxon world of postwar America. He therefore decided to anglicize it. Thus, the Bastelns became the Tinkers.

Heated arguments between father and son only began to cool when Fred met his future wife, Jill, at a party in New York, many years later. She proved to be a quieting influence on his extreme personality. Over time, he mellowed enough to become Fred, the great storyteller and, of course, the enormously successful Wall Street tycoon.

After three months of dating and a long engagement, Fred had finally proposed to Jill, knowing that somewhere deep down in his soul, something was not quite right and that he needed a loving woman's care. Jill had intuitively soothed his troubled heart to the point that he became infatuated and then obsessed with her. She became for him a kind of mother figure he never had. Jill saw in him a deep, terrible pain and anger, enough for her to decide that he would be her life's work. Their extremes of personality collided and, as opposites, somehow fused them together.

The result was that within two years of their marriage, Jill bore their first child.

At first, father and mother had struggled over a suitable given name for their first born. Fred insisted that it must begin with the letter A so that the boy's name would always top any list of forenames. As she demurred, he made her decision for her. "The first man was Adam, so let it be him."

She meekly agreed.

A Bit about Adam

Adam could not escape the polarizing influence of his authoritarian father and his tolerant but always fussing and artistically inclined mother. Torn between both personas, he landed somewhere in the middle. Though he himself held strong opinions, he managed to appear open to the opinions of others, even if he disagreed with them. This attribute made him popular enough at college that he ran for student president and only narrowly lost the election.

He was not someone who stood out in a crowd. In fact, his natural ability to blend in to almost any gathering of human beings gave him a kind of chameleon quality. He was neither anyone's closest friend, nor was he their foe. His apparent air of neutrality made him no threat to others and so enabled him to become a gregarious and even a popular fellow.

Perhaps his shock of curly, brown hair was his hallmark, even more so than his deep-brown eyes and pale skin. His build was average but manly enough to attract the attention of college girls. He was taller than both parents at five feet ten. At school, he excelled neither at academics nor at sports, for better or worse.

While still a college student, Adam had found himself increasingly engaged by the teachings of certain professors of history whose backgrounds hailed from faraway places. These included a visiting professor, Tibor Lantos. His specialty was tracing the history of Jewish persecution in 20th-century Hungary, his mother country. Another was a visiting lecturer, Yussef Bitar. He was allegedly an Egyptian and a "past member" of the Muslim Brotherhood. His focus was on the history and future of the Middle East.

Adam, though no A student, showed interest and curiosity in other parts of the world. He struck up a notably close rapport with Professor Lantos, whose current focus was on helping surviving members of Hungarian Jewish families to recover the artwork, jewelry, gold, and other valuables stolen from their families. The thieves were members of the pro-Nazi Hungarian regime that had purged Budapest of its Jewish community in the 1940s.

Lantos was Adam's favorite lecturer: he captured Adam's attention by pointing out that, by the year 2018—more than seventy years after the end of World War II—little restitution had been made to those whose property had been brutally pilfered and whose lives were so cruelly and prematurely cut short.

Having recently graduated, Adam was anxiously awaiting news of a job offer from several possible employers. There had been interviews with a large bank, a lesser-known management consultancy, and an oil company. All seemed to like his resume. However, the delay in hearing from any one of them was starting to gnaw at his confidence—even though his father had put in a good word for him at all three prospective employers.

"Boy!" Fred had said, "Before you even think of working for me or even dream about taking over the family business, one of these days…I want to see you earn an honest living based on your own wits!"

Fearing that no offer might be forthcoming, Adam sought counsel from Professor Lantos. "Don't worry! Something will come along before you know it!" Lantos had reassured the young man. "But, worst case, I may have something part-time for you that I'm working on now. Let me know in a week or two how things are going."

A month had already passed since Adam had attended his graduation ceremony. He bravely assured his college classmates that he was looking at various job offers when, in fact, none were forthcoming. His father offered no further help.

"Go get a job in sales somewhere! That's where I started. Look what it did for me!" he snorted, adding to Adam's sense of dejection.

Another month passed. Adam decided to call the campus, only to learn that Professor Lantos had already left for Hungary. He emailed Lantos asking for details of the part-time job the professor had mentioned.

Two more weeks passed. Adam now felt even more desperate.

He then opened his email one morning to find a short note from Lantos and a link to several websites. He felt a flicker of renewed energy at last, and eagerly began to wade through the material.

The first piece from Lantos to catch his eye was dated 2018. It had a byline of A. Lantos, perhaps a relative of the professor. It was an updated analysis of a book called *The Gold Train*, first published in 2002. The story centered on a freight train that had left Nazi-occupied Budapest in 1944, on the eve of the Soviet army's occupation. It was packed with valuables that had been plundered ruthlessly from the Jewish community of the city by the Nazis and their Hungarian supporters. The occupying Germans had ordered the haul to be shipped to a secret destination, somewhere in either the German Alps or in Switzerland.

But the train never arrived.

The Allies eventually captured it. However, by then, much of its contents had already vanished without a trace. According to a current valuation, the residual contents had a value of almost two billion dollars.

The Hungarian commander of the so-called Gold Train was a key person behind the Hungarian Holocaust named Arpad Toldi. He was a virulently anti-Semitic Hungarian Nazi sympathizer serving as Hungary's Commissioner for Jewish Affairs. He bore personal responsibility for the deportation and murder of four hundred thousand Hungarian Jews. Though briefly arrested by the Allies at the end of the war, he served just a few months in jail and then disappeared for good.

A second web link lead from Lantos was to a recent edition of *Inspire*, an English-language online jihadist magazine reportedly published by the Yemeni arm of Al Qaeda and known as Al Qaeda in the Arabian Peninsula, or AQAP. As Adam ran his eyes over the text, he noticed that someone had highlighted a certain text inside with a yellow marker. The words read:

> *By God's will, we may have found at last the treasures of the Hungarian Jew that the American infidels stole from the Germans. These treasures will be the key to supporting our jihad against Western culture and its immoral ways for years to come.*

The yellow highlighted byline of the article bore a single name: *Wazir.*

What could this mean? The references to the "treasures" meant nothing to Adam.

He replied, "Professor Lantos, it looks like there is no full-time job for me here at home right now. If I understand correctly, the material you sent me has something to do with that part-time position you mentioned some weeks ago?"

He hit the send button.

To his surprise, a response came back in minutes. "Yes. Can you meet me in Budapest next Monday? I'll tell you more then."

Adam was startled at this offer and breathed a big sigh of relief.

When he told his father that he had an interview for a part-time job in Hungary, Fred bellowed, "*Hungary*? Why *on earth* Hungary? And just for *part-time* work?"

But Adam persisted, knowing that some job was better than none and that he had at least shown his demanding father a small sign that he could stand on his own two feet.

Fred's retort was tart and to the point. "I'll give you one thousand dollars for your air travel to get you there, boy, and a few days' room and board. I expect you to repay me within one year! Now, get out of here!"

Surprised at his father's atypical but predictably brusque form of generosity, tempered, of course, by his mother's cries of protest at her son's "crazy" idea, Adam promptly went online with credit card in hand. He bought a one-way economy ticket from Montego Island to New York and an economy seat for a flight from New York's JFK to Budapest's Ferenc Liszt airport.

The nonstop flight to Budapest took eight and a half hours. Adam drank water like a fish to counter the dehydration. He had swallowed a single capsule of melatonin before boarding the first flight to help him sleep.

Even so, when he emerged at his destination, he was thoroughly bleary-eyed and tired. He barely noticed the modernized airport building and the beckoning Burger King and KFC outlets that might otherwise have warmly embraced a visiting young American.

Someone outside Customs was waving an arm at him. It was Lantos, a tall, lean man with a full head of graying hair and a slight stoop. He wore his trademark thick lens reading glasses perched precariously, as always, on the bridge of his aquiline nose.

After the usual preliminary niceties about the various flights and delays, Lantos shoved Adam's suitcase into the trunk of his black Opel. "We don't have a lot of time," he said. "I'll drop you off at your hotel so you can get a good night's rest. Then we can meet tomorrow, when you are refreshed."

Adam had chosen the Hilton Budapest City. It offered a special deal on the internet and was located close to the BarCraft Nyugati where he and Lantos would meet for a drink at noon the next day.

Lantos knew this bar would be busy at that hour and that no one would be able to overhear them talking. He wasted little time to bring Adam up to speed.

"Adam, there's something I need to tell you—but you must keep it to yourself, OK?" he began almost as soon as they met at the bar. Adam noticed how Lantos looked around and quickly scanned the crowd before saying more. "You already know that I'm a visiting professor on the history faculty at Columbia. But what you didn't know until now is that I'm also a member of a certain government agency—a Hungarian agency, that is."

"No, of course I wouldn't know." Adam's eyebrows rose. "So then, what's this all about?"

Lantos sighed, gazing into his beer and searching for words. The place was filling up, and the noise level was rising. Lantos looked up quickly and darted a glance from left to right to make sure that Adam was still his only audience.

"You see, I have a mission. I'm part of a team from the Hungarian Information Office that's trying to locate stolen property."

Adam frowned in puzzlement. "What's the Hungarian Information Office?"

Another quick glance to left and right before Lantos spoke. "Well," said the professor, "it's a civilian intelligence agency that conducts nonmilitary intelligence, mainly outside the country."

Adam nodded. Realizing that his questions might be just as sensitive as Lantos's answers, he too began look to his left and right before speaking.

"And the stolen property you've mentioned, Professor? Does it have something to do with that book about the gold-train link in your email?"

Lantos nodded. "Oh yes, it does. In fact, my niece Agnes has been helping me with some research."

"Aha! So, is she the one who wrote about hidden Nazi gold? She's your niece?"

Lantos smiled. "Yes, and very bright too. I think she may be getting close to finding where a large amount of stolen Nazi loot is hidden."

The professor glanced around once again and then suddenly froze. "We have to get out of here! There are some people arriving now who you and I don't need to meet."

Adam turned his head to survey the crowd, but he saw nothing unusual.

"Hurry! Go to the restroom in the back. There's a street exit there. I'll meet you at my car in the alley."

Adam suddenly felt his adrenaline and heart rate rise. This wasn't the kind of job he had been expecting. He headed hurriedly to the rear exit door and flung it open. Three minutes later, Lantos's car screeched into the alley.

"Get in, fast!"

Adam dove into the passenger seat, gasping at the sudden change of pace. "Where are we heading, Professor?"

Lantos hesitated for moment and checked his rearview mirror and the alley ahead before pulling away into the roadway.

"We are going to Szentendre. To you, that's St. Andrew. We say 'Sant Andre,' with a soft *a*. I have a house there."

"Where's that?" asked Adam, clearly puzzled.

"It's about a half an hour's drive north-northeast of the city. You'll like it. It's on the Danube. Lots of cobblestone streets and history. Many artisans."

"But why are we going there?" Adam was baffled. "And who was it you were trying to avoid?"

Lantos's face looked tense. "It's a long story. Let's get something to eat. Did you ever try *langos*?"

"Is that, like, *Lantos*?" Adam was hopelessly in the dark. He realized too late that his remark was well off the mark.

Lantos chuckled. "No, I said *langos*! It's fried dough, smothered in toppings like garlic sauce and cream cheese. Not so healthy maybe, but like most things you eat that will eventually kill you, they taste pretty good. It's a kind of Hungarian comfort food."

Tipping Pointers

Jill adjusted her golden, shoulder-length hairpiece one last time before the mirror. Then she came down to breakfast. She did not yet know it, but her tranquil life on the island and Adam's in Hungary at this moment could not have been heading further apart.

Fred had made scrambled egg whites and turkey bacon. He sat waiting for her in his study, eyes buried in yesterday's newspapers. Jill's light footsteps on the stairs told him it was time for him to provide breakfast service. As he plated their two dishes, he began to regale her with a litany of complaints as she entered the breakfast room next to the kitchen.

"Had a miserable time at the island's supermarket this morning. Traffic was terrible, people were pushing and shoving and milling about, only one half of the Sunday paper had arrived, and they were out of yogurt! Terrible! This island is not what it was!"

Jill rolled her eyes. "Now, dear, don't dwell on the unpleasant to start your day. Look out there! It's another beautiful sunny day for us both to enjoy. Let's enjoy our breakfast."

Fred growled, burped loudly, and shuffled off to the kitchen to fetch freshly brewed coffee, his slippers whooshing along the carefully painted white pine floors. Outside, he noticed three crows flying by, each conversing with the other in a series of caws, cackles, and clicks.

"I wonder what they're saying to each other?" he mused. "Maybe that the bull market will turn into a bear market before too long?" Such was the extent of his appreciation of nature.

He entered the kitchen and continued to vent, but there was nothing Jill could say to change his grumpy frame of mind. "The crowds get bigger by the day, thanks to that discount airline bringing in half of New York City! Thank God we can escape here to our little oasis! We pay all these hefty local taxes, and they still can't figure out how to handle all the tourists!"

Being a summer resident, of course, Fred wasn't a tourist but a mortal of much higher pedigree; and almost as thoroughbred an islander as one of the genuine year-round locals.

He continued to vent. "And on top of it, you can't pass those wretched, slow-moving motor scooters that the tourists use, thanks to all the double yellow lines!"

Jill broke into his negative monologue with a cry of excitement. "Oh! Look! We have an email from Adam! He's with one of his professors on the Danube, some island with a name I can't even pronounce!"

"Danube…er, yes, was that the…Danube Equity Investment

Fund?" said Fred absent-mindedly, half-listening to Jill as he returned to rereading yesterday's opening stock prices. He failed to notice the bottom of his broadsheet newspaper sinking silently into a mound of scrambled egg whites.

Neither Fred nor Jill had any inkling of what lay ahead.

Agnes and the Ecstasy

Years later, Adam would remember Szentendre, Hungary's well-known artisan community along the Danube, with its brightly colored houses, contrasting colored window frames and painted sills, all huddled together on cramped cobblestone streets.

He would recollect his brief visit to the Szentendre marzipan museum where there were all kinds of models, buildings, and busts of people—kings, queens, princesses, pop singers, cartoon characters and teddy bears—all created out of marzipan.

How could he forget Lantos's rattling old Opel as it bumped rapidly along the cobbled pavement and swung suddenly into a long and shaded alley of Hungarian ash trees? They had pulled up to the door of a small house with bright-yellow walls and beige outer window frames.

He would always remember how a curtain moved on a second-floor window of the house; and how a beautiful young woman's face appeared for a fleeting moment before vanishing.

Barely a minute later, the front door opened. The tall

4

silhouette of a breathless, willowy girl emerged from inside and was bathed in the bright light of a huge black door lantern. She was a stunning brunette. Her shoulder-length, silky hair flowed like a shiny brown river over her shoulders. It perfectly framed her oval face. Her slightly olive complexion shone under the lamplight.

She bore a small but distinctive birthmark, a beauty spot perhaps, on her right cheek. Striking dark irises defined her greenish-brown, almond-shaped eyes. Graceful and slender at about five feet eight, she held herself erect like a ballet dancer. Adam saw at once in her an elegant glamour. As their eyes met for the first time, he felt a sudden surge of excitement rush into his body.

"Uncle Tibor! You're back!" To Adam's surprise, she spoke in good English, and Adam guessed she already knew from Lantos that he was coming. She looked warily at Adam. "Hello," she said, "I'm Agnes." It sounded to Adam like a short A-vowel with a long *shush* sound at the end of it. "*Aaghne*shhh…" Her voice instantly bewitched him.

Agnes was all of twenty-one. She would later tell him she had just graduated near the top of her class with a degree in business from Corvinus University in Budapest. Her uncle knew her as smart, interested in history, and so an ideal candidate to help him with his research.

Her parents had raised her in the town of Asottalom in the southern plains of Hungary, some two hours' drive from Budapest. But lately, leadership of the town had publicly asserted its dislike for a multicultural society and had put up signs banning Muslim clothing and mosques. The current mayor had gone on the record saying things like, "We can see large Muslim communities in Western Europe that haven't been able to integrate—and we don't want to have the same experience here. I'd like Europe to belong to Europeans, Asia to belong to Asians and Africa to belong to Africans. Simple as that."

Agnes however disagreed strongly. To her parents' dismay, she had moved away permanently to Budapest, believing that she could learn from others, including Muslims, and from within a much more cosmopolitan and worldly community. She simply refused to accept a generalization that all peoples of other cultures would refuse to integrate.

Almost as soon as all three sat down, she began to talk with some agitation. The expression on her face showed that something else was on her mind. She decided to speak in fluent English, if only for Adam's benefit.

"Uncle Tibor, there's something odd going on. As you know, we get lots of tourists here in Szentendre. After all, it's well-known as an artisan's village. But I keep seeing one particular couple everywhere I go."

Lantos frowned and then smiled at his niece. "What's so special about that?" he asked.

"Well, they stand out. The man looks like he may be an Arab. There's not many of them around here. He has a bushy black beard. He wears a gray suit and a white shirt, open at the neck, and no tie. The woman with him, presumably his wife, always wears a headscarf, a *hijab*, that covers all but her face. Even though I've never had direct eye contact or a conversation with either of them, they keep turning up these

6

last few weeks everywhere I go."

Lantos continued to smile, as if challenging her to explain herself.

She pressed on, regardless. "For instance, I drove over to Visegrad the other day to see a friend. It's about a thirty-minute drive or twenty-three kilometers from here—oh, excuse me, Adam, that's fourteen miles or so. And sure enough, there the two of them were taking photos and looking like tourists. But something about them was odd, because I kept seeing them."

Lantos at last interjected. "Agnes, my dear, this may surprise you, but I think these people are in fact looking *out* for you, not watching you."

The look of disbelief and surprise that crossed her face made her even more attractive to Adam.

"Why don't the two of you get to know each other while I make some phone calls in my office," said Lantos.

It was an offer that Adam could not refuse.

A Short History Lesson

Jill was a woman of considerable ability and many skills, but basic history was just not her forte. She and Fred were glancing through Sunday's *New York Times*, while trying to ignore the unrelenting gray fog that had descended without warning on the island early that morning.

Her eye caught a series of atrocities on the front page. There had been one in Afghanistan, another in Saudi Arabia, and a third in London.

"Fred," she exclaimed, "I just don't understand this thing about Muslims and terrorism. It seems to go on forever. Look at all these dreadful stories—honor killings of sisters by their own brothers, fathers, and uncles; people being hanged, beheaded, stabbed in broad daylight or run down by madmen driving cars like maniacs onto the sidewalks."

Fred, consumed as always with the financial news, remained silent as she turned a few pages and pretended to peruse the Style section. After a few moments, she put down the paper and tried again to get Fred's attention.

"Well, honey, when you read today's paper and all the awful things people are doing to one another all around the world, it makes even a gray day here on the island bearable. Anyway, why is this thing about Muslims and violence always in the news?"

Fred gave a sigh of resignation. He knew that Jill's distraction away from what he really wanted to read about demanded an answer, and that she would persevere until she got one. He decided to make the best of it and show off to impress his wife.

"Jill, honey, let me share a bit of history with you to help explain what's going on today. You do remember, don't you, the Ottoman Empire?" He paused, suspecting, with good reason, that she did not.

He then decided to forge ahead. "Well, anyway, the residue of that empire, or what we call Turkey today, first emerged in the thirteen hundreds. Under Islamic leadership, it succeeded in conquering a huge area including North Africa, Western Asia, much of Southern Europe, including the Balkans, and all the way up to the gates of Vienna. But as I recall, by the late 19th century, Ottoman rule had weakened through corruption and inefficiency."

He paused once again, then drew a deep breath. Jill still appeared to be listening. He just couldn't resist the opportunity to give a lecture. "At that time, the British were still fighting off the prospect of a possible Russian invasion of India—the jewel in the British Crown. The Brits had colonized and exploited India commercially for its raw materials and cheap, plentiful labor. The British navy claimed to rule the waves and command the seas. But then, in the early 20th century, the Germans came along and persuaded the Ottomans to let them build a railroad between Berlin and Baghdad. You know where Baghdad is, right, honey?"

"It's in...Lebanon, isn't it?" said Jill, whose wavering tone gave away her uncertainty.

Fred pursed his lips. "Well, in fact, it's in *Iraq*. Now, this was a big deal, a game changer because the Germans could now move their troops and munitions at greater speed on land than by sea. Relations grew deeper between Germany and the Ottomans. Relations also became more competitive between Britain and Germany. The Brits saw the German railway project as a strategic threat to the British navy's control of access to India by sea, because the Germans' armies could now potentially travel faster by land toward India than could British ships."

Jill nodded, gazed lovingly at her spouse, and seemed absorbed by Fred's command of history.

His voice rose as he moved toward his dramatic climax. "The competition grew fiercer as the British, Germans, Russians, and French all jostled for world colonial power. The British, the French, the Dutch, and the Germans each set up colonies in Africa. Many of them also tried to extend their influence into what we call today the Middle East. By the early 20th century, the British were much more concerned about the rising militarism of Germany than about Russia. In fact, by 1907 the Brits had joined with the Russians and the French in a military alliance called the Triple Entente."

It was overload for Jill who was starting to gasp. "This is so much to absorb!"

But Fred pressed on. "Anyway, in 1914, the Archduke Ferdinand of Austria-Hungary and his wife, Sophie, were assassinated by a Serbian sympathizer in the Balkan town of Sarajevo, which was then governed by Austria-Hungary. This event gave Austria-Hungary a pretext to declare war on Serbia. Germany became Austria-Hungary's ally in a war against Serbia, which not only wanted control of Sarajevo but then, as now, was pro-Russian. That war launched World War I.

"Yes, but why?" asked Jill.

"You ask why?" replied Fred. "Because Germany then declared war on Russia, which backed Serbia. This had a domino effect: France declared war on Germany because of the Triple Entente Treaty, the Germans invaded Belgium to get easier access to France, and the British, as fellow members of the Triple Entente, declared war on Germany. All in all, a very bad deal for everyone. Some seventeen million people—military and civilian—were killed in World War I and twice as many were injured until a peace was signed in 1918."

"What a waste of human life!" sighed Jill.

Fred nodded in agreement. "Shall I go on, dear?" he asked.

She said, "Why not? I'd like to hear more. What a story!"

Fred reached back into his memory for moment and then said, "You asked why there are Muslim terrorists today. Well, I think that the roots of Muslim terrorism today may lie in an alliance which the Germans formed with the Turks in 1914. That alliance was meant partly to prop up the Turks' military and partly to give Germany a springboard into British areas of influence like Mesopotamia, Palestine, and eventually India."

Jill broke in. "Fred, dear, what is or what was this 'Me-so-pot-a-mi-a' exactly?"

"It was an area along the Tigris and Euphrates rivers that today covers parts of Iraq, Kuwait, Syria, Iran, and northern Saudi Arabia."

"I see," said Jill, though Fred wasn't sure that she did. But there was no stopping him now.

"And as for Palestine, the Brits issued a declaration in 1917, the Balfour Declaration, that favored the creation of a Jewish homeland in that area—lands that today we call Israel and Jordan."

Jill broke in once again. "But what about America?"

"Well, the US meanwhile was shipping supplies to the Allies to support them against the Germans. When German submarines started destroying American support ships, the US declared war on Germany, in 1917."

Fred fell silent for moment. He looked up, and his eyes turned toward the window and into the distance as he searched his memory before continuing.

"When the Allies forced a German surrender in 1918, part of the spoils of war was the Ottoman Empire. Back in 1916, British and French diplomats had drawn up a plan called the Sykes-Picot Treaty. This treaty was all about how to divide up that empire between them if the Allies won the war. And so, based on that treaty, a crop of so-called 'nation-states' was created in the early 1920s by the Allies. We call these countries today Syria, Iraq, Jordan, and Lebanon. The French wanted what we now call Syria and Lebanon. The British asserted a 'mandate' in Palestine—thinking at the time that Arabs and Jews would get along just fine, under British 'guidance.'"

Fred stopped to sip some coffee, to let this hefty dose of history sink into Jill's mind. But he was still not done. "But for all their differences and national interests, the victors of World War I had two things in common. They collectively imposed their own Western notion of 'nationhood' on Middle Eastern peoples, that is, on folks who were by nature tribal and whose first loyalty was, and probably still is, to their clan and their family."

"That's interesting," said Jill.

"Yes," said Fred. "The victors also installed what they hoped would be strong men as rulers of the new nations. The remains of this 'strongman leadership structure' prevail even today across the Middle East. It runs completely counter to centuries of tribal and family tradition that makes 'nationhood' in the Middle East about as good as oil is to water. Once the leadership, the so-called caliphate, of the Ottoman Empire disappeared as the keystone that had linked the disparate families and tribes together, Islam lost its leader."

Jill piped up again. "So then, the Muslims have no pope or top leader?"

"Right," said Fred, plopping a mouthful of scrambled egg

white into his mouth. "Now, fast-forward to today. The world of Islam is where religion and politics, church and state if you like, are one and the same. Until the Reformation in the West, church and state were also one and the same. But Islam never experienced a Reformation where the secular leadership broke away from the religious center."

Fred was now on an unstoppable roll. His voice rose for dramatic effect. "Where Western law was an entirely man-made idea to govern Western nations' behaviors and customs, Islamic law remained what it had always been since the time of Islam's founder in the 8th century—an immutable law given by God to Mohammed. It has endured that way for centuries. In the 17th century, the most traditional form of Islam, Wahhabism, joined forces to govern with the warlords in what has since become Saudi Arabia. It's still that way there today."

"Stop!" Jill cried out. "How do you pronounce that word, *wha-ha-something*?"

"It's pronounced like *wa-ha-bis-m*. Anyway, the Allies had in effect cut away a key link in the one chain that bound diverse Arab peoples together—the single leadership of Islam through a caliph, the chief Muslim civil and religious ruler, and someone regarded as the successor of Mohammed. Since the early 1920s and to this day, Islam has not had one single leader for its worldwide community, or *ummah*, as Muslims like to call it. There's also a wide disparity of interpretation within Islam of the Muslims' single source guide for life, the Quran."

"Amazing, dear, how you describe centuries of history...in

14

so few words." Jill watched Fred beam with pride at the compliment.

"Anyway, Jill, honey, let me get back to the paper and internet news. Oh! Look here! A story from the BBC about a bird, a pied crow, that speaks with a Yorkshire accent. And here's another one about rooks in France that they train to collect and deposit trash. Don't you wish our birds were as advanced as theirs?"

Much Ado about Something

"Why don't you light a fire?" said Agnes. She pointed to a pile of firewood and old newspapers. It was her way of letting Adam know who was in charge. He readily obliged.

The two of them sat together silently. Adam slipped into a kind of timeless bliss. Neither was ready to admit it, but it was clear to both that a powerful attraction was already drawing them close together.

"What do you think Uncle Tibor meant about two strangers, two foreigners, looking out for me? I told you both I never said a word to them, nor they to me."

"Well, er, *Aaghne*shhh," stammered Adam, "Perhaps they don't speak Hungarian?"

"So what? If they are there to protect me—and from whom or from what, I've no idea—why not say so?"

"How would I know? All I can say right now is that your English is very good and makes me embarrassed that I don't know a single word of Hungarian."

"*Aaghneshhh*, my girl!" The voice of Tibor Lantos broke into their dialog as he emerged triumphant from his kitchen. "I have much to tell you—and Adam too. Let's sit down and talk while we eat."

Lantos had magically produced a piping-hot plate of chicken and sour cream. "This is *paprikas csirke*, a classic dish here! It's chicken simmered in sweet paprika, with some red and yellow peppers and just a bit of olive oil and fresh tomato sauce. And those are egg noodles on the bottom. My favorite!"

He took a mouthful before speaking again. "Now, let me tell you what's going on. The two people Agnes thinks were following her—well, yes, they were. But they are part of a team that changes from time to time to avoid detection."

Agnes broke in, sounding alarmed. "Team? What team? What are you talking about?"

"Agnes, I told Adam here already that, in addition to my work as a lecturer at Columbia, I work for a civilian government agency here in Hungary. It's the Informácios Hivatal, the Hungarian Information Agency. Most people here have never heard of it. Its role is to gather nonmilitary intelligence, mainly abroad."

Agnes gasped, then said, "I would never have guessed!"

"You weren't supposed to," said Lantos with a wry smile. "Anyway, I have a special focus these days and that's probably why you, as my research assistant, are being watched by our people just in case you run into the wrong kind of characters."

"You have us mystified, Uncle, so tell us more," begged Agnes.

"There's not a lot more to tell," Lantos replied. "At least, not yet. My point is, did either of you ever go treasure hunting when you were little?"

"Sure!" interjected Adam. "My sister and I were usually the ones who found the hidden treasure."

"Then you have a sister, Adam?" said Agnes.

"Oh yes, but that's another story."

Lantos's expression now became serious. "There's several types of treasure. What you looked for as a kid was hidden by someone for fun. Maybe you even read lately about a treasure hunt that's been going on in France for twenty-five years: it's for a bronze owl hidden in 1993 by the author Max Valentin with a promise to award the 'real owl,' made of gold and silver, to the finder? But what I'm looking for is quite different."

He looked away for a moment and his eyes became sad and downcast. He paused and took a deep breath.

"There are plenty of stories about lost or stolen gold or other precious things. My focus in just on one of them. You've heard of Adolf Eichmann—the one who came up with the Final Solution, resulting in the Holocaust? Well, in December 1944 he gave orders to fill a freight train with property, stolen mainly from Hungarian Jews, and send it away to safety, apparently to somewhere in Germany or Switzerland. As you know, the Israeli secret service, the

Mossad, eventually caught Eichmann in Buenos Aires, then tried and executed him."

He took a large mouthful of *paprikas csirke* as if to give himself the energy to go on.

"There were more than fifty carriages filled with loot on that train. More than half of the carriages were heavily armored freight cars, complete with machine gun turrets to ward off any Allied air attacks. The contents were packed in over fifteen hundred cases, each classified and registered. They included at least five tons of gold ingots seized from the Hungarian National Bank. They also included gold literally ripped from the teeth of doomed or murdered Hungarian Jews, including former residents of Budapest. There were hundreds of kilos of diamonds and pearls. There were at least three crates filled with gold bars, gold wedding bands, silver-handled walking sticks, coin collections, fine porcelain, furs, watches, coats, typewriters and even silk underwear."

He took a drink of water and noticed that the expressions on Adam's and Agnes's faces had also turned from awed to grim.

Lantos continued. "The train left Budapest in December 1944. It made its first stop in Győr, a major town some sixty to seventy miles northwest of Budapest, about halfway between Budapest and Vienna. Here, Nazi sympathizers loaded aboard one hundred old master paintings stolen from the local museum."

"Those alone must have been priceless!" said Adam, his jaw dropping.

Lantos nodded and resumed his tale. "Yes, they were. The train journeyed on for three months but for less than a hundred miles, thanks to multiple robbery attempts, including those by rogue elements of the German SS, and to aerial attacks by the Allies. It avoided the Russians moving in from the east and almost reached Salzburg, Austria, while the Allies kept advancing from the west. In mid-April 1945, when the Americans' Fifteenth Air Force blew up a rail bridge at Brixlegg, a town near Salzburg, they destroyed the rail tracks to Switzerland. At this point, the train became immobilized. Its military escort and passengers then simply left the train and vanished."

"Is that all?" asked Agnes with a frown.

Lantos shook his head. "In May, an American infantry unit found the train hidden in the five-mile long Tauern Tunnel near Salzburg. They estimated the value of the remaining contents—excluding what guards and other passengers aboard may have stolen for themselves—at over two hundred million dollars, or what would be many billions of dollars today."

"You mean, the *Allies* looted the train?" said Adam incredulously.

Lantos replied, "I'm afraid so, yes. The Americans and the French moved the train back to Salzburg and secured the contents in warehouses. But they decided that it was impossible to determine the ownership of all this property; and in addition, due to shifts in Hungary's postwar borders, there was no way to return anything to the Hungarian government. Instead, it all became 'enemy government property.' This interpretation meant that high-ranking American officials, including the military, could treat the train's contents simply as the spoils of war."

"Did anyone challenge this decision or return anything stolen to their rightful owners?" Agnes asked.

Lantos again shook his head. "To their credit, the French later returned two carriage loads of property to the Hungarian government. But despite repeated requests and protests, the United States declined to do so. It insisted that its position met international law. Instead, most items went to auction in New York in 1948, and the proceeds went to war relief. Austria was able to recover many paintings, but not Hungary."

"That's not a pretty story about the Allies," commented Adam.

"Agreed," said Lantos. "It took another fifty-one years—yes, I said fifty-one *years*—until a 1999 American Presidential Advisory Commission report challenged the position taken by the US military. Then, in 2001, a class action suit brought against the United States resulted in a settlement of over a mere twenty-five million dollars from a class action suit. However, this was pocket change compared to the stolen billions reported to have been on the train when it was found."

"So, Professor, what does all this have to do with you?" asked Adam.

Lantos looked up and shrugged. "To make this long story short, my job is to trace the thieves and retrieve what I can for the Hungarian government. Any Hungarian who can show proof of ownership will then have a chance to recover what was stolen from his or her family."

"Quite a story, Uncle." It was Agnes who now spoke. "Then why is someone shadowing me?"

"Simple. There are others out there who are also looking for this missing stolen property, to help finance violent actions today and tomorrow against the West. I'm speaking specifically of certain Arab criminal gangs who like to use Islam as a cover for their activities. They're here right now in Hungary, doing what you, Agnes, have been doing— researching how to locate the hidden treasure. They aren't people any of us ever wants to meet in person."

Adam felt a chill down his spine. *What am I getting myself into here?* he wondered.

Agnes caught his eye and stared at him. He feared she might be reading his thoughts.

United States of Awkward

"Have you heard anything from Adam in the last day or two?" Jill asked Fred while stirring a stewpot for the evening meal. "I mean, he always was so good about staying in touch."

Fred replied through a mouthful of breakfast toast. "Not since that email earlier this week. Probably a good sign that he's hard at work." He was sifting through a group of financial magazines, as usual, to glean titbits of news that might yield a stock tip or two.

The phone rang. "Who would be calling us on a Saturday morning?" Jill glanced at the clock in the kitchen-dining room. It read ten o'clock.

Fred rose slowly and on the fourth ring picked up the receiver.

"Eve? You mean Eve Tinker?" He covered the mouthpiece and whispered, "It's the police."

Jill froze. Thoughts raced through her mind. *Oh God! Has Eve been hurt somewhere? All these shootings lately among schoolchildren...Did I even check that she was up this morning?*

23

Oh my God, I don't even know if she came home before we went to bed last night!

Fred noticed she went so pale that she might faint.

"I'll be right over!" He slammed down the receiver. "Eve's in trouble. No, no, she's not hurt but she is sitting in a cell in the island police jail. They told me she went out on a boat with some friends into the harbor last night. The police caught them using drugs, something called fentanyl."

"Oh no!" cried Jill. "I just read about that in the local paper! That's the stuff that causes respiratory failure and even death if used with alcohol!" She was rapidly losing control.

"Honey, Eve's all right. They checked her out. She's woozy, but that's it. Now I need to get over to the police and sort this mess out."

Fred fretted at this unwelcome news of Eve's possible involvement with opioids. A story like this might leak to the press and impact his business. *Would the police insist on making her name public? Would they put Eve away behind bars for goodness knows how long? Oh, Lord!*

To his surprise, the local police were empathetic. The lead detective on the case was reassuring. "Your kid got mixed up with the wrong bunch, sir. We have the ringleader who likes to take girls out on the harbor at night and do drugs. He gets them on the water, gives them beer to drink, and then dares them to do drugs. Sometimes there's a problem. Anyway, the hospital is checking your daughter out. We don't think there's probable cause to arrest her because she didn't knowingly join the kids to do drugs and because early tests show she took nothing other than one light beer."

Fred felt a surge of relief. "So, should I go get her back from the hospital and…is there anything else I need to know?"

"Sir, this was a close call for Eve. We think her detention here for a few hours will scare her away from messing around like this ever again."

It was true. When Fred picked the girl up, her face was pallid and clearly shaken. "Dad, I feel so terrible, so *stupid*!"

"Well, my girl, you got off lightly this time—but let's not see this happen ever again."

Father and daughter tacitly agreed not to discuss the subject further, but that did not dissuade Jill from delivering a long and tedious lecture over dinner to her daughter.

After Fred returned with the repentant Eve, it wasn't long before he returned to scanning the financial news. As he skimmed over the pages, he could barely fail to miss a lead story about the owner of a well-known internet shopping service, the richest man in the world and, by definition, far richer than the current president of the United States.

Fred continued sifting through to the financial news. He then remembered to check his email and reached for his laptop. There was the usual glut of unwanted emails (*How on earth do these people ever find my email address?* he pondered) and some mundane updates from his lieutenants at the hedge fund. Someone, a stranger allegedly from the Central Bank of Nigeria, was offering to share with him half of a fifty-million-dollar deposit "from a deceased relative of yours": all that Fred needed to do was share his bank account details and social security number. Just another phishing effort and a recipe for identity theft. Fred promptly deleted it.

He was just about to sign off when he caught a text message that had earlier escaped his attention. The sender was someone he knew well in the City of London, a place where financial people were getting more jittery by the day as the deadline for the British departure from the European Union, known as Brexit, was fast approaching.

> Fred: please call. I have something important to share with you about an exciting investment opportunity. I think you'll like it. There's to be a meeting in the City in ten days' time with all the interested parties present. I think you should be one of them. Yours ever—Charles.

Charles Martin Fortescue was a rainmaker and investment banker. His father was British and his mother was American. He and Fred had met twenty years ago and had since become periodic business partners and good friends. Charlie had never let Fred down: his word was truly his bond, and he had a great eye for financial deals.

Fred reached for his smartphone. The line to London was busy at his first try. He waited, tried again and then got through.

"Mr. Fortescue's office, can I help you?" It was a woman's voice with a pronounced London accent. Fred couldn't remember the name of Charlie's female assistant from years ago, but no matter.

"Mr. Fortescue, please. Tell him it's Fred Tinker calling from the United States." There was a crackling sound and then muffled voices in the background.

"This is Dick Harvey, Mr. Tinker. I'm his personal assistant. Mr. Fortescue is away on business now. How can I help?"

Fred outlined the contents of the mail. Presumably this Harvey fellow either knew something about it, or if not, he could put Fred in touch with Charlie.

Harvey responded, "Mr. Fortescue told me to check your address and to send you something by overnight courier."

Fred thanked him, provided his home address on the island, hung up the phone, and gave the call little more thought.

Next afternoon, a padded envelope arrived by international courier. A small, hard object was inside along with some documents. Fred assumed the object might be a zip drive containing a financial presentation. He was wrong.

Carefully wrapped in bubble wrap was what looked like a small gold ingot, the size of a matchbox. A handwritten letter accompanied it, uncharacteristically signed "Chad." That struck Fred as odd. In all the years they had known each other, Fortescue had never used that nickname. Fred turned his attention to the letter itself, typed neatly on heavy, cream bond paper but with no letterhead or date.

Dear Fred,

As I mentioned to you in my text message,

we have an exceptional investment opportunity that might interest you.

You may know that there are still billions of dollars of property stolen by the Nazis in World War II which are still unaccounted for to this day. Among these massive thefts were valuables looted from the Hungarian Jewish community, mainly residents of Budapest, and sent off from Budapest by train. The Americans eventually found some of this stolen property and valued it at over two hundred million dollars in 1945. That's about three billion dollars today.

When the Americans made the discovery, they warehoused the train's contents in Salzburg. It remained there where it was all unloaded and locked away securely. Eventually, and except for two freight carriages taken over by the French and later returned to Austria, the Americans labelled the rest "enemy government property." They claimed that the rightful owners couldn't be identified; and that postwar territorial boundary changes in Hungary made it impossible to return the contraband to the Hungarian government.

Fifty-six years later, in 2001, a class action suit by claimants was filed in the United States. It resulted in a settlement of $25 million in 2005 for the benefit of the some of the owners.

This brings us to today's project.

The settlement award made in 2005 would be about $32 million in today's dollars. Simple math therefore suggests that there is still an unaccounted value remaining out there somewhere of some $2.9 billion.

We know that part of that hoard was probably hidden by escaping Nazis deep underground, but we don't yet know exactly where. We have a reputable team already at work using modern tools to locate the site or sites. It's like drilling for oil: it requires exploration of multiple potential sites. We think the high-tech tools of today can help narrow the most likely burial sites to a minimum, at relatively little cost.

Let's assume that we can find only about one half of the lost property, or about $1.5 billion. The governments of countries where we discovered a hoard would likely claim or reclaim the majority of that discovery. But we think our financing group could reap a finder's fee of up to ten percent of that value, or an estimated $150 million. We just need ten investors to put up $150,000 each, for a total $1.5 million, to cover exploration costs. That could mean a $15 million payout per investor and so a substantial return on investment.

Fred, if this proposal interests you, please read carefully the more detailed prospectus attached to this letter and let me know as soon as possible if you want to join the investor group,

Yours sincerely,

Chad

There was a postscript below the signature.

P.S. Enclosed is a 10 Tola bar. I know—it sounds like and looks like what Americans might call a "candy bar." (The term tola is an Indian—East Indian, that is—unit of weight, in this case 3.75 troy ounces.) This bar is said to be made of 99.9% pure gold. A small gold ingot like the one enclosed feels heavy because its atomic structure is very dense. Gold is also soft, so <u>please take care not to drop or damage it.</u> Also, if you decide to become an investor, be sure to return this ingot to me personally to authenticate your decision. Otherwise, it's yours to keep.

Fred sat back in his chair, gazing blankly at the letter. It had done its work and gotten his financial juices running. Ever hungry for a great investment opportunity, his mind began racing with thoughts and ideas. How great was the risk?

After all, a mere one hundred and fifty thousand dollars was pocket change if the actual return was even a fraction of what "Chad" had indicated. Odd, though, that Charlie would send him a solid gold ingot out of the blue. Odd too that he would sign off as "Chad."

Fred scanned the prospectus quickly, then made his decision.

Anonymity

A dam stared blankly into space, a look of palpable fear on his face.

"Here's the good news, Adam," said Lantos. "Sooner or later, the other   parties interested in finding and taking their cut of the stolen Hungarian property will identify Agnes and me. But my idea is that you, Adam, become as invisible as possible—and that you also keep an eye on Agnes, in particular. I can't guarantee that my department here can afford to keep watch on her every hour of the day."

The fear on Adam's face turned to relief. He now felt a surge of excitement at the prospect of becoming Agnes chaperone. "Happy to help!" he said, inviting a shy smile from Lantos's niece.

Lantos's tone shifted as he asked Agnes to give her latest report. "Now, let's get down to work."

Agnes was ready and eager to share her findings. "Well, Uncle, here's what I have. Two main things—that is, about our search for looted property of the Hungarian Jews in World War II; and the financing of terrorism, including by people like those said you saw earlier at the New York Café."

She paused, evidently for Adam's benefit. "We know that various governments around the world have tried for years to cut off funding for terrorism, especially extreme Islamist terrorism."

"Right," said Lantos.

He glanced at Adam to check his attentiveness as Agnes continued. "These terrorists need large amounts of money to buy weapons, equipment, various services and food and related supplies. Much of the funding for Islamic terrorism comes from what appear to be charitable donations, or *zakat*: that's typically a percentage, usually about two-and-a-half percent, of a practicing Muslim's income. The proceeds officially support education, social services, and health care for needy members of the Muslim community."

Lantos liked her analysis so far. "Go on, please."

Agnes flicked her long hair back before resuming. "However, some of these so-called charitable donations end up supporting extremist Islamic violence. The extremists often link up with organized crime groups engaged in drug and human trafficking, extortion, and kidnappings for ransom. Such alliances can amount to powerful forces of instability and insecurity. In turn, this really hurts economic development and upsets financial markets around the globe. I suppose that's what terrorists want to do so that they can take power from chaos?"

"That sounds about right," said Lantos.

Agnes smiled and resumed. "Anyway, more and more governments are now criminalizing terrorism financing, but they're challenged to detect it and prosecute it successfully. They need proof of intent to use funds for terrorism to get successful prosecutions. The pressure from many governments to find funding for terrorism has reached a point where Islamic extremists now feel forced to find new sources of money to finance their attacks."

When Lantos asked for details of the attacks, Agnes was quick to respond. "There were more than twenty fatal civilian attacks in Europe alone over the past few years, resulting in several hundred deaths and many more injuries to innocent people. The number of attacks doubled between 2015 and 2017 alone. European states have since stepped up their vigilance."

"What examples do you have, please?" asked Lantos, eyeing his niece watchfully.

Agnes noted that the British had five hundred ongoing investigations into at least three thousand jihadist extremists residing in Britain as potential terrorist attackers. Another twenty thousand British citizens were "subjects of interest." She added that Islamic hate preachers in mosques and on the internet, as well as personal contacts between Muslim extremists and other Muslims in Western prisons, had turned certain prisoners into radicalized attackers. The attack planners, typically based in Syria and Iraq, used the term"The Westerners' Crusader war against Muslims" as the pretext to inflame their followers and attract new recruits, including some lone wolves.

Lantos interjected. "So, this brings us to today. We're getting closer to finding a large amount of property stolen from the Hungarian Jews in the closing days of World War II. Our team of experts is almost certain to have located one or more sites where hidden gold and other valuables stolen by the Nazis and their Hungarian supporters might be found. Meanwhile, we think we have also identified an Islamist gang that is intent on getting to these finds before we do."

Adam interjected. "That's quite a story!"

"Oh, yes, and there's more," said Agnes between sips of coffee. "There have been many failed efforts recently to locate the stolen property, as well as some successful ones toward the end of World War II."

"Tell him about Merkers, Agnes," said Lantos.

"Well," Agnes continued, "In 1945, the Americans found a hoard of gold and platinum bars, gold bullion, gold coins, silver objects, one bag of platinum bars, bags of gold rings and valuable artwork in a salt mine located in Merkers, a town some 120 miles southwest of Leipzig in Germany. Much of this stolen wealth probably originated in Hungary. There are many other examples of priceless hidden Nazi loot. But most of it just disappeared or remains hidden."

She paused and cleared her throat. Her concentration and focus made a strong impression on Adam, who found his mind wandering as she continued her report.

"Some say the Merkers gold found its way to the Swiss National Bank. Switzerland was one of the main gold distribution centers in Europe. It's rumored that the Swiss laundered almost a hundred tons of Nazi gold. Others reported that stolen Nazi gold was 'in safekeeping' in the Vatican Bank, though the Church denied it. Other such alleged destinations included Portugal and certain Latin American countries."

"That's amazing!" Adam commented. "I wonder how many people know all that?"

Agnes cast a glance at him that made him blush at his ignorance. She then looked up from her notes. "Let me tell you about some more recent searches. In 2016, a Nazi treasure trove valued at almost six hundred and fifty million dollars was allegedly pinpointed by a treasure hunter in a privately-owned Bavarian forest near the German town of Arrach. The landowner declined to give permission, as required by German law, for the treasure hunter to excavate it. The two parties are at a stalemate: the landowner has the land but not the map leading to the loot, while the treasure hunter has the map but no access to the land."

It was Tibor who spoke next. "Tell Adam about your technique and how it differs from other hunters and searchers."

"Fine," she said, shuffling her notes. "Most hunters of hidden Nazi gold like to research possible sites, and then they rush to get a permit to dig. For example, there were two guys who just recently split up after a long and costly search in what had been a German town until the war ended. That town is called Walbrzych. Today, it's in southwestern Poland, near the Czech border. Here's what happened."

Agnes pulled out some current photographs of what looked

like a disused railroad track set in an urban wasteland but surrounded by modern office buildings and workshops.

She explained how in 2015, two Germans, Piotr Koper and Andreas Richter, thought they had found a promising site in Poland. Using ground-penetrating radar, they detected a three hundred-foot long train-like object concealed about one hundred feet underground. The two treasure hunters wanted ten percent of the "find." They dug for a week, spending over one hundred thousand dollars. They then reluctantly identified the images as natural ice formations. So, the real "find" turned out to be good for the town's tourism, but nothing else.

"I thought about this a bit and then I had an idea," she said. "Most Nazis active in the Second World War are either already dead or are quite elderly. People assume their secrets died with them. But many had families and descendants who are still alive and who might be aged anywhere between their early-seventies to their mid-eighties. Many might still be living in Germany today. Others might be in various Latin American countries like Argentina to which many Nazis fled after the war to avoid prosecution. I thought, why not trace some of those family members to see if they know something that could help our research?"

Tibor broke in. "When Agnes suggested this to me, I liked the idea. Somehow, I managed to persuade my department in Budapest to finance a search from this angle. Believe me, it wasn't easy. As the world knows, we have a politically right-leaning government administration here whose members seem to prefer not to wake sleeping dogs. But fortunately, my boss has some discretion to direct funds where needed, regardless of the current government in power. We have up to about twenty-one million Hungarian forints at our disposal, or some seventy thousand dollars."

Tibor reached for his worn leather briefcase. He entered a code on the combination lock, opened the case, and drew out a red folder. Peering down his nose over his eyeglasses, he flipped through several sheets of paper and headshots of men and women while his niece and Adam watched him with mounting curiosity. At last, he drew a deep breath.

"You two need to pack some clothes and gear. I want to you take a trip. You will appear to all the world as young newlyweds on a honeymoon."

Adam stole a quick glance at Agnes whose eyelashes fluttered. It was her turn to blush, uncontrollably. "But Uncle…" Her voice trailed off as Tibor shot her a severe look, one that Adam had never seen before.

Lantos frowned. His tone was serious now. "This is not a game, Agnes. There are many players who want to find what we want to find first. Some of them will stop at nothing to get it. You and Adam have been handpicked as part of your assignment to help with this project. Provided that you follow my instructions carefully, you'll not come to any harm, because someone from our team will be watching out for you. Someone will warn you in time if any danger looks like it's coming your way. But the name of the game here is for you two to appear to be just two anonymous innocents enjoying a wonderful honeymoon. The rest you can leave to us."

Tibor glanced at his paperwork. "So, here's the plan. You'll take your 'honeymoon trip' in Argentina. Yes, that's right. You'll have ten days there to do what you need to do, then you'll just return here to Hungary. We've booked a hotel for you in Buenos Aires. It's very nice. Of course, you'll have a three-bedroom suite 'in case a friend joins you.' That's your cover story, just in case one of our people needs to be present with you. Agnes, you can have the Honeymooners' Master Bedroom all to yourself, so you'll be completely private. You, Adam, will have the other smaller bedroom."

Agnes blushed again but said nothing. Adam almost burst out laughing. *This is beginning to sound like a fun first job after all*, he thought to himself.

But Tibor was all business. "I have here your plane tickets: two business class tickets on Lufthansa. It's a direct flight but with one stopover. Our own Hungarian airline, Malev, has no nonstop flights. We need you to get there as quickly as you can and get refreshed. It's a long flight, about seventeen hours. You'll leave tomorrow at 7:10 p.m. with a stopover in Frankfurt, which is in the same time zone as we now are here. There, you'll have an hour to change planes to another Lufthansa flight to Buenos Aires's Ministro Pistarini airport. Get some food, then get on the plane, and go straight to sleep. You'll arrive in Buenos Aires at about seven the following morning, which is four hours behind our time here. Any questions?"

Adam was still struggling to understand the change in time zones. Agnes now looked surprised and excited.

"What then?" asked Adam.

Tibor replied. "Adam, remember you have German ancestry on your father's side. That's a natural asset, because you'll receive a letter of introduction to the Club Clarion in Buenos Aires. It's at 23 Avenida Corrientes. Go to the gym. Someone there will contact you. Remember: this is an old school German social club, mostly for men only. Don't take Agnes there unless invited, but remember she too has German ancestry, through her mother. That may come in handy later."

"How will I know the person to contact me?" Adam frowned, clearly puzzled.

"Don't worry about that. Someone in the gym will know what you look like. Just remember to say, when asked about where you are staying, 'At the Anselmo Hotel.' The contact will ask where you're from, and you'll say, 'New York.' He'll then ask for your help in translating a German word: 'What is *basteln* in English, please?' You'll say, 'That's "tinker." That's my family name.' He'll then pass you an envelope and politely move away. Don't open the envelope there but take it back to the hotel and then open it up. Show it to Agnes."

Two days later, Adam and Agnes found themselves in Buenos Aires.

Tangled Tango

Agnes and Adam had checked into their Buenos Aires hotel. They were pleasantly surprised by the Honeymooners' Suite. There were indeed three bedrooms and a spacious living room. Large vases of flowers, a chilled bottle of champagne and a tempting bowl of fresh fruit and chocolates all signaled arrival of the "newlyweds."

Adam decided to follow his instructions from Lantos promptly and to the letter. A taxi dropped him off at the Club Clarion, housed in the basement of a grimy building set in an inconspicuous side street. The gym was in the basement. There were only four other men there.

Just as Tibor had predicted, one of the men got off a nearby treadmill and sauntered casually over to Adam, only minutes after he had begun to pedal away on a stationary bicycle. They exchanged some pleasantries and smiles. Adam felt himself stiffen when the man asked where he was from and where he was staying. He felt an adrenaline rush when the stranger asked for help with translating a German word, *basteln*, into English. He uttered the "tinker" name, holding his breath. The man smiled and turned to leave. As he did so, he dropped a large white, sealed envelope at Adam's side.

Adam turned to tell the stranger he had dropped something, but the man had already disappeared. Looking down at the envelope, he saw his own initials on it and a blue wax seal at the back. The letters "A. T." were written in neat handwriting in black ink on the front.

Back at the Anselmo Hotel, Adam and Agnes eagerly tore open the envelope. It contained an invitation to a dinner in two days' time. It was handwritten in English on heavy, cream-colored bond paper. The dinner venue was to be the Club Clarion's own Rhombus Restaurant.

There was a note attached, including an email address for a response to the invitation and a street address. The note indicated that "Dr. Otto Weber from the Goethe-Institut in Berlin will present some of his latest and most important rediscoveries of German heritage and will invite your support."

The New German Family Union cordially invites

Mr. and Mrs. Adam Tinker

to attend an exclusive special private dinner

and presentation on

Friday August 29, 2018,

at 8:00 p.m. precisely

at the Rhombus.

The topic of the evening will be as follows:

The Consortium Plan to retrieve

Our Lost Inheritance

Adam looked at Agnes and asked, "What's that funny-looking sign on the invitation?"

Agnes smiled. "You obviously have a poor musical education! That's a notation from sheet music called *dal segno* or D. S. for short. It's Italian for 'from the sign.' In other words, it tells a musician to return to an earlier passage in a musical score that has this symbol."

"But why use a musical symbol here? What has that got to do with the topic? And what is this reference to a lost inheritance about, anyway?" The invitation clearly puzzled Adam. "And, while we're at it, what does the word *rhombus* have to do with anything?"

Agnes was about to respond when the living room phone rang. Adam saw a momentary look of alarm cross her face. He too felt a sudden pounding of his heart. But why feel afraid? After all, they were just two innocent newlyweds enjoying a honeymoon in Argentina. Perhaps it was just the front desk calling.

Adam reached for the phone. "Hello?"

"Adam? Adam Tinker?" said a familiar voice.

"Yussef? Professor Yussef Bitar?" It was unmistakably one of his other favorite lecturers from Columbia—an Egyptian, the alleged past member of the Muslim Brotherhood, and expert on the Middle East.

"Where are you?" Adam asked nervously, caught off guard.

"Right here in the lobby. I know this is short notice, but please may I come up to your room? I'm only here for a short while. I must catch a plane later tonight."

"Sure. Come on up!" Agnes met his glance with a scowl of

silent disapproval.

Five minutes later, there was a rapid, insistent knock at the door. Adam looked through the peephole. There indeed was Bitar. Adam let him in.

Agnes noticed that Bitar didn't shake her hand when Adam introduced him. The man seemed agitated as he spoke.

"Let me get straight to the point," said the visitor. "It's no accident that I'm here, and that I'm contacting you. Things are moving very fast, and I can only tell you a little about what I'm doing and why."

"What things do you mean?" asked Adam in genuine surprise.

Bitar glanced at his watch. "Adam, you know that my focus as a lecturer is on the past, present, and future of the Middle East. What you may not know is that I'm involved with people who are shaping the Middle East and trying to bring peace and prosperity there."

Adam was confused. "But what brings you here? What people are you talking about? I mean, you're a long way from the Middle East."

"I'm much closer to it now than you might think. It's a long story. But I'm here for one reason only—to warn you both."

"*Warn* us? About what?" Agnes said nervously as Adam looked on stunned.

"There are people here in Buenos Aires from the Middle East. They may be looking for you."

45

"But why?" said Adam.

"They think you have information they need."

"What information? We don't have any." Adam looked at Agnes. She said nothing but was clearly thinking.

"They want information about vast amounts of wealth—stolen wealth. I'm talking about stolen property hidden all over the world. These people want to get their hands on that wealth to fund their activity."

"What people, what activity?" Adam was now feeling frustrated and lost.

"Adam, and Agnes too, you may not realize it, but you're about to get close to the center of a very dangerous conspiracy involving individuals, governments, terrorists, and possibly life-threatening circumstances. Let me tell you a little of what I know."

He took a deep breath. Adam noticed he seemed very tired and edgy.

Bitar resumed. "You have heard of a Nazi named Martin Bormann? In short, he became Hitler's *de facto* number two. He did some terrible inhuman things resulting in the death of millions of innocent civilians—mostly Jews and Slavs. Before he died in 1945, Bormann had secretly set up an organization to accumulate stolen Nazi wealth in preparation for a resurgent Nazi effort in the event of a German defeat in World War II."

"I know a bit about that," said Adam, choosing his words carefully.

46

Bitar nodded before continuing. "Bormann called this organization the *Hacke*, meaning the 'Pickaxe.' He set up Pickaxe cells in neutral countries like Portugal, as well in Nazi-friendly countries like Italy, Japan, Spain—and here in Argentina. The *Hacke* probably controlled over five hundred million dollars of wealth, most of it stolen from victims of concentration camps."

Bitar again glanced at his watch before continuing. "The story is that the Russians blackmailed Bormann by threatening to reveal his secret plot to Hitler and his associates. But even this didn't stop Bormann from encouraging top German industrialists in 1944 to get their money out of Germany to a safe place. All they had to do was set up companies in countries like Turkey, Switzerland, Spain, and of course, Argentina. Then Bormann made sure that the key Nazis would get jobs in such countries after Germany's defeat and access the wealth needed to finance a Nazi comeback. Several hundred companies like that were formed, and presumably a great many Nazis who escaped prosecution found work when the war ended."

Adam piped up. "I still don't see what this has to do with us here today in Argentina?"

Bitar continued, clearly anxious to tell his tale. "I happen to know that you and Agnes are here posing as newlyweds. I also know that there are people from the Middle East here right now who want to do business with certain German Argentinians. Both parties want the same things: among them, prompt access to as much stolen Nazi wealth as possible; and use of that wealth to exterminate not only Israel but also as many Jews as possible, everywhere."

"How would you know that we are 'posing' as newlyweds?" asked Agnes. She was clearly suspicious and worried at this revelation.

Bitar looked at the floor before responding. "I can't tell you now, because that would only put you in even more danger. But I can tell you that certain German Argentinians you plan to meet have already checked you out, Adam, and they know about you and your family. Specifically, they know that your father Fred Tinker was once interested in joining the Hitler Youth. There's constant communication between the Argentinian German community here and the Argentinian Department of Home Affairs."

Adam felt a familiar surge of fear as Bitar continued to speak. He noticed too that Agnes seem startled and shocked at hearing about Fred Tinker's past attraction to the Hitler Youth.

Bitar had more to share. "I know that certain Middle Easterners are trying to locate Agnes. They think her research into hidden Nazi gold may help them find it. The good news is that the Germans aren't telling their Middle Eastern friends about you, Adam; and the Arabs aren't telling their German friends about you, Agnes. In fact, we don't think that either party has identified Agnes yet, which means that you're safe for now, but not necessarily in the future."

"Who is this 'we' you're talking about, Professor?" asked Adam, by now clearly alarmed.

Bitar thought for a moment, then said, "Again, I can't tell you—at least, not now. It's best you know as little as possible
48

about me outside of my teaching activity at Columbia. That way, you can play dumb if certain people start asking you questions."

Adam had another question for his former college lecturer. "I don't grasp the Middle East. Can you give us a quick look at what's going on there and why it seems such a mess today?"

"I can also give you plenty to read on the subject. But not now. I can just give you a very quick and superficial overview, if you still want it?"

"Fine with me." Adam glanced at Agnes, who nodded her assent.

"Well," began Bitar, "the recent history of what we call the Middle East today has its roots in developments during the mid-to-late 19th century. You know that the Ottoman Empire ruled for six centuries over most of Southeast and some of Central Europe, North Africa, and Western Asia."

Adam nodded in agreement as Bitar continued. "The Ottomans were Turkish, not Arab. They became targets for emerging and restive Arab and Turkish nationalist groups within the Ottoman Empire. Concurrently, the Germans were building relations with the Turks, in order to destabilize British, French and Russian overseas interests. The result was World War I and the defeat of both Germany and the Turks."

"OK," said Adam.

Bitar was now getting into his stride. "The Arab nationalists discovered common interests with the German National Socialists when they came to power in the early 1930s. One such common interest was the complete extermination of the Jews. Simply put, you could say that the roots of today's radical Islam lie in the collapse of the Ottoman Empire after World War I. Both the Nazis and the Arabs picked on the Jews as the cause of their troubles. For the Arabs, this meant the loss of their leader, the Caliph, at the head of the Ottoman Empire. For the Germans, it meant the loss of their leader, the Kaiser, and massive reparation payments imposed on them by the victorious Allies."

"I remember my dad telling me that," said Adam.

Bitar once again stole a glance at his watch, as if his time was running out. But he still had more to share. "Today, there are still long-standing relationships between surviving Nazis and the Arab communities. There are thousands of Nazis all around the world who escaped prosecution and fled to countries like Switzerland, Austria, Syria, and of course, Argentina. Some of the most dangerous are here. I've barely scratched the surface of a much more complicated history, but hopefully this gives you some idea of it."

Bitar turned and made for the door, saying, "Now, that's as much as I can say for now. But one last thing. If you see me with anyone else, treat me as if you're meeting me for the first time. If you appear to recognize me, you may put all of us in danger. Is that understood?"

Before either Adam or Agnes could respond, Bitar had grabbed his coat and slipped out the hotel room door.

London Fog

Fred Tinker booked a first class seat on a flight from JFK to London. His arrival at dawn was greeted by the typical gray sky and cold, damp, bone-penetrating weather. The car service driver was there outside Customs with a sign reading, "Mr. Frederick Tinker."

Within an hour, they had reached the West End and a small boutique hotel in Chelsea.

He failed to notice the plain-looking woman reading a newspaper in the small reception area of the hotel. Nor did he see her slip out her cell phone and make a quick but discreet call.

Upon entering his room and throwing down his briefcase and overcoat, Fred reached for his phone and placed a call. "Mr. Fortescue, please." He put his phone into speaker mode so he could start to unpack while still on the call.

There was a pause. A female voice answered, "And who's calling please?" Fred thought it was the same woman's voice with the London accent that he had heard when he called Charlie previously from the island. Once again, he thought he heard muffled voices in the background.

"Mr. Tinker?" said a somewhat familiar man's voice.

"Yes. Who is this, please?" said Fred, continuing to empty his suitcase.

"Dick Harvey, Mr. Tinker. We spoke a few days ago."

"Oh yes, of course. I want to speak with Mr. Fortescue, please."

Harvey hesitated for a moment before responding. "Yes, well, he's still traveling I'm afraid. But I have good news. He asked me to meet with you and fill you in a bit more about the investment idea he shared with you. Would you care to have dinner with me at my club?"

The Army and Navy Club, known as the Rag, oozed with tradition. It had been in the same location since 1851. Fred announced himself at the door and was promptly directed to the Smoking-Room Bar. He was surprised when a young athletic-looking man with blond hair and piercing blue eyes greeted him.

"Dick, Dick Harvey, sir. A pleasure to meet you in person, at last!"

After some preliminary small talk, Harvey said, "Let's get some dinner. I have a nice table for two in the club's Coffee Room."

Fred was impressed as they took their seats by the portraits of stiff-looking but impressive royal and military figures in their full military uniforms that adorned the walls.

"I suggest the Signature Menu," Harvey chimed in. "They

do a really good Essex beef bavette steak with slow-cooked tomato, onion rings, and chips—fries, I think you call them!"

The dinner dragged on and Fred wondered when this talkative British guy would get to the point of their meeting. He did not realize that Harvey was carefully sizing up his guest and assessing his reactions. Fred felt growing impatience as his host prattled away about his family, the artwork on the walls, and that most obscure subject of all called "cricket."

Sensing finally, that it was time to get to the point, Harvey sipped a mouthful of black coffee and said, "Now, then," his piercing-blue-eyed gaze suddenly fixing in a hard stare at his guest. "Mr. Tinker, to be serious for a moment. You need to know that the investment under discussion is not without its risks."

"I know! I know!" said Fred, a little more huffily that he intended. "I *did* read the prospectus."

"I'm not talking about financial risk, Mr. Tinker." The charming host's face had now turned into a grim mask. "There's risk to life here. In other words, if you commit to invest in this project, you put your life at risk—and possibly the lives of your family as well."

The color drained from Fred's face. "But no one told me…" This was a new insight that wasn't indicated in the prospectus. He began to fidget uncomfortably.

Harvey continued, unfazed. "You see, ours is not the only group looking to harvest this investment. Other consortia are working hard to beat us to the punch."

"What other consortia do you mean? I don't recall reading about that in the prospectus," Fred asked, clearly puzzled at this second revelation.

Harvey smiled a cold smile, shifting uneasily in his chair. "Precisely, and that's why we are meeting here tonight so I can acquaint you with the bigger picture—beyond just the prospectus alone. There are two other main groups who are after what we're after. One is a syndicate of former Nazis, with a global network of members at its disposal. The other is a loosely aligned group of Arab extremists who are on a mission to fund a long-term goal, namely, to restore the caliphate that ended a few years after the defeat of the German and Ottoman Empires in 1918."

Harvey paused and studied Fred's face for a reaction. His guest seemed unfazed by what Harvey had told him.

"Our job," continued Harvey, "is to get hold of the lost treasures before either of these groups do so. Meanwhile, we understand that both groups may now be working together—and there's a long history of Germans and Arabs making common cause. Our latest reports suggest that they are making their final plans, possibly in Argentina, and that execution of those plans is imminent. So, we don't have time on our side."

Harvey now observed Fred's reaction of dismay. "Now that I have told you this, are you still interested in becoming an investor?"

Fred rubbed his chin. "Well, I don't want to put my family at risk, of course. However, and depending on the level of risk, I might still be interested."

Harvey interjected. "Please understand, Mr. Tinker, that no one is compelling you to become an investor. But if you do join the investor group, you and all other investors will potentially become marked men. Your lives and those of your families may possibly be put at risk. You'll have no protection if something bad happens. On the other hand, as you know, the potential rewards of this investment are significant."

Fred continued rubbing his chin. "Let me think about it overnight. Then I'll call you in the morning."

"Fine. Here's the investors' agreement. Please read it over carefully. If you still want to proceed, sign it, make a copy for yourself and mail it back to me by overnight courier at the address shown."

Fred flipped through the document, only half noticing that the return address was simply a post office box number in London.

An Empty Chair

Agnes emailed an acceptance note to the address on the Clarion Club invitation. Her next thought, of course, was *What should I wear?* But Adam's mind was elsewhere.

He wondered how this invitation had come about? Professor Lantos had indeed alerted him to its likely appearance in Buenos Aires, but was that all? Meanwhile, Bitar seemed unaware of it, maybe because he was in a rush to catch a plane? Where to, by the way? And why would Bitar of all people suddenly turn up out of the blue in Buenos Aires of all places and seek out Adam, especially when in a rush to catch a plane?

Something here didn't quite add up. While he was pondering these loose ends, Agnes reminded him that they had two days to kill before the dinner date at the Club Clarion. She suggested that they do some sightseeing with a local guide.

They toured Buenos Aires' 16th century Plaza de Mayo with its impressive Presidential Palace, the Casa Rosada, at its eastern end. Opposite it was the Cabildo, the old town hall.

It was still guarded by members of the Regimiento de Patricios wearing their traditional red, white and blue uniforms from more than two hundred years ago when, as the Legión Patricia, the Patricians' Legion, they had defended Buenos Ares from British invaders in 1806.

Agnes reminded Adam that the same Plaza de Mayo was where the mothers of Argentine's Disappeared Ones or *Desaparacidos* protested the loss of their children during the so-called Dirty War between 1974 and 1983. Backed by the United States, Argentinian military and security forces joined forces with right-wing death squads to hunt and "disappear" any political dissidents.

She remembered reading that leftist guerillas murdered over one thousand people in the ten years leading up to 1979. The guerillas included students, trade unionists, writers, journalists, or anyone suspected of being a left-wing activist.

In response, the military had launched something called Operation Condor to silence any opposition to the rule of the military junta. Adam saw tears well up in her eyes as she continued speaking. "That operation swept up thousands of Argentinians, including some thirty thousand people who were murdered or 'disappeared.' That left a big ugly stain on Argentina, even though some junta members are still in jail for crimes against humanity and genocide."

They went on to visit the flea market at San Telmo, and then, after sampling the antique shops tucked into the narrow streets of brightly colored houses, they found a cramped bar where they learned to dance the tango.

The guide insisted on showing them the famous Café Tortoni, proudly reminding them of the many Hollywood and other celebrities who had visited it since it had first opened in 1858.

When the night of the Club Clarion dinner presentation arrived at last, Agnes donned a simple black linen dress. It flattered her figure and artfully displayed just a hint of cleavage at her breasts. Adam gaped in amazement as she entered the living room of their suite.

Both were blushing. "Wow!" he said. "You look stunning!"

Shortly afterwards, a cab dropped them off at the Club Clarion. A stone-faced and unsmiling doorman greeted them there. He checked their invitation, took a long, hard look at Adam and said, "Guten abend, Mein Herr und Meine Dame! Hier ist der Rhombus," pointing to a dimly lit stairwell in the rear of the building.

At the top of the stairs were two well-built security guards. Adam noticed that the shorter of the two bore a diagonal scar from his left ear to the corner of his mouth.

The taller one spoke. "Arme hoch! Beine auseinander!" ("Arms up! Legs apart!") The security men frisked them both, lightly but carefully.

The shorter man reached for Agnes's purse. "Öffnen bitte!" ("Open, please!")

Satisfied, the guards pointed to a facing door marked *Privates Treffen*. Agnes whispered, "That means 'Private Meeting.'"

They entered a medium-sized hall. There were about eighty chairs lined up and already occupied. Most members of the audience were gray-haired men and women and many looked like octogenarians. Sprinkled among them were a few younger-looking men and women.

But what caught Adam's attention was a chair. An empty chair.

It was high backed and located in the center of a stage that rose a few feet above the audience. A bright spotlight shone down on it at an angle, intensely illuminating two gilded numbers on the seat back.

What does the number "88" mean, I wonder? Adam asked himself.

He turned to ask Agnes, but she was talking to another guest. He then noticed a door off the meeting room. It bore a faded sign reading *Rhombus*. Presumably this was the adjoining dining room where dinner would follow.

He was wondering how well he could interpret the upcoming presentation and whether anyone present spoke English when, as he was about to turn back to Agnes, he felt a light touch on his arm.

"Welkommen! Ich bin die Vorsitzende!" ("Welcome! I am the Chair of the meeting!") An elegantly dressed older woman with long, silver-gray hair was smiling at him.

The puzzlement on his face gave him away.

"So, perhaps you're the young American we invited to our meeting?" Her English was almost without an accent.

"We're delighted you can join us as our guest! Are you here with your wife?"

Adam blushed uncontrollably. "Well, yes. Let me introduce you."

As only women can, the two were soon chatting away in German, like old friends. Finding his courage at last, Adam couldn't resist asking a question.

"What's the significance of the empty chair on the stage?"

The chairwoman seemed surprised at the question. "Oh! You don't know? The numbers 8 and 8 each represent the eighth letter of the alphabet."

He said, "You mean HH?"

"Yes."

"I see," said Adam. Except that he didn't.

"We will tell you more over dinner, but now we must hear the presentation."

Adam struggled to understand what the presenter, a Dr. Otto Weber, was saying in German. He couldn't fail to notice the excitement and passion behind the man's initial words. Dr. Weber had started out calmly enough but as he warmed up, his voice began to rise. His expression changed, abruptly from that of a warm, avuncular white-haired speaker to that of a fierce demagogue. Adam caught angry words leaping from the man's mouth like bullets, such as, "Unser recht!" ("Our right!")

Adam shot a quick glance at Agnes beside him and noticed

how the muscles tightened in her face. The speaker was now screaming almost hysterically, and the audience was joining in with him. When Agnes turned to face Adam, the look on her face told him that the speaker's message was one of hatred. At last, Dr. Weber's rant ended. His remarks drew loud applause from most members of the audience.

It was then that Adam spotted a younger woman, perhaps old enough to be his own or Agnes's mother. The woman did not applaud. He wondered why not. She simply stared expressionlessly at the speaker.

Her blond hair was set in a bun. She wore a simple gray dress with a black belt and flat shoes. Adam studied her profile. Her high cheekbones and finely carved nose were striking. As if she knew she was being watched by him, she turned her head suddenly and fixed her clear-blue eyes on Adam. He felt himself blushing with embarrassment. He looked away.

The chairwoman rose and stepped up to the podium. In German, she appeared to invite the audience members to the dinner by pointing to the door marked *Rhombus*. The "newlyweds" edged their way through the throng. There were place cards on each of the ten round tables.

Each diner had a member of the opposite sex on either side. A tall, distinguished older man with a distinct military bearing stood to Agnes's left and politely pulled out the chair for her. A short, fat fellow with a double chin and thick glasses sat to her right.

Adam found himself seated to the right of an elderly lady whose limited ability to speak English became rapidly apparent. As he settled into his seat, and much to his surprise, the blond woman with the bun at whom he had been staring only minutes ago alighted to his right. He smiled and introduced himself, as if to reconfirm the name on his place card.

The woman smiled back. "Schon Sie zu treffen, Herr Tinker," she said. "Pleased to meet you, Mr. Tinker."

Just as everyone began small talk, the chairwoman rose to her feet once again, tapping her wine glass for silence. "I wish to speak in English in honor of some of our guests here tonight." (Adam wondered if he was the only person present whose mother tongue was English.) "As most of us know, the day is coming when Germany will once again rise as a great, and perhaps the world's greatest, power. While America is being 'made great again' (this remark drew a soft chuckle from the room), our mother country is preparing to rise to heights never before seen. Dr. Weber's talk tonight underlined our progress so well. Thank you, Dr. Weber!"

This remark drew loud and prompt applause. A beaming Dr. Weber, seated at the head table, nodded his approval.

"Now," said the chairwoman, "as is our custom, I would like to offer a toast to Number 88."

On cue, all present stood and silently raised their glasses. Adam and Agnes blindly copied their neighbors. Adam glanced to his right. He noticed that the blond with the bun reached for her wine glass and stood but did not lift her glass with everyone else. Then everyone sat down.

A team of waiters dressed immaculately in black tuxedos

and crisp white shirts and black bow ties emerged silently on cue out of the adjoining kitchen and filed in with military precision to serve dinner.

A clunky first course of burrata, prosciutto, and tomato arrived. It was followed by a huge juicy Argentine steak adorned with mushrooms and roast potatoes. The dessert was a rich apple strudel with vanilla ice cream that melted in the mouth. Bottles of deliciously fruity Argentine red wine were emptying at each table at a rapidly rising rate. Everyone was loosening up and having a good time. Or so it seemed.

The blond woman to Adam's right chose her moment to lean over to him and ask, "What brings you to Buenos Aires, Mr. Tinker?"

Adam explained that he and Agnes were newly married and on their honeymoon.

"That's nice. But you're a long way from America, yes?"

They chatted about Argentina and Buenos Aires; and then, moments later, she invited Adam and his "new wife" to visit her at her home a few miles outside the city center. She gave him her card with her telephone number.

"My name is Isolde Rauff," she said. "Maybe I can show you both some things that typical tourists never see here?" The invitation sounded innocent enough.

Adam, by now feeling at ease with his new acquaintance, decided to revisit the question he had earlier posed to the chairwoman. "What was the significance of the empty chair with the numbers 8 and 8 on it—not to mention the toast to Number 88?"

"Oh, you didn't know?" said his dinner companion. "Well, the two numbers each represent the eighth letter of the alphabet. That's 'HH.'"

"And that means?"

"Heil Hitler, of course."

A Deadly Investment

Fred slept well at his London hotel. He rose at his customary 6:00 a.m. Turning on the television, he struggled to find a newscast with the latest business news.

'Why on earth do these Brits televise so many games of snooker and darts, especially at six in the morning?' he pondered.

The investor agreement lay on his bedside table, next to his glasses. He sipped a tumbler of water. As usual, his mind began to churn about the pros and cons of the investment. It seemed to promise a generous return. Worst case, he might lose a hundred and fifty thousand dollars.

'You win some, you lose some,' he mused.

On the other hand, what exactly was the risk to him personally, and to Jill and the two children that this guy Dick Harvey had mentioned? Fred had no idea. But if the real level of risk was low enough, and not a significant threat to his family after all, at say five percent or less, then why not have a go?

He picked up of a copy *The Times*. The cover photo that morning was of a large extreme right-wing demonstration in Chemnitz, a German city known for its textile production dating back to the Middle Ages. ('Hadn't a famous female ice skater been born there when it was still part of East Germany? What was her name? Oh yes! Katerina Someone...Katerina Witt. Of course!' he muttered out loud). The Chemnitz demonstration had been prompted by the alleged murder of a white German male by two Middle Eastern immigrants, an Iraqi and a Syrian, both of whom had been arrested and charged. The nature of this extremist demonstration in modern Germany was unprecedented, at least in recent memory, if only for the unabashed Nazi salutes from the crowd.

Fred looked up and, while staring out the bedroom window, thought back to his early life in Germany in the 1940s. How ironic that Germany had worked so hard to build relations with the Arabs back then, in the hope that they could jointly drive the British and French out of Palestine and Syria. Yet today, here was the extreme right reacting violently to the various Arab immigrant communities who now represented most refugees arriving in Germany over the past few years.

The phone rang and broke his train of thought. It was Harvey.

"Good morning, sir. Just calling to let you know that the deadline has been moved from noon today to 5:00 p.m. which should give you a bit more time to make your decision."

"That's fine." But Fred had one question. "How would you

measure the personal risk to me, my family or all of us if I decide to join your consortium? What would you say is the percentage level of risk?"

There was silence on the end of the phone. Harvey was going to pick his words carefully.

"Well, sir, it's not for me to say, as far as you and your family are concerned. But based on what I know, if it were up to me, I'd say it's about fifty percent."

Fred knew he should have stopped at that point. But he could not. The temptation of a high return on investment was too great. This time, it was his turn to pause for moment.

Then he said, "I may as well tell you. I'm in!"

Warning Signs

Adam and Agnes took a cab back to the Anselmo Hotel as Buenos Aires was starting to settle down into the small hours of the night. They were both exhausted. Adam knew he had drunk more glasses of fruity Malbec wine than he should have done. But through his partly woozy mind, he still noticed that Agnes had become quiet and withdrawn.

"Agnes, are you all right?" he asked, sensing that something was bothering her.

Agnes looked up and stared at him. "I'm fine. It's just that some things I heard tonight upset me."

"What things?" asked Adam. But she remained withdrawn and held her tongue until they were back in their quarters.

"That Dr. Weber guy really bothered me," she told him. "He spoke about Aryan purity and about how Germany had come so close in the 1940s to cleansing entire populations of Jews, gypsies, handicapped people of all ages, old people — in fact, anyone who dared to stand in the way of the 'great social experiment' of the Third Reich. Then, as if that were not enough, he proceeded to talk with glee about the coming emergence of a 'Viertes Reich,' a Fourth Reich, a Fourth Realm, thanks to financing from networks of families of former Nazis who are pooling their knowledge of hidden Nazi loot."

Adam attempted to change the subject and calm her down. "Agnes, I could barely understand a thing he said. Look, let's not get upset about this and talk instead about something more pleasant. For instance, I sat next to a woman who invited both of us to her home and offered us a special tour of Buenos Aires."

"What woman? Oh, *that* one. Did you like her?"

"Come on, Agnes," he said. "She was just my dinner partner and way too old for me anyway. I didn't pick her. Now, why don't we both get a good night's sleep? Then maybe we'll give her a call tomorrow."

The next morning, they rose later than usual and decided to go to breakfast in the hotel restaurant. The perfect weather invited them to explore the city further. Adam placed a call, with Agnes's consent, to Isolde Rauff, his dinner companion of the night before.

A woman's voice answered on the hotel speakerphone. "Bitte?" The voice had the deep baritone sound of a heavy smoker. Adam was sure it wasn't the woman calling herself Isolde.

"One moment please, I will get Isolde for you." The accented voice spoke good English. Moments later, Adam remembered his dinner companion's lilting tone and recognized it immediately. "Mr. Tinker, this is Isolde. How nice to hear from you! Why don't you come over to our house? It's probably not far from you. And, of course, please bring your wife."

The house was set back off the road. Its gravel driveway led into a circular courtyard. The building's architecture was modernist. Its huge glass windows were embedded in massive concrete walls topped with a sloping roof. The open-plan interior was supported by several sweeping white overhead concrete beams.

A housekeeper answered the door. She led the couple toward a terrace at the rear where there was a long swimming pool, shaded in part by two large mesquite trees. The sparkling blue water danced under the sunlight of a brilliant, clear-blue sky.

Alongside the glistening pool sat Isolde and, presumably, the woman with the baritone voice who had answered the phone. Isolde rose from beneath a huge blue market umbrella to greet her guests and to perform the introductions. "This is my older sister, Monica." She offered the visitors something to eat or drink. "Please, take a seat and be comfortable."

The group spent a few minutes getting acquainted.

Adam remembered his observations from the previous evening. "I sure don't mean to be rude, but I was curious about last night and have several questions."

The two hosts nodded politely and waited for him to continue.

"Well, Agnes and I wondered about all the symbols. There was that one on our invitation which Agnes thought looked like a musical sign known as *dal segno,* or D. S., for short." The two sisters glanced at one another. "Then the number 88 on that spotlighted chair in the meeting room." Adam noticed as he said this that Isolde shifted uncomfortably in her chair. He continued anyway. "And the *Rhombus* sign on the door to the adjoining dining room."

It was Isolde who spoke next. "Yes, well…I already told you about the number 88 and what that stands for. The *dal segno* sign is the club's discreet way of reminding its members to 'go back to the sign.'"

"I told you so, Adam!" said Agnes.

Isolde elaborated. "*That* sign," she emphasized, "is the swastika, commonly known today in the West as the symbol of the German National Socialist Party founded by Hitler. Now, there's nothing inherently wrong with the swastika, as such. After all, it's an ancient symbol of divinity and spirituality in Indian and East Asian religions."

"Now that's something I didn't know," said Adam.

Isolde took a deeper dive on the topic, given Adam's evident limited knowledge. "Did you know that it originated from the Sanskrit word *svastika,* which means 'well-being' — and so it came to mean good luck? It's also a twelve-thousand-year-old symbol of good fortune, prosperity, abundance, and eternity in the Far East among Buddhists. In fact, to this day, you will find it carved on statues of Buddha's feet and on his heart. But once the German Nazi Party adopted it as their symbol in the 1930s, it became associated in the West with racism and stigmatism."

Adam shot a glance at Agnes to see if she, like him, was learning something new, but her expression was an enigma. He turned back to Isolde as she continued her lesson in expatriate German customs in Buenos Aires.

"Now, you also asked about the *Rhombus* title for the club dining room? That represents a four-sided, diamond-like shape. It is supposed to represent the alliance of four groups in a common cause."

"Which groups and what common cause?" Adam decided to persist.

"Well, it's said that the four sides represent first and foremost, the resurgence of the Nazi dream of a Fourth Reich. Second, the Arab hope to restore the Muslim Caliphate. Next, the destruction of Israel. And finally, the extinction of all the world's Jews. But no one is absolutely sure if this is accurate."

It was Monica's turn to speak, in her deep baritone, throaty, cigarette-smoke-coated voice. "You see, most of those people you saw last night are living a fantasy, that one day they will return to a glorious, united Germany, to enjoy its prestige as it rises once again as the world's greatest power. However, these people are powerless. They may seem dangerous and their speakers may seem inflammatory, like that Dr. Weber that Isolde told me about. But, to our knowledge, they are most, if not all, quite harmless."

She paused, lowering her eyes. A silence descended for a few moments on the group.

"However," she continued, "there are dangerous German people living in this country and in others nearby. For example, there's a town in Argentina called San Carlos de Bariloche. It's on a lake about thirteen hundred kilometers, maybe eight hundred miles, from here as the crow flies, but you have to change planes to get there. It's known as Little Switzerland because of its many alpine chalets. Evidence suggests that many Nazis fled there to avoid persecution after World War II. There were even rumors that Hitler and Eva Braun were smuggled by submarine to Argentina and lived near Bariloche into the early 1960s—but there's no conclusive proof! The town is a big tourist attraction these days—which is perfect cover for certain people who want to blend in while they plan conspiracies."

At that point, Isolde interrupted.

"Yes, but if you want to meet more German communities a bit closer to Buenos Aires, there's also the town of Nueva Germania in neighboring Paraguay. It's only a direct two-hour flight from here. You can get a Paraguayan visa at the airport when you arrive. It's quite interesting, if only because there are whole German families there with past associations with the Nazis. Paraguay's time zone puts it one hour ahead of us here, so it would feel like you arrive there at the same time as you left Buenos Aires! Isn't that funny?" She laughed.

Agnes interjected. "This all sounds very interesting," she said, darting a glance at Adam. "But may I ask how each of you feels about the possible emergence of a new Fourth Reich?"

"Let us put our cards on the table," said Isolde. "Would you agree that it is not necessarily right to blame the children for the sins of their fathers? And that children may not necessarily agree with what their fathers or mothers think or do?"

Agnes was surprised at the questions. "Well, yes, I suppose I agree." Adam nodded, wondering what would come next.

"Then what would you say if we told you that our father wasn't only a Nazi but also a leading officer in the *Einsatzgruppen*, the paramilitary death squads responsible for mass killings of civilians—men, women, children, old, or handicapped people from all non-Aryan races—during the war?"

Adam and Agnes sat in stunned silence for a few moments, not daring to look at one another.

"We don't mean to shock you or alarm you," said Monica in her throaty bass voice. "But, in answer to your question about a Fourth Reich, we saw enough as children of the Third Reich never to want to see it or another one ever again."

This comment gave Adam the cue that he needed. He turned to Monica's sister and asked, "On that note, Isolde, I wondered last night why you didn't applaud the speaker, and why you didn't offer a toast to Number 88."

"That's right—and I'm known quite openly for that here in the German émigré community of Buenos Aires. Even though I'm the daughter of 'one of them,' they see me as powerless, and so they ignore me because they think I'm not a threat."

Monica sat up in her chair. "I have an idea. Why don't you two visitors take a short trip to Nueva Germania in Paraguay, as Isolde suggests? Do you have time? We can get you booked to fly there in no time, thanks to friends at our air charter company."

Agnes glanced at Adam as if to say, "Why not?"

The time had sped by, and it was now late morning. The young couple politely took their leave and asked to postpone the proposed special tour of lesser-known Buenos Aires.

Back at the hotel, Adam suggested sending a quick text to Agnes's uncle. "Visit to Nueva Germania suggested by a German woman named Isolde Rauff: Do you know of her? Do you recommend we go or not?"

The reply came back in minutes. "Don't know of anyone named Rauff, but yes, do it."

When Adam called Isolde back, she had already reserved two round-trip airline tickets for the couple to and from Nueva Germania.

Oktober Fest

He was about to confirm his return flight from London Heathrow to New York when Fred Tinker's phone alerted him to an incoming email. Normally he would ignore such alerts, but perhaps this had something to do with the paperwork he had just signed and sent off by courier to Harvey at the post office box address a few hours ago.

The email was from Charles Fortescue.

> Fred, so sorry to have missed you in London. Hope Dick H. took good care of you. I gather you told him you're 'in' on our deal. That's good. But there's one more thing. I wanted to catch you before you return to the States. There's an important meeting in Munich with some key members of the investment group. You need to attend it. Let me know by return email if you can. Yours ever, Charlie.

Fred didn't fail to notice the signature. No "Chad" this time but the more typical "Charlie."

He called Jill back home, this time remembering the need

when in London to dial 001 before the area code and number. "Honey, they want me to go to Munich, like right now. That may mean delaying my return home for a day or two. Is that OK?"

The groan at the end of the phone line indicated that a reluctant "OK, dear!" was coming. "You would pick a time when our generator has gone on the blink! Anyway, don't worry. I'll sort it out," said Jill.

Fred felt a slight relief. He was curious about this investment meeting in Munich. What could it be about? It sounded important.

Minutes later, he replied to Charlie's email with an affirmative, "I'll call my office to make the arrangements."

Next morning, he was on a two-hour Lufthansa flight from London to Munich.

A black Mercedes with tinted windows whisked him efficiently to the Mandarin Oriental Hotel on Neuturmstrasse. When Fred notified Charlie by text of his arrival, his almost instant text reply gave Fred instructions to meet a driver in the hotel lobby at noon. It would be a woman in a gray, two-piece suit.

This time, a different, smaller black Mercedes picked him up. "Where are we going, please?" Fred asked.

"To Pullach, Mein Herr. It's about thirty minutes from here." Even though her flawless English sounded British, the next thirty-minutes passed in silence.

The saloon car pulled up at an anonymous-looking concrete

building that was part of a large new business complex. A sign at the entrance read simply BND. Fred had a vague recollection of seeing those initials before. He entered the lobby and announced himself at the reception desk, behind which seemed to be a solid concrete wall. He could not fail to miss the two military men in combat fatigues standing at ease on either side of the desk. Each carried at the ready a Heckler & Koch MP7 compact submachine gun. He began to feel uncomfortable.

"Where the hell am I?" he whispered to himself under his breath.

Moments later, a thick concrete door slid open in the wall to his left. A voice called out "Welcome, Herr Tinker. Please come this way and follow me." A tall blond and blue-eyed young man emerged wearing a well-cut, two-piece, dark-navy suit. He beckoned Fred toward a doorway and escorted him down a long, narrow hallway to a small meeting room.

Inside, a single sheet of paper and a pen lay on a round table. "Please kindly read this document," said the anonymous greeter. "If it is acceptable, then please sign it. There is a buzzer on the table. Please press it when you're ready."

Feeling somewhat dazed, Fred sat down and began to skim the paperwork. It was in English.

Dear Mr. Tinker,

You are at the Munich office of the BND, the Federal Intelligence Service of the Federal Republic of Germany. Your signature below will mean as follows:

> 1. You will forget the address of this building and the names and descriptions of everyone you meet here on your visit.
>
> 2. You agree not to divulge to anyone any material or information whatsoever that you obtain while on this visit or any others.
>
> 3. You understand that this is an unofficial visit by you to an unofficial meeting which the record will show never took place.
>
> 4. You understand that the Federal Republic of Germany offers you no guarantees whatsoever, including guarantees for your personal safety and that of your immediate family.
>
> 5. You agree that you are giving your full consent below to the above by signing this document.

If satisfied with the terms above, please sign and date this document below.

However, if you do not wish to proceed, then please alert our representative accordingly who greeted you on arrival. He will then arrange for your prompt return to your hotel.

It was clear to Fred that he had already passed the point of no return. He took a deep breath, signed the paper, and pressed the buzzer.

The tall blond greeter reappeared. Glancing quickly at the signature on the sheet, he swept it up, smiled, and once again directed Fred to follow him.

They returned to the corridor and continued further along until they reached a steel door. The tall greeter bent forward and positioned his left eye in front of an optical scanner. He then entered some numbers on a coded panel. He placed a finger on a pad which beeped cheerfully in recognition. There was a loud *click*. The heavy steel door swung open. The two men proceeded down another but narrower corridor whose only features were a series of other steel doors, each protected by a trio of security features like the ones at the entrance.

One such door opened into a medium-sized, oakwood-paneled room. Two men in suits rose to greet the visitor.

There was no sign of Charlie Fortescue.

The tall greeter discreetly withdrew, closing the room's steel door behind him.

The shorter of the two men spoke first. His thickset, muscular build suggested barely concealed physical power. His face was lined and leathery, as if he had been hardened by rigorous military training. There was something that Fred found vaguely menacing about his manner. His eyes were a pale cold blue. His German accent was pronounced.

"Herr Tinker, I'm Ludwig Farben, the Deputy Director of Operations for Europe, the Middle East, and Latin America.

My colleague here is Herr Doktor Thiel from our headquarters in Berlin. Please, sit down. Would you like some coffee or tea?"

"Thanks, I'll just take a glass of water." Fred's mouth was starting to feel dry.

Before he could say anything more, the man called Farben reached for a bright-red folder with black edging, marked *Streng Geheim*. Fred's German was still fair despite its minimal use since his youth: he recognized the words *Top Secret* on the cover.

Farben spoke first. His manner was friendly enough but businesslike. "Herr Tinker, we appreciate your willingness to meet with us. Thank you for your signature on our document. You must be wondering, quite naturally why you're here?"

Fred nodded. "Well, that's right...but also, I was expecting to meet someone in Germany today who I know personally."

"Ah, perhaps you mean Mr. Fortescue?" This time, the man called Dr. Thiel spoke. The "Herr Doktor from Berlin" was tall, gray-haired, and might easily have been mistaken for an academic. He too possessed a pair of pale blue eyes, peering from behind a wire-rimmed pair of eyeglasses. Though he spoke with a soft voice, there was an undeniable intensity about the man.

Fred took an instant dislike to them both.

"Yeah, now that you mention it," said Fred as casually as he could. "He asked me to come to Munich for a business meeting."

"Quite so," said Thiel, whose English was impeccable. "You see, Mr. Fortescue had planned to join us here today. Unfortunately, his travel plans changed quite suddenly, and so he was unable to join us. I'm so sorry."

Farben picked up the conversation at this point. "Herr Tinker, we're working very closely with Mr. Fortescue with whom we have a long-standing relationship. The nature of our work is highly sensitive. In fact, no one else in this building — except Gunther, the young fellow who brought you to this room — is aware of our project or why you're here with us."

"I don't understand," replied Fred, looking baffled. He was feeling more and more uneasy and it was beginning to show.

But Farber appeared not to notice and kept talking. "Naturally, you expected your old friend Chad to be here with us. As we said, he would have been with us but for urgent business in another geography."

When Fred heard the word *Chad*, he felt his muscles stiffen. Something felt not quite right. But his instinct told him not to challenge the speaker's choice of nickname.

Farben added, "We have to very careful, Herr Tinker. Even here in the BND, there are many different factions. Some are Social Democrats. Some are supporters of both the extreme left and right. That's why we're meeting here under high security."

"Well, gentlemen, perhaps you could come to the point." Fred was beginning to feel trapped and ready to leave.

Thiel spoke this time and Fred thought he felt growing tension in the room. "We may have some things to share with you, Herr Tinker. In exchange, we also have a few questions for you, if you don't mind. So, as you say, to come to the point, we understand you are aware that several parties are presently engaged in locating valuable property, much of which has been carefully hidden—some of it in Germany and Austria, and some in other countries around the world. We're working with the rightful owners of this property to help recover it. That's the story, how do you say, 'in a nutshell.'"

"What does that have to do with me?" asked Fred innocently.

"We also understand that you're interested in becoming a member of a consortium interested in locating at least some of this hidden cache. Is that not so?"

"I don't discuss my personal business affairs with third parties. But I can tell you that Mr. Fortescue told me to come here promptly for a meeting in Munich to hear about a private investment opportunity. That's why I assumed he would be here now with us."

"So, he gave you no details of the meeting or even who would be here?" This time, it was Farben popping the question.

"Nope. I'm completely in the dark on those details." Something told Fred he had said enough.

Farben and Theil exchanged glances.

"Ah, well, Herr Tinker," said Thiel. "It seems that we brought you here for nothing after all. Now that you're unable to meet with Chad and his people, perhaps you will now have a little time to take advantage of our Oktober Festival, here in Munich?"

Fred felt it was time to leave. "Gentlemen, thank you for your time and for that suggestion. I think I should be getting back to my hotel."

"But of course." Farben pressed a buzzer.

The three men shook hands. Gunther entered. He escorted Fred back to the reception desk where the woman in the gray, two-piece suit was waiting. She led him to the car and drove him back to the hotel. Neither driver nor passenger uttered a word until Fred arrived and thanked her. She nodded and drove off.

On entering his hotel room, he noticed the telephone message light blinking.

A familiar voice, though barely audible and sounding far away, had left him a message. "Fred. It's me. Be at the Augustine-Keller tonight at nine o'clock. My friend Kurt will meet you there. He knows how to find you. This is most important."

The voice was unmistakably that of Charles Fortescue.

"The concierge booked a table for two at the restaurant. It's well-known for its authentic Bavarian dishes," he told Fred.

The Augustine-Keller was a ten-minute cab ride from the hotel. Its beer garden was full of people of all ages, merrily downing huge steins of light-colored, frothy beer. Fred got to his table just before nine o'clock.

A few minutes later, a nondescript man approached, wobbling slightly as if he had already drunk too much. As he reached Fred's table, he dropped a small white calling card on the ground at Fred's feet, then stooped to pick it up. He then looked up, stared at Fred, and placed the card on the table. Fred glanced at the card and recognized it instantly as Charles Fortescue's calling card.

Before he could say a word, the stranger said softly in English, "Sir, I think this card may be for you. I'm Kurt. May I join you?"

The man with the wobbly walk seemed suddenly to have sobered up. He looked quickly around him, then continued to speak.

"Charles needs to know who met with you today at the BND. He also advises you to take the first flight possible back to New York. He needed to take a long trip on short notice and sends you his apologies."

Fred had to decide rapidly whether he could trust this stranger named Kurt. "I met two people today, one called Farben and the other called Thiel. That's all I can tell you."

"Herr Tinker, you have no idea how helpful that information is. I know Mr. Fortescue will value it very much." To Fred's surprise, his table companion stood up almost as soon as he had sat down, picked up his stein of beer, and shuffled away while resuming the wobbly walk that had first caught Fred's attention.

Nueva Germania

The local guide sounded bored. "There is little to see now and even less to learn from the aging German community here in Nueva Germania," she said. "A relative of the German philosopher Nietzsche founded this community in the late 19th century. He planned to create a new utopian Germany in South America, free of all racial impurity. But the harsh life and later intermarriage with the country's natives led to his suicide. He was later to be described by Hitler as the father of Nazism."

Adam and Agnes had hired Hilde Bauer as their local guide. The Paraguayan policeman who issued their short-term visas at Nueva Germania's tiny airport had recommended her.

She continued her lament. "There are fewer and fewer visitors these days, considering what had started over a century ago as a vibrant new home for German immigrants. When Bernhard Förster and his wife, Elisabeth, the sister of the philosopher Friedrich Nietzsche, first came here in the 1880s, they had an ambitious plan: nothing less than the establishment of a colony from which an advanced contingent of Aryans could forge a claim to the entire South

American continent. But within two years, Förster not only gave up in despair but committed suicide. Meanwhile, his wife Elisabeth returned to Germany. There, in contrast to her brother Friedrich, the philosopher, she supported the Nazi party and was a famous anti-Semite until she died, in the 1930s."

Agnes asked about the remaining descendants of "Germans who arrived in Nueva Germania in the mid-1940s." She hoped that her coded language would suggest mere curiosity and not put the guide on the defensive.

"Well, a few remain. You will see the occasional grandchildren around, distinguished by their blond hair and blue eyes. If you're staying overnight, perhaps you would like to join in a German celebration here tonight in the Volksplatz Meeting House. It's a birthday party. There will be a group of German descendants there. Why don't you come?" The invitation was accepted.

Frau Bauer was right. Sure enough, there were several families present at the party that evening. It was obvious that the original "pure" Germans had long ago married local girls. There were a few heavy, older blond women and a handful of small, fair-skinned, blue-eyed boys and girls running about.

Agnes decided to talk with some of the children. She picked two, a boy and a girl who spoke good German. Agnes caught the eye of the little girl. "Hello," she said. "Are you two related?"

The little girl quickly replied with a toothy smile. "Yes, Hugo here is my brother. I'm Anna. I'm six years old. Where are you from?"

"I'm visiting from Hungary," said Agnes.

The girl frowned and looked puzzled. "Where's that?" she asked.

"It's in eastern Europe, a long way from here."

"Hugo and I only know Nueva Germania. We always lived here, with my grandmother."

"Oh really? What about your mother and father?"

"They went to heaven."

Something about this remark grabbed Agnes's attention. "What happened?" she asked sweetly.

"They went away when I was born," said little Anna, in a monotone.

Agnes decided to probe. "Why do you think they went away?"

"Because some men came and wanted some papers that were secret. Our grandmother says the men took our mother and father away," said the boy called Hugo.

Agnes thought for a moment. "So, what did your parents do with the papers?"

"They gave them to Grandma before the men came to take them. She hid the papers in our house," said Hugo in a matter-of-fact voice.

Agnes decided to pursue her line of questions further. "Does your grandma still have those papers?"

"Yes. I have seen them. But I don't know what they are," said the boy Hugo.

"Are they newspapers?" Agnes asked.

"No," said Anna. "Grandma says they are things called maps."

Agnes curiosity was piqued. She probed again. "Maps? Maps of what?"

Anna's face lit up, and she gave a broad smile. "Grandma says secret treasure. All over the world!"

Agnes felt a chill in her spine. She had to ask the next question. "Can I meet your grandma?"

Anna was enthusiastic. "Yes. She is at home now. She does not like to be here with the others. She stays up late at night and reads books. You can come now. It's not far."

Agnes looked around for Adam. He was talking to a small group of men. She decided to slip away for a short while. There was something her instinct told her about the child's mention of maps that she needed to know.

The little girl was right. She took Agnes's hand and led her out the hall. A ten-minute walk brought them to a drab, single-story, chalet-style house, accessed from the street by a small, white wooden gate. The garden was small, overgrown, and clearly neglected. The girl Anna tugged at Agnes's hand and led her into the house.

An elderly woman rose to greet them. It was apparent from

her slow movements that she had limited mobility. Her t-shirt was worn and dirty. Her blue pants were wrinkled. She had on a well-worn pair of cheap sandals.

"Ich bin Eva," said the disheveled woman with a gap-toothed smile. "I'm Eva."

She offered the visitor a glass of *tereré*, a tea-like infusion drunk cold through a straw called a *bombilla*.

"What brings you here, fräulein?"

"Well, I'm just visiting Paraguay briefly. I'm on my honeymoon. Someone told me that I must visit this special community. It's one of kind, they told me."

They talked for a while—and for longer than Agnes had planned. Then little Anna piped up.

"Grandma, I told this lady about the secret papers. She would like to see them."

"Oh, those! It's been so long since I put them away. In any case, they mean nothing to me now."

Agnes felt this was a good moment to ask, "Could I see them?"

The grandmother gazed intently at Agnes, then slowly rose from her white plastic chair and shuffled off into an adjacent room. When she returned, there was a large worn plastic bag in her arms.

"They are just maps of places I have never seen, in countries like Argentina, Bolivia, Germany, Austria..." The grandmother's voice trailed off. "I have no need for any of them now and they are taking up space I need. Do you want to take them?"

"I'd be glad to!" Agnes felt her heart beating faster. "I should be going as I'm sure my husband is looking for me." She politely took her leave, thanked Anna, and then returned to the Meeting House, with the maps tucked under her arms and a feeling of great excitement.

The birthday party was winding down, even though the accordionist was still playing what sounded to Agnes's ears like rustic German songs. She looked around for Adam.

He was nowhere to be seen.

An Unofficial Visit

There was something fishy about his trip to Germany, thought Fred. Why had Charlie not shown up? Who were these people from the BND, and what were they after? And why would a stranger called Kurt want to know their names, and then counsel Fred to return promptly to New York? Nothing made sense. It seemed as if his entire trip had been a waste of time.

Above all, why was Charlie playing all these games? It was so out of character. Why would he lead someone on and then not appear as expected?

It was pointless to remain in Munich. Fred booked the first direct flight out and arrived tired and grumpy the next day at JFK. He took the next available flight to Montego Island.

Jill had good news. The generator vendor had come and installed a more modern replacement that would be more efficient than their old one. "It just died of old age!" she exclaimed.

Eve was still wearing that ring in her nose. Everything seemed orderly as before. Jill had been painting away and eagerly showed off her latest work to her husband.

"Not bad, honey! You are getting better and better. I could never figure how you mixed all those oil paints to get *amazing* results like that! Maybe you should have a show somewhere?"

Fred soon resumed his daily rhythm of scouring the financial press for tips. But a nagging feeling remained in his mind that something was amiss.

One morning a few days after his return from Germany, while Jill was out running errands and Eve was already at school, there was a knock at the front door. Fred saw two men he didn't recognize standing at the stoop. They both wore dark suits. Their briefcases gave them a professional-looking appearance.

"Can I help you, gentlemen?" Fred asked prudently from behind the closed door.

"Mr. Tinker?" a voice asked. "May we have a few moments of your time? We're here on government business and have something important to share with you."

Jeepers! thought Fred. *Could it be the IRS? But why? The outside accountants had checked all the company books and told us everything was squeaky clean.*

Fred hesitated. "What is this about, please?"

"Sir, we don't have much time and we don't mean to waste yours. We're with the State Department. We have news about your son."

Fred's mind was now racing, in a different direction. *Adam? Why would the State Department have news about him? Had*

94

something bad happened to the boy? Better let them in. He ushered the two visitors into the living room and pointed them to the couch.

The older looking one of the two spoke. "Mr. Tinker, my name is Field. My colleague here is Jones." The other man was looking around the room. Fred started to feel nervous.

Field continued. "Mr. Tinker, we believe your son is in Argentina."

"*Argentina*? But…I thought he was in Hungary, doing some part-time work?" The news stunned Fred.

"Yes, he was, sir," said Field. "But we think he is now somewhere in Buenos Aires. We were hoping you might know where."

"Not a clue," said Fred. His prompt reply and tone of voice must have told them he was telling the truth.

It was Jones's turn to speak. "Hmm. Well then, we don't need to waste another moment of your time, sir."

Fred blurted out "Wait a minute. What's this all about? Why is the State Department interested in my son?"

Before he replied, Field glanced at Jones as if to say, "Let me do the talking now," then spoke: "We have reason to believe he now has in his possession or may acquire some sensitive information that is vital to the United States government. We want to find Adam. He may be in danger."

Fred was thinking, *Thank goodness Jill isn't here! She'd go crazy hearing all this!*

Jones, the younger man, now spoke again. "Here's my card, sir. Please call my number as soon as you get word from your son about his location. We can then arrange to pick him up and get him out of any possible danger."

The two got up and took their leave.

Fred's mind was churning again. First, the Munich mess. Now this. *And why on earth would Adam be in Argentina when he was supposed to be in Hungary?* What was the name of that professor he was working for? Somebody called Lantos? *Better give him a call.*

The office person at Columbia University was unhelpful at first. "So sorry, Mr. Tinker. Professor Lantos is away in Hungary and won't be back on campus until the next semester." At last, evidently convinced that Fred's request was legitimate, she reluctantly provided the professor's email address.

Fred put down the receiver and promptly emailed Lantos, demanding to know what was going on with Adam.

Two days passed without a reply from Lantos. Fred's anxiety was rising, but he dared not mention anything to Jill. She meanwhile noticed he was irritable and snapped at her for no apparent reason. She decided to hold her tongue, at least for now.

Wazir

It surprised and relieved Adam to find some English-speakers among the younger men at the Volksplatz Meeting Hall. They were as curious about him as an American as he was about them as descendants of 19th-century German settlers here in Nueva Germania.

He had not noticed Agnes leaving with the little blond girl. Instead, he found himself telling his new audience about the wonders of New York City. He learned fast enough that there were few jobs and prospects in Nueva Germania and that most young people there dreamed of going to North America.

While he spoke, Adam noticed an older man who joined the group. He looked out of place, dressed in narrow jeans and an open-necked white shirt as if he had come from some civilized country to this decaying backwater. The man chose his moment, waiting patiently for Adam's audience of local residents to tire of his tales and move on.

To Adam's surprise, the man spoke perfect English as he introduced himself. "Hello. I'm Charles. Charles Fortescue. Pleasure to meet you, sir."

"Hi, I'm Adam Tinker."

"Ah, yes," said the stranger. "Are you just visiting here?"

Some small talk followed. Then Fortescue dropped a hint. "Funny thing. I used to know a Fred Tinker who ran or maybe still runs a hedge fund in New York."

Adam expressed surprise. "Wow! Now that's a coincidence. What a small world! He's my dad!"

"Really?" said Fortescue.

Adam was intrigued. He asked, "Yes. How do you know him?"

Fortescue paused, scratched his ear and simply said, "We've been business partners over the years."

Adam's face broke into smile. "Now, that's something! So, what brings you to Nueva Germania? I mean, there doesn't seem to be much going on around here."

Fortescue paused to pick his words carefully. "Oh, just some soil tests for minerals excavation and things like that."

They chatted briefly and Fortescue shared some of his knowledge of the area. "A descendant of Bavarian farmers called Alfred Stroessner ruled Paraguay some years ago. You may be too young to remember, but he was one of the people who gave refuge to many Nazis at the end of World War II. Same thing, in Argentina with Juan Peron. There are still some elderly Nazis around, along with their descendants."

After a few more minutes talking, Fortescue looked at his

watch and said "Anyway, I must be going. Got to get back to Argentina tonight to catch an early flight back to Heathrow tomorrow. Glad to have met you."

Adam looked around. He was starting to feel tired. The trip from Buenos Aires had sapped his energy. He was ready for bed.

As he turned to leave, he glanced around the hall. No sign of Agnes, but as he did so, he felt a light tap on his shoulder and swung around. To his astonishment, there was Bitar, his former Columbia professor.

Adam was clearly stunned. "Man, what are you doing here, of all places? We thought you took a plane somewhere the other day. This is so weird! You're the second person I've run into here who knows either me or my dad."

Bitar mumbled. "Yes, well, I've been doing some research for my project here in Paraguay. I flew to the capital, Asuncion, the other day to meet some friends. They suggested I visit Nueva Germania."

Adam sensed this was a small part of why Bitar turned up so unexpectedly. "But what's here that could possibly have anything to do with the Middle East? And I don't mind saying you were secretive when you mysteriously 'dropped by' out of the blue at our hotel room in Buenos Aires. In fact, how did you even know we were there, or was it just a coincidence that you showed up as the same hotel as ours?" Adam was at a loss for more words.

"You've asked a lot of questions. Where can I begin? Do you have time to talk now?"

"I'm about ready for bed, but anyway, fire away. Let's go somewhere where we can talk in private for a bit."

They found a small, almost deserted bar nearby. Bitar began his explanation. "You know that I'm originally from Egypt, right? My father is Egyptian, but my mother is Israeli. You may not have known that. I don't broadcast it. But I got my education in Israel, thanks to a momentary period of cooperation with Egypt. I then got a job in research when I graduated from Tel Aviv University. That's how I became a student of the Middle East. I became an employee of the Israeli government and have been one since. Let's just say that my mission here is to research some exploration projects in the area."

"That's interesting. I was just talking with an English guy who also said something about an exploration project."

Bitar's eyes stared at Adam. "Did he introduce himself, perhaps, as Charles Fortescue?"

"Why, yes he did!" said Adam innocently.

Bitar collected himself and remarked "Remember what I told you in Buenos Aires? About not appearing to recognize me, and putting us in danger? Well, this guy Fortescue is not just the businessman he appears to be. He too is a government agent, except he works for the British government."

"What are you saying? He's a spy?"

"In short, yes. Just like me. He and I are after the same thing."

"And that is…?" said Adam.

It was Bitar who now chose to pick his words carefully. "Information, about stolen property that Israel wants to find. Let me spell it out. You may know that the retreating Germans hid a vast amount of property stolen from the people they sent to the concentration camps. It's hidden in many countries and in many locations—under mountains, in various train tunnels, and in the basement warrens of several castles in Austria, Germany and elsewhere. They often dynamited the entrances to make it hard for anyone else to access the hidden loot. We think that one of the worst Nazis, Klaus Heilmann, created a series of maps for the left-behind Nazi troops, the so-called *Werewolves*, who would go into hiding and await orders to rise up and fight another war, this time to win it and launch a Fourth Reich."

"I don't get it," said Adam as he struggled to piece a jigsaw together in his mind.

"Look," said Bitar," many governments want to know where this stolen property is located. This includes the British, the Americans, the Germans, and the Israelis. Most of the wealth in question came from the Jewish communities of central and western Europe, as the Nazis embarked on their murderous quest to annihilate Jews everywhere. That's why it's so important for me, as an Israeli citizen, to find this information. Remember: the Germans pilfered over three billion dollars of personal and public property. The most that Jewish concerns ever recovered, at least in name, was a tiny twenty-five million settlement in 2012, through a class action suit and a court settlement in New York."

Adam saw a movement out of the corner of his eye. It was Agnes walking past the bar window.

"Excuse me, Professor, but I have to let my wife know that I'm here."

"Ah yes. I remember. The newlyweds, right?" Bitar smiled. Adam rolled his eyes, realizing that Agnes' reappearance now deprived him of asking Bitar why he seemed to know so much about him and Agnes.

He darted through the bar's front door and called out. "Agnes! Over here! You remember Professor Bitar? Well, he's here too! I'll tell you more later, but I'm dead tired! So let's go get some sleep. Good night, Professor. I can't imagine our paths won't cross again!"

Back in the hotel room Agnes revealed the contents of her plastic bag. They were a bunch of maps, stained and yellowed with age, but still clearly legible.

"Just look at this stuff!" Agnes exclaimed in amazement. She rattled off a long list of countries, castles, hidden train tunnels, and even basements of private homes containing looted valuables. The volume of data was staggering. There were detailed inventories of gold and silver jewelry, diamonds, pearls, priceless oriental rugs, and lists of paintings by old masters. Each map bore a swastika sign, a signature that appeared to read 'K.Heilmann,' and the date of December 1944.

Adam asked the obvious question. "What do you think we should do with all this? I mean, it seems that the British and the Israelis among others are very anxious to get their hands on this material."

"Adam, I'm not sure," she replied. "The only one I can trust here is my uncle Tibor, and maybe you." She looked sternly at Adam, then smiled. "OK, I think I trust you!"

Adam thought for a moment. He looked her straight in the eye and said, "We have to get away from here. I sense that something is heating up and that we don't need to be part of it. I suggest we get back to Buenos Aires tomorrow and then catch a plane back to Hungary."

The next morning, they packed and ate a light breakfast. A decrepit cab took them to the Nueva Germania regional airport.

As they landed in Buenos Aires, Adam checked his email. There was a message from Tibor Lantos. "Call me as soon as possible. Most important. It's about Wazir."

The Anselmo Hotel switchboard helped them place the call to Lantos, moments after they returned to their suite.

Agnes cried out in an excited voice, "Uncle Tibor! It's so good to hear your voice! We're just back from Nueva Germania. We found something special there."

Tibor interrupted. "Agnes, you aren't on a secure line. Whatever you found can await your return. But I must ask one thing. Did you encounter any Arab on your trip, anyone at all?"

"No, not really. I mean, we ran into Professor Bitar a couple of times. Once here at the hotel and then in Nueva Germania. That seemed a bit odd."

There was a pause.

"Remember the research you did for me," said Lantos, "about internet messages proclaiming *jihad* and talking about funding it from gold stolen from Hungarian Jews? The byline for the article was Wazir."

"Yes, of course."

"I have reason to believe Wazir and Professor Bitar are one and the same. I think you need to return to Budapest as soon as you can."

The line went dead.

Parental Paranoia

Neither Fred nor Adam were accustomed to communicating with one another by email or text message. It had to be either face-to-face or by telephone. As Fred had no other idea how to reach his son, his only option was email.

Jill, by contrast, was a recent convert from a flip phone to a smartphone. She delighted in emailing and texting everyone she could. Someone had shown her lately how to create a Favorites List so that all she had to do was touch a name on her smartphone and, presto, the number would ring.

Fred called out from the upstairs bedroom. "Honey, do you have Adam's email address? I don't seem to have it. And I misplaced his mobile phone number."

What he didn't tell his wife was that he had inadvertently deleted all of Adam's contact data from his own phone a week earlier. He was kicking himself for doing so, now that he had an emergency on his hands.

Jill, her sixth sense rising to the occasion, wondered out loud why her husband would suddenly want to email or text their son. Fred mumbled something almost incoherent about needing Adam's contact data for a business matter.

Descending the staircase and then closing the door of his study behind him, he decided to dial his son's mobile number, only to hear a voice mail greeting. The sound of Adam's voice gave him some reassurance that his son's phone was still working and that he would eventually pick up any email message. He snapped "Adam! This is your father. Call me please as soon as you get this message."

As he feared, Jill was hovering at the study door, seemingly arranging flowers in a vase. "Did you reach him?" she asked nervously.

Fred swallowed, rolled his eyes upward, and said, "I left him a message to call me."

But Jill wasn't satisfied. She asked, "Is everything all right?"

Fred, trying to sound confident, replied "Sure. As far as I know, everything's fine."

"Fred, level with me," said Jill. "Tell me what's going on. The neighbors are talking about two men in suits who came to the door this morning while I was out doing errands."

Fred was cornered, and his cover was blown. He declared, "Honey, there's nothing to be concerned about."

Years of marriage had primed Jill on her spouse's habits. She always knew when he was withholding something from her, he would predictably call her "Honey" whenever there was bad news to come.

"Something bad has happened to Adam, hasn't it? I know

it!" she stated baldly, her voice rising.

"Did I say that?" parried Fred, hoping that Jill would back off.

"Tell me who those men were today!" she demanded.

Fred's defenses were crumbling. He knew Jill would not let go until she extracted the truth from him.

He gave it to her, but in small bites. "They said they were from the State Department," he said, with a matter-of-fact tone that suggested that the unexpected visit from a government agency was quite normal.

"The *State Department*?" cried his wife.

"That's what I said. They told me Adam was in Buenos Aires."

"Oh my God! *Buenos Aires*! And we thought he was in *Hungary*!" shrieked Jill.

Fred knew he had to try to calm her down. "Jill, don't get upset. All they wanted was for me to let them know where Adam was—when he calls."

"What do you mean, 'when he calls'? There's something you're not telling me!"

"I've told you everything I know."

"No, you haven't! You've barely spoken to me since you got back from Munich. Was that a productive trip?"

Fred filled her in, carefully omitting any mention of his visit to the BND building and his mystery meeting in the beer garden with a stranger named Kurt.

Jill seemed satisfied and appeared ready to relent when the phone rang.

An unfamiliar voice spoke as she picked up the receiver. It wasn't at all reassuring.

"Mrs. Tinker, your son is in immediate danger. We aim to find him, very soon. He has in his possession something that does not belong to him. Tell him to give it to us. Otherwise, we cannot guarantee his safety—or yours."

The color drained from her face. She stood frozen for a moment as the message sank in. Fred watched helplessly as she lifted her head, rolled her eyes upward, and collapsed on the floor in a fainting fit.

As she came around, she mumbled, "Where am I? What happened?"

Fred told her, "You fainted, honey. Who was that on the phone?"

"It…it was some man's voice," she said." I don't know who. He was threatening Adam and us too if Adam didn't give him something. Yes, that's it. He just said 'something.' He didn't say what."

"I'd better call the police to report this." Fred reached for the phone.

"Police emergency line. Please state your name and telephone number." It was a woman's voice. "Your address, please?"

Fred waited, his heart rate rising.

"We'll send someone right over."

A squad car and two local police arrived minutes later. Both looked young enough to be schoolkids dressed as cops at a high school costume party. One was a young woman, evidently the senior of the two.

After lengthy preliminaries about names, addresses, telephone numbers, dates of birth, and other tedious questions, the young woman asked what had happened. Jill responded with the message word for word, as best she could remember it. Fred explained that Jill had fainted after the caller hung up.

The young woman cop tried to sound helpful. "If you need medical attention, we can call an ambulance. Did you hit anything, like your head, when you fell? Do you think you broke anything?"

"No," said Jill," I think I'm all right. Just a bit shaken up. But I'm worried that our son is in danger, and we can't seem to reach him."

The younger cop piped up. "We have our notes, ma'am. Give us a call if you get any more calls like this. Before we go, can we see your phone? Let's see if we can trace the caller's phone number."

The young cop examined her smartphone. "Did you make any calls after that unwanted call came in?" he asked.

"Only to the police emergency line," said Fred.

"Gee," replied the girl cop. "Well, let's try dialing star sixty-nine for the last incoming call."

A recorded voice uttered words no one wanted to hear. "We're sorry. Your last incoming call was from an unlisted number."

Bad Press

The "honeymooners" decided to stay in and order room service for dinner on the day of their return to Buenos Aires from Nueva Germania. Both were exhausted. Both shared the same concern about Tibor's message. Was Professor Bitar really the very same person as Wazir, the terrorist peddling violence and mayhem against the West on the web who Agnes had discovered in her research?

"If so, then he already knows where we're staying," she said, her voice quavering. "Adam, I think we ought to switch hotels. I don't have a good feeling about staying here after what Tibor just told us."

Agnes, whose Spanish was only a little better than Adam's, placed some calls. The Palacio Duahu Hyatt Hotel in the Avenida Alvear offered a special rate and promised the newlyweds a two-bedroom penthouse with a staggering view toward the waterfront. She gave a credit card number to guarantee the room. It would be available next day after three.

After dinner, they turned on the television and tuned in to

CNN. A newscaster was delivering the daily diet of fires, murders, crooks going to jail, and some political commentary from the White House. Adam was about to change channels when he heard this report.

"Our correspondent in Buenos Aires reports that a Columbia University professor was the victim of a hit-and-run driver in the capital earlier today. The victim's name is Professor Yussef Bitar, a specialist in Middle Eastern studies. He is said to be in stable condition at an unnamed hospital."

Before he could say a word, Agnes put a finger to her lips to signal for silence. The next item on the news hit her like a blow.

"Our reporter in central Paraguay learned today of the grisly murder of an elderly woman in the community known as Nueva Germania. The name of the victim was Eva Heilmann, said to be the illegitimate daughter of the infamous Nazi, Klaus Heilmann. There have been no arrests so far. The motive for the murder is a mystery. Nueva Germania is a former colony of German immigrants founded by anti-Semites in the later 1800s to launch a new German utopia of pure Aryans in Latin America."

Agnes was almost certain that the murdered woman had to be the same grandmother who had given her the bag full of maps, literally just the night before.

"Look, Adam, let's get out of here tonight!" she cried, clearly scared out of her wits. "I'll call the Hyatt hotel and see if they can get us in tonight. I think it's time to leave Buenos Aires, as early as tomorrow evening. I'll also check the flights to Budapest with the airline. I'd better do it directly, too, and

112

not through the concierge, just in case."

They were in luck. The Hyatt fitted them in, but only to a two-bedroom suite. Agnes cancelled the penthouse suite booking, with regret. The airline called back and confirmed them on a flight to Budapest the next evening.

They called for a taxi. There was only one waiting in the hotel's taxi rank. Once their luggage was on board, they promptly entered the cab.

As they did so, a large black Audi screeched into the courtyard and braked hard to a halt. Three large men jumped out and raced into the lobby.

By the time they figured that their two quarries had left, the couple's cab was already well on its way to the Avenida Alvear.

Hungarian Rhapsody

Tibor Lantos took his time to reply to Fred Tinker. It was important to know for a fact that both Agnes and Adam were on their way back to Budapest. A text message from Adam gave him the assurance he needed.

Lantos suggested by email that Fred call him on his mobile phone. The call came in almost immediately.

"Professor Lantos? This is Fred Tinker, the father of Adam Tinker, who I gather has been working for you?" The voice sounded agitated.

"That's right, Mr. Tinker," Lantos replied calmly. "Your son has been doing some fine research for me. And I'm happy to report that he is in the air on his way back here to Budapest."

But that wasn't good enough for Adam's father. "Then what the hell has been going on? People tell me my son was in Buenos Aires, of all places. Did you send him there?"

Lantos's voice remained calm and reassuring. "Adam was helping me and my niece with my research. I suggested that he visit Argentina to gather some materials. That's about it."

Fred remained on the warpath. "Do you know, sir, that I've
114

had people from our State Department here making inquiries about my son, and telling us he's in danger? Do you also know that my wife recently got a threatening phone call that also seems to have something to do with my son?"

"How could I?" said Lantos plaintively. "I've hardly been in contact with Adam since he left. But I'm sure he'll call you the moment he is back. I will see to it personally."

The calm academic's voice seemed to mollify Fred. "Well, tell him his mother is all upset and wants to hear his voice. I'm so confused now I can't figure what's happening!" He hung up abruptly.

Breathing a sigh of relief as he replaced the receiver, Lantos began to settle down for the evening. He had earlier gone out to dinner and had then walked home to his house in Szentendre. There were few pedestrians about that evening. It was midweek and quiet, unlike the weekends when tourists would flood the town looking for artwork for which the place was famous.

However, he had barely noticed a black sedan parked a few hundred yards from his front door.

Lantos loved music and had built a diverse collection of classical and jazz pieces. He scanned his CD collection and selected Liszt's Hungarian Rhapsody Number Two to accompany a small glass of Furmint, a dry wine from the Tokaj region of northeastern Hungary. He could almost taste the red-and-brown clay of the region, with its delicious hint of lime.

There were school papers to read and edit. There was a new

novel he had started to read. He thought to work a little, read a little, and then turn in for the night.

He was marking up a student's paper when thought he heard a sound. He thought to himself. *Might it be glass breaking? Why worry, anyway. There are no break-ins or burglaries in Szentendre.* He returned to his student's paper.

Out of the corner of his eye, he caught a slight movement in the doorway to his living room. He turned slowly, to see the silhouette of a tall, masked male facing him. He was about to say something when there was a short hiss.

The bullet struck Lantos's forehead. He fell motionless to the ground.

The shooter slowly replaced his weapon into his jacket pocket and slipped out, almost as silently as he had entered.

Return of a Prodigal Son

Adam knew to call his parents the moment he and Agnes were through the Immigration and Customs process at Budapest's Ferenc Liszt International Airport and before they set out from there to see Lantos at his home in Szentendre.

He heard and felt the enormous relief in his father's and mother's voices.

"How *could* you!" Jill vented at her son, then told him about the threatening phone call. "We think you had better get on the next plane and come back home." Neither Jill nor Fred was going to give an inch.

Adam's protests fell flat. "But, Dad, I need to finish my research project here. It will only take a few more days."

Fred bellowed, "I don't care! You take the next plane to New York, or you will forfeit every dime I gave you for this 'research trip' of yours. You hear me? Your mother and I have been worried stiff about you. We even had the State Department here trying to find you."

"Why me? What do they want from me?" said Adam.

"They didn't say. But I'll call them to say you will be back in day or two. Now get back here fast and before you get all of us into serious trouble." The call ended, as expected, abruptly.

The young couple hurried through the Arrivals terminal and took a taxi to Szentendre. It was getting late, and it had been a long flight. They would get a light snack at Lantos's house and then get a good night's sleep.

The taxi dropped them, took the fare, and then slipped away into the darkness.

As Agnes approached the front door, she felt a crunch underfoot, like broken glass. She rang the bell. No answer. It was then that she noticed the front door was ajar. She pushed it and went in.

"*Olstenem!*" she shrieked in Hungarian. "Oh my God! Uncle Tibor! Uncle Tibor!"

Adam gasped at the bloody figure lying on the carpet. There was what looked like a nasty wound on one side of his forehead. "We'd better call for help, fast! I think he's been shot!"

The local police arrived moments after Agnes had called the emergency number. A white ambulance then appeared. The police offered the couple a lift to the local hospital.

"He's lost a lot of blood. He may not make it," said one of the cops. They had evidently seen this kind of thing before.

The surgeon on duty was less than optimistic. "Most people don't survive this kind of wound. Maybe five percent do,

118

and only about three percent resume a reasonable quality of life."

Both Agnes and Adam were so tired at this point that they could barely stay awake. After they gave a brief statement of the episode to the police, Agnes groaned, "Where can we sleep tonight? We have nowhere to go." It was out of the question to sleep at her uncle's house.

Fortunately, one of the nurses saved the day. "You can stay with me. I have two small bedrooms. Are you two married?"

"No, we're just friends of the patient," muttered Agnes, by now ready to sleep anywhere. The nurse touched Agnes's arm and said, "OK. I can help. I'll meet you shortly in the parking lot."

As they were about to leave the hospital, the police demanded that they visit the local gendarmerie the next morning to make a full statement.

The next morning, a bright dawn light broke through a crack in the curtains and woke them up early. Luckily, their host the nurse was an early riser. She made them a hearty breakfast of bread, cheese, cold cuts of ham, and piping-hot sausages, all helped down by strong black coffee. Agnes whispered to Adam that he should leave the nurse some money, preferably in dollars, on the sideboard in his bedroom.

When the nurse drove them back to the hospital, there were two armed policemen at the entrance and three more outside the private room where Lantos lay inert and heavily bandaged in bed. Miraculously, the wound on his forehead turned out to be superficial. It would be some time later that the police would determine that the bullet that struck Lantos and lodged in his living room wall had missed his brain by just a few millimeters.

The surgeon, clearly exhausted after a long night's bloody work, seemed more optimistic than he had been the night before. "This is one tough guy. We think he might pull through," he said.

The last thing that anyone had expected was to find Tibor shot and almost dead in his own home. Who would do something like this, and why? The episode left Adam and Lantos's niece fearful and in a quandary. Adam wondered if he should do as his father told him and return immediately to New York. Agnes was at a loss to know what to do next for her uncle.

But other matters took precedence. They barely saw Tibor that morning, for the local police now wanted them to go to police headquarters in Budapest and make a statement there too. Less than an hour later, they found themselves sitting in a small, bare gray interview room whose only features were a metal table and some fold-up wooden chairs.

The wait was interminable. They could hear animated conversations and arguments coming from an adjacent room. Eventually, a stocky man with a heavy black mustache, a shock of unkempt black hair, and a grim look on his face arrived at their door.

"Good morning. I'm Andras Kiss." The pudgy man's face was dark, pockmarked, and jowly. Agnes could not help thinking he was the last person she would ever kiss, despite the name.

Kiss eyed the couple with a look of disdain on his face. "I'm the detective in charge of this case. As you see, I speak English so you can both understand me. OK?"

The usual preliminaries followed. Name, address, date of birth, country of residence, telephone number, and, for Adam, his passport number. Then a host of questions.

"What is your relationship to the victim, Lantos?"

"Why were you there at his house?"

"When did you last speak with the victim?"

"Did you see anything suspicious, at or near the house?"

"Who do you think might have committed this crime, and why?"

"Did the victim have any enemies or problems that have something to do with last night's event?"

"How soon did you contact the police after you found the victim?"

The interrogation dragged on. The weary looks on the couple's faces reminded the cop at last that he should offer them something to eat or drink. After all, these people were just witnesses at this point, until or unless they were charged with attempted murder.

A pot of tepid black coffee arrived. "Please, enjoy. I will be back shortly."

Detective Kiss left the room. A longer wait followed this

time. When he returned, the expression on his face had turned from grim to alarm.

"We have just received a ballistics report on the bullet fired at Professor Lantos. It's a nine-millimeter caliber. This suggests it is from a certain type of weapon. Do either of you own a weapon?"

The couple stared at each other in disbelief. "No, sir!" said Adam. Agnes shook her head.

The detective consulted his notes. "That does not surprise me," he mumbled. Eyes still focused on his paperwork, he elaborated further. "We think the bullet in question probably came from a specific type of pistol with a built-in silencer called a Maxim 9. It's a fairly new technology, designed to suppress the sound of a shot. Professional marksmen like to use them on firing ranges to protect their hearing. But…Professor Lantos's home is not a firing range, is it? There's another thing. We don't see many of these type of weapons in Hungary today."

He paused to let the point sink in.

"Are you aware of anyone else in Hungary who knows the victim?"

This time, there was a look of mutual puzzlement on the interviewees' faces. It seemed enough for the detective.

"Well, enough for today. Please arrange to stay in Budapest. We may need to talk with you again soon. I do not recommend that you stay in your uncle's house. If you need to call the hospital, please, use our phone." He then left the room, this time with the self-locking door wide open.

Agnes knew of a nearby café where they could get a late meal. Planning next steps was now urgent. They left the police headquarters building and made for the café.

There was no reason for them to notice the tall, blue-eyed, blond-haired young man who settled down at a nearby café table, shortly after they had arrived and had ordered two cups of strong black Hungarian coffee.

Great Expectations

Jill lay stretched out on the living room sofa, struggling to regain her composure. Fred tried to reassure her that there was nothing to be concerned about. After all, they had spoken to Adam. But Fred could not also resist telling her how he planned to give "that boy" a piece of his mind the moment he came in the door. He then set about making coffee, in the hope that it would refresh them both and clear their minds.

There have been so many odd things happening lately, he thought.

His visit to Munich had been a wild-goose chase. He still had no idea who the people were that he met at the BND. They had referred to his London business associate as "Chad," just like the odd nickname used in the cover letter that had originally come with the gold bar. What about Charlie not showing up at that meeting near Munich? Then, two federal government types knock on his door, right here in Montego Island where that kind of thing never happens. And now, his wife gets a threatening phone call.

Nothing made sense.

The police were of little help. He could call Jones, the man from the State Department. After all, he had left his calling card. But what could Jones do? He seemed to be just as much in the dark. Perhaps another call to Charlie's London office might help? What did he have to lose?

The kettle shrieked as if alarmed by his troubled thoughts. Fred poured the boiling water into the coffee pot to brew. Then, ducking quickly and furtively into his study next door, he dialed Charlie's London number.

Once more, he heard the now familiar voice of the woman receptionist with the London accent who connected him, not to Charlie but, once again, to Dick Harvey.

"So nice to hear your voice, sir," purred Harvey. "I'm sure you'd like to speak with Mr. Fortescue. I think he's in the air right now returning from abroad. He should land soon at Heathrow. Can I give you his new mobile number?"

Fred placed a call. No answer. Charlie must still be in the air.

The letter from "Chad" had said something about the consortium meeting in ten days. A week had now passed, yet Fred had heard nothing more. He remembered clearly that he had signed the paperwork and sent it back by courier to the London address as indicated. It was beginning to look as if someone had either let him down or led him up a garden path, to nowhere. He decided to wait for an hour or two and then try another call to Charlie.

It was Charlie who called first. Presumably his man Harvey had alerted him to Fred's earlier call.

Charlie sounded full of remorse. "Fred! Terribly sorry to have played hard to get. I just got back from overseas. I hear that you signed up with our investor group. That's good news indeed. How are you?"

"Charlie, where do I begin?" He rattled off a list of all that had happened and ended with a request for some explanations, like why did Charlie ask him to go to Munich in the first place and then not show up.

"I can't talk about this over the phone, except to tell you I think I met your son, in Paraguay."

"In *Paraguay*? He told me he was in Argentina! He was supposed to be in Hungary. How was he? What was he doing?"

"Just visiting for a day or two, I think. We came across each other at a town called Nueva Germania. He seemed fine."

Charlie sounded reassuring to Fred. It was time to get down to business. Fred pointedly asked, "Well, now that we're talking at last, what's happening with the consortium? Wasn't there going to be a meeting in a few days for all the investors?"

"Unfortunately, that meeting had to be postponed," said Charlie. "There was a delay in getting all the documentation together, I'm afraid. But I will let you know as soon as I can about next steps."

"What about that guy who approached me in Munich? Kurt, was it? He asked me who I met at the BND, and I told him. Why on earth was I meeting with people from the BND in the first place? Anyway, I assumed the two fellows I met there represented the German government and had something to do with the investment project. Did the man Kurt give you their names?"

Charlie paused.

"Yes, he did indeed. But for reasons I can't tell you now, avoid any further contact with them whatsoever. If you do hear from them, phone me or Harvey at my office and just say you're calling to wish me a happy birthday."

"I still don't understand. Who are these people?" Fred's question hung in the air, begging for a clear answer.

"Fred," said Charlie, "You really don't need to know — and the less you know about them, the better. Now, please excuse me. My driver is waiting for me, and I'm already late for a meeting."

Before Fred could utter another word, there was a click, and the call was disconnected. *Funny,* he thought, *that's not the Charlie I used to know.* There was an unfamiliar tension in his voice, as if he were under some great pressure. Meanwhile, Charlie had now delayed this investor meeting.

Nothing made any sense.

He Who Hesitates Is Lost

Agnes and Adam had booked two separate rooms at a modest hotel overlooking the Danube in Buda. After leaving police headquarters, they sat in the nearby café sipping their coffee. They checked the web for the latest status of flights from Budapest to New York. LOT, the Polish airline, had an early morning departure that might work. Despite the police request to remain in Budapest for more questioning, Adam was thinking about making a tentative airline reservation.

Then someone tripped and fell while passing their table. It was a tall blond-haired and blue-eyed young man who looked to be in his early thirties. "Oh, I'm so sorry!" he said in English. "How clumsy of me! There was something slippery on my shoe. I couldn't help it. You speak English? Yes?"

Adam helped him up.

"Thank you, thank you! I'm visiting from Bavaria. I don't always look where I'm going. I'm Gunther, by the way. And you?"

"Adam. And this is Agnes." They all shook hands.

"Where are you staying? Can you recommend somewhere good? And any good restaurants?"

Adam had a moment of hesitation. Why tell a stranger where you're staying, especially now in the aftermath of the attempted murder of Agnes's uncle and his former college professor? And anyway, why would a stranger ask such a personal question so early in a first conversation? But then again, why not? The man seemed pleasant enough. Adam darted a quick glance at Agnes. He noticed how she stared hard at the young man as she sized him up.

Then, before he realized it, Adam had blurted out the name of the hotel they had booked for the night. "We're at the Hotel Kempinski Corvinus."

"I've heard it's very nice. But I must return home late tonight after dinner, so no hotel for me this time. Do you like Budapest?"

The blue eyes were now staring hard at Agnes who remained silent for a moment before she said, "I live here," forcing a smile.

"And you, Herr Adam? You have an American accent?" The blond inquisitor was unperturbed by Agnes's coolness.

Adam played along before his belated intuition kicked in and made him abruptly switch gears. "Yes, I'm a New Yorker. Tell you what, sir: we've had a tough day, and I don't mean to be rude, but we must go. Hope you enjoy the rest of your day."

There was something about this Gunther's line of

questioning, after so conveniently tripping up next to their table, that didn't feel right.

They paid the bill, got up, and left.

"Adam, there was something odd about that man. Why did you tell him where we're staying? You know, I think we must be very careful. Let's cancel the Kempinski and find somewhere else for tonight."

Adam knew Agnes was right. He had been an avid reader of John Le Carré novels and had learned from that writer about something called "tradecraft," a series of methods used by certain types of government agents to shake off anyone who might be following. They decided to take the Metro, change trains, take a bus and then a cab, and alight near a small hotel in Pest on the opposite side of the river. As far as they could tell, there was no one on their trail.

The police called next morning to request another round of questioning. When Adam explained that his family urgently needed him to return to New York, this only served as a red flag.

Detective Kiss was firm. "Please bring your passport with you, Mr. Tinker."

Once again, they returned to police headquarters. They soon found themselves back in the same room with the steel table and the self-locking door. Once more, they waited for what seemed more than an hour.

When Detective Kiss reappeared, this time a woman accompanied him. Dressed in a white blouse and black pants, with short, brown hair and no makeup, she looked to be in her forties. She had a warm and reassuring manner. She introduced herself.

"I'm Dr. Hanna Nagy. I'm a police psychologist. Perhaps you can help us with our inquiries?"

A long list of questions followed.

Had either Adam or Agnes any insight into Professor Lantos's state of mind around the time of the "event"? Was he of sound mind? Had he ever threatened anyone, to their knowledge? Was he a drug user? Did he owe anyone money? Was there anyone who bore a grudge against him? The questions were exhaustive and exhausting.

Detective Kiss had a final request. "Mr. Tinker, please show me your passport."

Adam obliged. Kiss flipped through a few pages and then, to Adam's dismay, slipped the passport into his jacket pocket.

"But that's *my passport*! I'm an American citizen! You can't do that!"

"I'm afraid I can, and I must. You and your friend here are still our prime suspects. We appreciate your cooperation now and in future. Rest assured that you will have your passport back promptly, once our inquiries are completed and we no longer have reason to feel you're a suspect. You are free to go, but you must remain in Budapest for now and report to us daily. I'm sorry, but those are the rules."

This was crushing news. After all, they had saved Lantos's

life in the nick of time, only to be treated by the police as potential murderers!

What an irony! What a mess! thought Adam. Now they had to think about where to stay. Adam also had to break the news to his family.

He began to wish he had never come to Hungary in the first place.

Guilt by Association

Fred was surprised to get a phone call later that day from Jones, the State Department person. He recalled that Jones had asked for Fred to call him, if he heard from Adam—not the other way around.

Jones's tone was that of a bearer of bad news. "Mr. Tinker, sorry to bother you again. We've learned some new information since our recent visit to you. You're probably wondering why I'm calling you, because I'd asked you to contact me once you heard from your son."

Fred's antenna told him to be alert, listen carefully, and say as little as possible.

"That's right. But I haven't yet heard from my son." Fred surprised himself by telling the lie. Something he couldn't put his finger on held him back.

Jones continued. "Sir, the purpose of my call today is to alert you to the possibility that you may receive some unwanted calls from strangers."

Fred's ears pricked up. "Funny you should say that, Mr. Jones. We got one already. The police are looking into it. My family was threatened."

Jones was undeterred. "Sir, you may get more calls like that. They may or may not be from the same person or people. But please be sure to note the time of any such call, and, if you can, keep a record of the callers' numbers. That will help us, and you too."

After a moment's reflection, Fred replied "Mr. Jones, I don't know what this is about, but my top concern now is the safety of my family."

"I understand, sir," said Jones. "But until we get to the heart of the matter, there's not much we can do to help you. I suggest you and family relocate for a few days and that you tell no one where you're going. We appreciate your help."

Jones then hung up.

It was about an hour later that another call came in. The caller identified himself as a retired US Army general. "Mr. Tinker? Hi! This is General Pugh. We've not met. But I'd like a few words with you privately. I happen to be on Montego Island right now with my family. Could you come over one afternoon for a private chat?"

Fred was unaccustomed to strangers calling him for a chat by anyone in the military at all, let alone in the peaceful haven of Montego Island.

"May I ask what this is about?" he asked, sounding as innocent as he could.

The general wasn't forthcoming over the phone. "It's a sensitive matter, sir," he said in what sounded like a conspiratorial voice. "Would tomorrow work for you, at three in the afternoon?" He then gave Fred a home address.

When Fred pulled up at the house the next afternoon, there were some small children playing by the entrance. Fred greeted them with a stiff smile and rang the doorbell. An attractive gray-haired woman who looked to be in her fifties answered. He identified himself. She ushered him in.

"The general is expecting you, sir." Fred noticed she had an accent, but he couldn't place it.

A voice called out from the hallway. "Welcome, Mr. Tinker! I'm George Pugh. Come into my office, please. Ursula, would you bring us some fresh coffee please and some of those donuts?"

Pugh had a stocky build and close-cropped white hair, was of medium height and had an erect military bearing. He looked tanned and fit for his age which Fred guessed was close to seventy. Pugh motioned Fred toward a deep armchair in tufted red leather.

The wood-paneled office walls were almost hidden by a cluster of group photographs, some faded in black-and-white, others in color. There were gold and silver trophies perched precariously on the shelf above a huge fireplace. A traditional green banker's lamp lit up an impressively large oak desk adorned with a red-leather blotter, a notepad, and a pair of pens in their holder.

Pugh began the conversation, to put his guest at ease. "I hope the kids didn't bother you on the way in? Sorry if they did. I'm on grandparent duty today." He gave Fred a winning smile.

"They look like great kids," said Fred, pretending to sound friendly.

Pugh rapidly began to turn the conversation to business. "Sure thing. Well now, I appreciate you coming over for a little chat. Where are you on the island?"

"We're in the bay, at the other end," said Fred. *What else could I say?* he thought.

Pugh paused, taking a deep breath before speaking.

"Let me get to the point, Mr. Tinker. I'm sixty-five years old and technically long retired from the military. Came from a family of army brats. My dad was with the US Army in Germany at the end of the war—World War II, that is. Traveled all over. Made it to general when I was fifty, like my dad. Did that for five years and retired at fifty-five. They just raised the retirement age to sixty-two, by the way. I guess that was to save pension payouts."

Pugh cleared his throat, as Ursula arrived with coffee and donuts. He waited for her to leave the room, before resuming his speech. "You see, there are parts of the military from which you never can really retire. I keep my hand in the game, now and again. Now, in case you're wondering why I contacted you, there's a dangerous game going on now that may involve you and your family."

He paused again, watching for Fred to react. But he remained impassive.

"Many years ago, toward the end of World War II, the Allies

captured a lot of property that was classified as 'enemy property.' Much of it found its way to the US military, for private use by the higher-ups. No one has ever held anyone else to account for it, even to this day. Worse still, the US went about hiring some of the worst Nazis you could imagine, many with the blood of thousands on their hands. The purpose was to use them to spy on the Soviets, in exchange for their freedom."

He cleared his throat. "The Americans were not alone doing this recruitment activity. The British, the French, and the Russians did it too. The Americans turned some of their Nazi prisoners round to spy on the East. Maybe you've heard of Reinhard Gehlen, one of Hitler's generals, who was the Nazis' chief of the German Army's intelligence operation. He wound up joining the CIA to spy on the Russians. He then became president of the postwar German Federal Intelligence Service, the BND."

Fred kept a poker face, even at the mention of those initials that he still knew so little about.

Pugh sipped his coffee and bit into a donut. He swallowed a wad of sugary dough, then continued his comments. "The thing is, much of the so-called 'enemy property' had once belonged to various European art museums and to millions of Jews who perished in the Holocaust."

The general took another bite of his donut, chewed it, and swallowed it in one gulp. "To this day, Mr. Tinker, relatively little of that property has been recovered, and even less has been returned to its rightful owners."

Fred was wondering, *Where is this guy going with his story?*

"But there's something else," declared Pugh. "You may have seen a lot of press reports lately about the extreme right demonstrating in Germany. Ever since the collapse of the Soviet Union began in 1989 and since West and East Germany reunited in 1990, the extreme right in Germany has tried to rebuild its dream of launching a fourth empire or 'reich.' You probably know that the ideas of Hitler and Nazism are still very much alive and well in Germany today."

"Yes, I think I'm aware," said Fred. He kept a poker-faced interest in the general's remarks. Then, for a fleeting moment, Fred had a flashback to his childhood passion for the Hitler Youth. But that would not be part of this conversation, he thought to himself.

Pugh had more to say. "To launch such a movement, the extremists now need funding to buy all the equipment they need. They can't get it legally. But they are hunting aggressively to find undiscovered wealth that their Nazi forbears hid all over the world. The architect of this concealment plan was Klaus Heilmann, a military official very close to Martin Bormann and to Hitler. We have reliable information that he compiled a group of maps showing the coordinates of the buried loot. We think it may amount in total to well over five hundred million dollars in today's money. As to Heilman, the record says he died in 1945 in Hitler's Berlin bunker. His remains were tested for his DNA in 1998, and his date of death was confirmed."

"I don't see what all this has to do with me." Fred was starting to feel impatient.

138

"Bear with me. Mr. Tinker, please." It appeared that the general now began to realize he was being long-winded. "Let me now get to the point," he said. "Heilmann was married and had children. One of them was a daughter named Eva. Perhaps she was named after Hitler's partner, Eva Braun. Anyway, a recent report stated that an Eva Heilmann, resident of Nueva Germania, Paraguay, was murdered. There was no apparent motive, nor has anyone yet been apprehended for the crime."

Fred's throat went suddenly dry. He took a long drink of coffee. The association of Nueva Germania with Paraguay and Adam sounded less and less like a coincidence. He noticed that Pugh had stopped speaking and was staring at him.

"Are you all right, Mr. Tinker?"

"I'm just fine," said Fred. "Please, continue."

Pugh gulped a mouthful of coffee, as if to drive the donuts faster into his digestive system. "My guess is that someone was after something they thought this Eva Heilmann had in her possession. Nothing of value was stolen, according to our friends in the Paraguayan police. The murdered woman was living in poverty anyway. But we learned that someone had visited her a few days before her death—a young woman, in her twenties. Then, we checked the flight manifests, and saw the name 'Tinker' listed. This didn't seem like a local name, so we checked it out. 'Tinker' turned out to be a young American named Adam Tinker."

"That's my son."

Pugh's face now became like stone. "We thought so. What took him to Paraguay in the first place? I mean, it's not exactly Miami Beach!"

"Darned if I know!" said Fred. "My wife and I just spoke with him the other day. He was supposed to be in Hungary. Then we learned he was in Argentina. And now Paraguay. I told him to come home immediately. I've no idea where he is or what he's up to."

Pugh's eyes now fixed on Fred with a penetrating stare. "Mr. Tinker, there are some very important people in this country who want to know the location of those maps I mentioned a moment ago. We think that Klaus Heilmann may have given his daughter safe custody of the maps. Someone killed her while trying to find them at her home. You can see this is a rather delicate situation for you and your family if, as we suspect, your son is involved."

Fred swallowed the rest of his coffee. He nibbled another donut, then took the plunge. "I wish I knew more and could tell you something. But I just don't know what's going on. There are a lot of odd things that have happened lately that I can't explain. I'm waiting to hear of Adam's arrival here anytime now."

Pugh stood and extended his hand. "I do surely understand, sir. But please give me a call once you hear from him again. I'm sure he's a fine young man and he won't have any trouble. Now, maybe you and your wife can join us for dinner some night?"

Flight Risk

"Uncle Tibor's sister has a townhouse in Pest. I will call her to see if she can put us up there for a day or two till this problem of ours, how do you say, 'blows over,'" said Agnes.

Lantos's ever-resourceful niece was in luck. Agnes's aunt was Lantos's older sister. She was about to leave on a trip overseas. They told her nothing about the shooting, hoping she would learn nothing from the Hungarian or foreign press. She was delighted to have a family member be a house-sitter for a few days.

They grabbed their few belongings and took a taxi to their new quarters as fast as possible. Once settled, in separate bedrooms and on different floors, they duly reported in to the police and informed Detective Kiss of their temporary address and phone number.

Agnes felt anxious. "We have to talk with your uncle and see what more he knows. Let's call the hospital." The duty nurse answered after a long delay. "Mr. Lantos is not to be disturbed, on doctor's orders. You can leave a message, and when he is ready to call you, then he can. Please know too that we do not allow visitors at this stage." She hung up.

Both Agnes and Adam were stumped. Who could they turn to? What could they do now except wait?

Agnes decided to change the conversation. "What did you think of that fellow who conveniently tripped next to our table? There was something about him I didn't like. He was too friendly, too fast."

Adam agreed. "I thought the same thing. There's something to be said for instinct."

Then Agnes remembered something else. "Did you remember to cancel the rooms we booked at the Kempinski? I guaranteed them on my credit card. Let me call them."

She reached the front desk, gave their names, and confirmed the cancellation. She was about to hang up when the reservation clerk told her that a young man had visited the hotel asking for them.

"Where should I say he can reach you if he contacts us again?" asked the clerk.

Agnes was shocked. "Oh, no matter," she said warily. "We know how to reach him. Thank you."

Adam saw the startled looked on her face. "Let me guess. Pretty boy from the café was looking for us. Not good."

"Well, I called on my cell phone," said Agnes, "so at least he won't know where we are now."

No sooner had she spoken than a buzz on Adam's mobile phone signaled an incoming text message:

Adam! It's me, Bitar. I had a little accident while traveling but I'm all right now. Where are you? I have something important to share with you.

"Uh-oh! That's all we need. Bitar wants to meet me."

"Text him that you're about to leave for New York. Ask if he can send you whatever he has by email." To their surprise, they got an email back within minutes.

There are people from several countries who think I have access to information about hidden stolen property. I'm in some danger so I can't tell you more yet. Let me know as soon as you're back in New York. I will be getting some medical treatment there within the next few days and will probably stay to recuperate.

Yours

YB

Deductive Reasoning

Neither spouse was known to be a star student of world affairs. Fred's habit was to focus his attention almost exclusively on the financial markets and their gyrations. He tuned in to current political and economic news only when it suited his investment interests.

Jill for her part was the consummate homemaker. Always presentable and attractive looking, she took great pains to ensure that everything about her and her household were always as close to immaculate and as perfect as possible.

But something was nagging at Fred. All these loose threads from his recent experiences, none of which made any sense on their own, or even as a whole, forced him to retreat to his study for reflection.

First, he had been somewhat impressed that Adam had found himself a part-time job on his own, and in another country too. Yet the boy had not been forthcoming about his travels, before, during or after them.

Next, the business of trying to reach the elusive Charlie Fortescue bothered him. Each time they were supposed to meet, whether in London or Munich, Charlie was supposedly "traveling" somewhere. Why then would he want from Fred the names of the people at the BND in Pullach? Why would Charlie use a cutout called Kurt to get those names from Fred, if, that is, the people he had seen at the BND were indeed members of the same investment group? And why would Charlie later warn Fred to stay away from those people?

What was all this talk from the State Department guys? What about the call from a semiretired US Army general? It sounded like something big and bad was afoot. But he just couldn't pull all the strands together. The man called Jones had even suggested that the family go into hiding because of possible danger ahead.

Fred's thoughts turned at last back to the financial news. He had never adjusted his reading habits. A day without a newspaper that he could touch was incomplete. Unlike his children to whom emailing, texting, and catching the news online were second nature, his world revolved around a cursory reading of national and world news in the *New York Times* and the *Journal*, and invariably on financial news at that. However, while he was thinking through all the loose ends of the past few days and weeks, a headline caught his eye: "Mystery Surrounds Attempted Murder of Two Columbia University Professors."

Perhaps it was just because Adam was a recent Columbia graduate that he read the entire article and noted that there were some unanswered questions.

Was it just a coincidence, or was there a link

between a hit-and-run episode in Buenos Aires and a shooting in Hungary that injured one and almost killed another member of the Columbia University teaching staff? The university remains tight-lipped about both incidents on the grounds that they still remain under investigation.

The piece described what had happened to each man. It noted the respective academic focus of both Yussef Bitar and Tibor Lantos, pointing out that while both taught at the same school, their academic work was unique in each case. There seemed to be nothing in common between them except a shared college campus. According to the article, the two men hardly knew one another.

And yet why would anyone violently assault two faculty members of the same university within days of each other? Was this drug-related? Were they tied in with some gang?

Eyewitness reports from Argentina noted that a black Audi had hit Bitar. The Argentine police report stated that the car had stopped momentarily after hitting its target and had then sped off at high speed. Later inquires revealed that the Audi had false number plates.

There were reports from Reuters that the shooter's weapon in Budapest was one used only by the German military. It seemed that the single shot fired may have been fired by a marksman whose job in this case was to injure, not kill—or, in other words, it was a warning. The article concluded that professionals seemed to be behind both incidents. Meanwhile, the reporters had so far been unable to locate either victim for an interview.

Try as he may, Fred remained bewildered. He put down the paper, closed his eyes, and took a nap.

Call of the Wild

Adam felt obliged to call his father again. He also knew he would be berated if he told him about his latest troubles. But he saw no other option. Watched by Agnes, sprawled among the cushions on her aunt's green leather sofa, he placed the call.

"Hi, Dad. It's me," said Adam meekly.

Fred delivered his first salvo. "Your mother's going crazy with worry about you. Where the *hell* are you?"

"Still in Hungary. In Budapest." Adam braced himself as he knew what would come next.

"When will you be here?" Fred demanded.

Adam took a deep breath and explained that there had been a traffic accident he had witnessed. The police wanted him to delay his departure to New York for a few days while they completed their inquiries.

But Fred remained on the attack. "Adam, I just don't get it. First, you tell me you're going to Hungary. Then I learn you're in Argentina. Then in Paraguay. And now back in Budapest where I read your Professor Lantos was shot.

What on earth are you doing?"

"Dad, who told you I was in Argentina and Paraguay?"

"That's none of your business," snorted Fred.

Adam felt provoked. "Dad, I could say the same to you, on my account."

"Don't be impertinent with me, boy!" There was an odd tone of threat and yet puzzlement in Fred's voice. "Look here, you had better know that some people in the government over here warned me that our family may be in danger. That includes you, not to mention your mother and your sister. In fact, I suspect you may be the cause of that threat. So, I want you to quit that damn part-time job of yours and come home as soon as you can."

This was a mild admonition for Fred and somehow, Adam recognized that behind the usual bluster, Fred was genuinely worried.

"OK, Dad. I hear you." Adam looked over at Agnes for a moment's distraction, then completed his sentence. "I'll let you know just as soon as I can about my return flight. Tell mother not to worry. Everything's all right. Talk to you soon."

His parting words sounded hollow and straight out of a bad Hollywood movie. Adam felt odd lying to his own father. The man was gruff and stern, but he meant well after all.

There was some cold chicken and a salad in the fridge, thoughtfully provided by Agnes's aunt. After what had happened, both Adam and Agnes were ravenous.

They were each munching an apple when the phone rang. A now familiar voice was on the line. "Hello. Detective Kiss here. I have some good news for you. We just got a final ballistics report. The bullet only grazed Professor Lantos's forehead and lodged in the wall. This leads us to believe that the shooter meant to wound but not kill him. Let me ask you once again. Have either of you ever fired a weapon, specifically a pistol?"

Adam glanced over again at Agnes who, overhearing the question, mouthed "No." Adam replied to the detective with a firm "No, neither of us."

"Well," said Kiss, "further research confirms our original suspicion. The shooter was a highly trained marksman. Also, the only people in Europe who typically use this type of weapon, the Maxim 9, are members of the German armed forces, the *Bundeswehr*. Do either of you happen to know anyone there?"

"No, sir." Adam was emphatic.

"Then I think we can now return your passport, Mr. Tinker. You are free to travel." The relief on Adam's face was palpable.

As he broke the news to Agnes, he sensed that she had conflicted feelings. They had bonded together this far, and both now faced the prospect of losing one another.

As soon as Kiss hung up, Adam emailed his father. Better to do this than have another tough talk by phone. "Dad, I just got clearance to come home. I'll email you the flight number and the itinerary as soon as I can. Love you both. Adam."

Early the next morning, Adam collected his passport from police headquarters. He wanted to find out more about the shooting but to no avail. "We do not discuss details of crimes under investigation," said Detective Kiss.

Agnes took him to the airport. Her face was downcast and her expression sullen.

"Let's stay in touch, Adam," she murmured.

Adam felt a sudden excitement as he told her "You know, I'm really going miss you, Agnes, but hopefully not for long. Your passport should allow you up to ninety days to visit the US as a tourist. Will you come over?"

She tossed her head and left Adam wondering whether she meant yes or no.

A Brick without Mortar

Adam's return flight to JFK was long and tedious but uneventful. He could have predicted almost word for word the lectures he would get from each of his parents and their lengthy interrogation. Why this? Who that? When did this? What was that? He was glad after all that he had described his recent experience as a witness in Budapest as related to a "traffic accident" rather than to a shooting.

Fortune mercifully intervened in the form of his sister, Eve. On top of her recent brief brush with the local police, and preceded by her return home weeks ago with a ring in her nose, she now presented her parents with a dismal high school report card where the letter C loomed large in almost every subject. She was downcast. Her parents were now distraught with both Adam and Eve.

An uneasy peace best described the atmosphere in the Tinker household over the next few days. Now that Adam was back home on the island, Fred started to badger him again about finding a "real job."

Playing along, Adam appeared to be searching away on the

internet for possible permanent work. But, in fact, he was discreetly surfing the internet for any mention of Bitar. The final words of Lantos when they last spoke still rang in his ears.

"I have reason to believe the Wazir and Professor Bitar are one and the same. I think you need to return to Budapest as soon as you can."

What had made Lantos say that? What evidence did he have? It would be a while before the two of them would speak again. Why not take the bull by the horns and confront Bitar in person, assuming he was now back in New York?

Dusk was falling one evening as Adam was about to text Bitar and suggest that they meet. He had barely started to type when he heard a deafening crash followed by a loud scream from downstairs. Had someone dropped something in the kitchen?

He scooted down the stairs to the living room. Before him stood his parents, standing dumbstruck and staring alternately at a broken windowpane and a large red brick on the carpet.

"Oh my God! Oh my God! It's happening again!" Jill was screaming. She was clearly losing her senses. Fred reached out and wrapped his arms around her.

"What do you mean 'again,' Mom"? Adam asked.

Jill stammered. "We got that threatening phone call the other day. And now... this!"

It was Fred's turn to speak, trying to sound in control and in command. "A man called Jones came here unannounced some days ago. He was with another fellow called Field. They said they were from the State Department. Jones later called and suggested we leave Montego Island for now and book a hotel on the mainland, rather than return to our Manhattan apartment. It now seems he had a point."

"Dad, that's really weird." Adam kept a straight face and held back his thoughts, knowing that to reveal them now would only aggravate the situation.

Fred took charge. "I'm going to book some rooms for all of us somewhere safe in New York, right now. Meantime, I suggest we keep this latest incident to ourselves. The local police are no help, and I just don't feel good about those guys called Field and Jones. The less they know, the better. And that includes the fact that you, Adam, are back with us."

Early the next morning, a charter plane flew the entire family into White Plains. A large SUV picked them up and, within an hour, had deposited them at the entrance to the exclusive Halcyon Club in Midtown.

While his parents and Eve were settling in, Adam returned to texting Professor Bitar.

"We're back in the US. Are you now in New York? I'd like to meet with you."

The family dined together in the Halycon's Red Room. Jill remained shaken and had little appetite. There were few other club members present. The place had an eerie and musty stillness about it. But is seemed safe and insulated just enough from the outside world to afford everyone some sense of security.

After dinner, Adam checked his incoming text messages. Bitar had replied that he was indeed in New York and was staying with a friend while undergoing further medical treatment.

He suggested that the two have coffee at a small café in Soho the next day.

The Dark Side

Bitar arrived by cab minutes after Adam, complete with his right arm in white plaster and a blue sling, and two small Band-Aids on his face. He explained how his upper arm had snapped like a twig as he tried to protect himself when a speeding car mounted the sidewalk in Buenos Aires and drove straight at him.

"The funny thing is" he said, "that driver could have killed me. But he didn't. So, I think this may have been a warning."

"A warning?" said Adam. "About what?"

"Adam, do you remember me texting you to say I had something important to tell you?

"Sure, I do."

"Let me tell you something, Adam." Bitar lowered his voice, glancing quickly around at the café's customers. "I think there's a plot developing between some factions in the German government and some extremist members of the Arab community to join forces and launch World War III. I know it sounds dramatic, even crazy. But there's strong evidence to support the theory."

Adam's mind began to spin. Bitar elaborated, almost in a whisper. "How do I know? Because the Israeli government sold a lot of special signals intercept equipment to Uncle Sam; and because, buried in that equipment are transmitters that enable the Israelis to intercept whatever is intercepted by the USA."

Adam raised his eyebrows. *Why on earth would the US government use foreign equipment in the first place to eavesdrop on its enemies?* he wondered.

But Bitar was still talking away. "It was from these 'shadow intercepts' that the Israelis learned about something called the *Familienverband*, which, when translated from German, means 'the family union.' Sounds innocent enough, right? But on close inspection, the membership of this 'union' proved to be unusual. It turns out that its leadership includes some extreme but powerful extremist factions in both the German and several Arab governments."

Adam remembered that someone had mentioned the *Familienverband* at the Clarion Club in Buenos Aires.

He remained silent as Bitar plowed on, noticing that his former lecturer was more than a little agitated. "But that's not all, Adam. There are also factions within just about every Western government that provide supporting roles. Together, they have a shared mission. It is to locate the maps created by Klaus Heilmann showing where most Nazi loot is hidden; and then, on the pretext of 'development and exploration,' to retrieve the loot, share a percentage among themselves, and help finance a Nazi comeback in a fourth empire or 'reich.'"

Adam had a question. "But, what does any of this have to do with you, Professor?"

"Look," said Bitar, "my business is to gather and process information about the Middle East. I get information, I pull it together, and sometimes I sell it to interested parties."

"But you told me you worked for the Israeli government, didn't you?" Adam was starting to probe.

"Yes, that's exactly what I told you." Bitar glanced quickly left and right. "But, you know, Adam, no country's government is an orchestra in perfect harmony. Every country has its factions within the government structure. Sometimes the factions go to war with one another, and not always publicly. So, I pick and choose those to whom I give my information. It might be a faction in one country and their supporters in another. But at the root of it all, I'm still an Arab at heart."

Adam decided it was time to stop beating about the bush. "Professor Bitar, if you're an Arab at heart, would that explain why some people think you're a past member of the Muslim Brotherhood and are therefore sympathetic to Muslim extremism? They also say you preach violence and terrorism in the name of Islam—and even that you write under the name of Wazir on an English-language, jihadist web magazine called *Inspire*."

Adam expected Bitar to react. However, to his surprise, Bitar was unfazed. "Adam, listen to me carefully. I will always deny what I'm about to tell you, if anyone ever asks me. I'm part of an international team whose mission is to destroy violent extremism in general, and, specifically, Arab extremism. Just because I'm an Arab does not make me a violent extremist. But then you understandably ask, 'Why preach violence on the web?'"

"Yes, I'd really like to know." Adam was unsure what would come next.

Bitar's expression became hard. "I'll tell you why. I do it as bait, to attract a credible base of followers. In turn, we can then trace, identify, investigate, arrest, and, as needed, prosecute and jail them." He clasped his hands together and leaned in toward Adam. "Most respondents to my blogs on *Inspire* are just misguided young people, desperately seeking a cause to believe in and to belong to a group. As you well know, it's a confusing world out there for young people everywhere. But on occasion, I hook a bigger fish."

"Really?" said Adam.

"Yes, really." Bitar seemed to be open and telling the truth. "That fish might invite me to a meeting, perhaps to a mosque somewhere. I might even attend such a meeting. There, I glean information for our team to assess for risk. In short, our job is to destroy violent behavior from within and to take violent people out of circulation. I can tell you that we have prevented an impressive number of terrorist incidents as a result. Does that answer your question?"

This was a new perspective for Adam. He nodded.

Perhaps Tibor Lantos had misjudged Bitar after all.

The Darker Side

They ordered another round of coffee. Adam sensed that his journey into Bitar's mind had only just begun.

His puzzlement must have registered with Bitar, for he now launched into greater depth to give Adam deeper insight into the mind-set of certain traditional Middle Eastern thinking.

"Look, Adam," he said, "it's important for you to understand just how deep the feelings run in the Arab world. You see, since the end of World War I, the people we think of as Islamists have long held a parallel, though different, view of the world from that of the Nazis."

"Wait a minute, Professor! Are you saying that Islamists and Nazis are one and the same?" Adam's frown confirmed the confusion in his mind.

Bitar felt compelled to spell out what to him seemed obvious, though clearly not so to his former student. "Fair question, but not exactly. The picture is not black-and-white. It has many shades of gray. But ask me what's an Islamist? Someone, perhaps, who advocates or supports Islamic militancy and religious fundamentalism, which also

160

includes the destruction of Israel and all Jews in general. Now ask me what's a Nazi? Someone, perhaps, who is highly nationalistic, welcomes dictatorial rule, participates actively in a mass movement of national unity governed by the strictest possible discipline—and wants to annihilate all Jews."

Adam nodded and said, "I think I see what parallels you mean."

The café was starting to fill up with a medley of customers. Adam noticed how Bitar carefully appraised each one of them. His recent experience in Buenos Aires had clearly raised his awareness of his surroundings and of potential aggressors.

"Well, I mean, just think of all the things they perceive in common, the Islamists and Nazis!" Bitar exclaimed. "Both welcome a single, all-powerful leader. Both see their own people as a single global community of the one true faith, which in Islam is called the *ummah;* and, for certain Germans, the pure and perfect blue-eyed-and-blond world of the Aryan *volk.* Right?"

Again, Adam nodded. He seemed to be joining the dots.

The deafening wails of a police siren started up, grew closer, and then a police squad car shot by the window. For a moment, all conversation was obliterated.

Bitar took the opportunity to gulp some coffee. He waited for the high-pitched scream of the siren to dissipate into the distance before continuing. "Both believe in violent struggle to achieve their goals. Both see the role of women is

161

essentially just to produce soldiers. Both use the scapegoat of the world's Jewish community to blame for all their problems. Both share a common goal to annihilate Zionists—those who believe in the development and protection of a Jewish nation called Israel—and Jews everywhere."

As Adam was nodding again in agreement, a waitperson nearby dropped a pile of plates that shattered in every direction. All heads turned in alarm. But Bitar barely noticed. "By the way, Adam, did you know that an estimated *four thousand* German officials or others involved in war crimes against Jews and others in World War II found refuge in the Middle East?"

"What are you saying?" asked Adam distractedly, watching the cleanup process out of the corner of his eye.

"What I'm trying to say," said Bitar patiently, "is that this *welcomat* for Nazi criminals didn't just happen out of the blue. Remember that history proves that German-Turkish relations developed in the late 19th century. Remember the German Chancellor, Otto von Bismarck, who pulled all the separate German principalities together to form a united Germany, in 1871? Well, thereafter, lasting relationships grew between the Ottoman Turks and the German military, long before World War I began in 1914."

A second approaching police car siren now began to wail in the distance. Its rising decibel level bounced off the café walls as the vehicle sped by with all lights flashing. Once again, all conversation stopped.

Bitar rolled his eyes at the noise as Adam smiled
162

sympathetically. As the sound of the siren at last diminished, the Israeli Arab academic resumed his lecture. "You know, Adam, that when the Allies won that first World War, they severely punished the Germans with massive reparation payments. They also dissolved the Ottoman Empire. The Germans lost their Kaiser, their emperor; the Turks lost their Sultan, their caliph, and their chief Muslim religious and secular ruler. But, nonetheless, many of those personal German-Turkish relationships endured well into and beyond the end of the Second World War in 1945."

"But hold on! You started talking earlier about German-*Arab*, not German-Turkish, relations."

"Yes," acknowledged Bitar. "That's right. It was German-*Turkish* relations that developed with the Ottoman Empire in the late 1890s, once British influence waned in Istanbul. The Turks urgently needed Western technology and military support. They were faced with the prospect of a Russian invasion. But always remember that, at that time, a wide assortment of Arab clans, tribes and families were still Turkish subjects."

"What happened after that?" queried Adam.

Bitar pressed on again. "All right. So, after World War I, the Ottoman Empire was dissolved and was replaced by a secular pro-Western Turkish government under Kemal Atatürk. The British and the French carved up the old Ottoman Empire. They proceeded to create a series of nations in the Arab part of the Middle East, using a Europe model of nation-states that were nominally independent but were in fact their puppets."

It was Adam's turn to dig deeper. "What happened to Turkey?"

"Well," said Bitar as he refocused his thoughts, "the last Sunni Caliph of the Empire and leader of all Muslims held on till 1924; but he was exiled when Kemal Atatürk's pro-Western Turkish government then took power. Atatürk wanted to dispense with tradition and remodel Turkey as a modern westernized state so that it could compete on an equal footing with the West. Does that make sense, Adam?"

"I guess so. Sure." Adam felt like he was back at school. He wished he had learned more from Bitar's courses back then. He cocked his ears, eager to learn more as the coffee-fueled lecture resumed.

It began to pour with rain outside. The sound of rainwater against the café's windows was almost louder than the wailing of the police sirens some minutes earlier.

"You can clearly see," said Bitar glancing out the window at the downpour, "that a vacuum for traditionally minded Muslims was created in and after 1924 upon the exile of the last Ottoman caliph, Abdelmecid II, and the disappearance of his administration, or the caliphate, as it was called. At the same time, many of his former Arab subjects were getting restive, notably under the new colonial rule of the British in Palestine and of the French in Syria."

"Yes, I see that," said Adam.

"Here's where it gets more interesting," whispered Bitar,

once again looking around the café to make sure that Adam was his only audience. "While some Arabs yearned for the return of the caliphate, others sought their own nationhood, but on their own terms, not on those of the victorious Allies. The group that wanted the return of the caliphate became the seedbed for Islamism: its goal was to convert the entire world to Islam, through violent *jihad*—as required of good Muslims, in its view, by the Quran."

"And the other group?" Adam asked.

"By contrast," said Bitar, "the second Arab group was all about building one-party Muslim nationalism. Even though both groups fought with each other, their common hatred of the Jews and Bolshevism drew them to Nazi Germany after Hitler came to power there in 1933."

"OK. What happened in the 1930s?" Adam would not let go.

"You want more, Adam?" Bitar asked. "More knowledge, more coffee or both?"

"Both!" said Adam, laughing, as they ordered more coffee.

Bitar then picked up again from where he left off.

"In 1922, the Allies' postwar association of states, the League of Nations, empowered the British to administer Palestine. They granted the Jewish and Arab communities the right to run their internal affairs. As a result, the economy expanded, and education and cultural life flourished. But by the late 1930s, and after considerable Jewish immigration to Palestine had occurred, Arab pressure mounted and, eventually compelled, the British began to limit Jewish immigration to Palestine. So far, so good?"

Adam nodded.

"Now, let me tell you about the godfather of Arab extremism. Did you ever hear of someone called Mohammed Amin Al-Husseini?"

"I'm not sure. Was he related to someone like Saddam Hussein, the dictator of Iraq, the one who was hanged?"

Bitar's expression hardened as he responded. "No, not by blood. But Saddam Hussein was related to a close associate of Al-Husseini who was, let's just say, an interesting guy. Want to know more?"

Adam was hooked as Bitar delved deeper and deeper.

"Husseini came from a prominent Jerusalem Arab family," said Bitar. "It traced its roots back to the Prophet Mohammed. Al-Husseini was a sworn officer in the Ottoman Empire's armed forces. He took part personally in the Turkish *jihad* against Armenian Christians between 1915 and 1917 in which one and a half million people died from murder and starvation. Nice guy, huh?" said Bitar with a heavy touch of irony.

He reached for another sip of coffee. Adam felt himself treading on unfamiliar ground as Bitar continued.

"Al-Husseini became the Grand Mufti of Jerusalem, the top Sunni cleric in charge of Muslim Holy Places like the Al Aqsa mosque. He saw Hitler come to power in 1933, after which the Germans came down hard on certain of their own citizens, most of whom were German Jews. When Husseini visited Germany in the late 1930s and met with Hitler, the führer explained that he wanted to kick all German Jews out of Germany. He needed to find somewhere else for them to go. Both Al-Husseini and Hitler also wanted to get the British out of Palestine. That way, the Arabs could take over Jerusalem and Hitler could expand his German Empire to the East. They found common cause."

"This is pretty scary stuff," said Adam. "Then what?" he asked.

"Al-Husseini made it clear to Hitler that he wanted all further Jewish immigration to Palestine to stop," stated Bitar. "This presented Hitler with a new problem. He had already let about a half million Jews leave Germany, many of whom opted for Palestine. Once Al-Husseini and his Arab followers successfully pressed the British to close the door to more Jewish immigration to Palestine in the late 1930s, Hitler felt he had only one option left—to plan the extermination of not only German Jews but all Jews in any country that the Nazis would conquer."

"Yikes!" cried Adam. "Then the Arabs indirectly played a role in creating the Holocaust?"

"Yes, *yikes!*" said an unsmiling Bitar. "And, in time, there were quite a few of those countries with large Jewish communities, like Poland, Czechoslovakia, Austria, Belgium, Holland, and France. Hitler even had England and America in his sights for this plan.

"This is a lot to take in," groaned Adam.

"It sure is, if you want to begin to understand the roots of

167

Islamic terrorism," quipped Bitar. "Anyway, long story short, Al-Husseini literally got away with murder. He was never tried as a war criminal by the Brits. They were handling an Arab revolt and didn't want him to become a martyr, because that would only worsen matters. They even granted him amnesty. He went on to help build a relationship between Iran and Germany, based on much-needed oil for the German military. The Nazis later made him prime minister of a Pan-Arab Government in exile, based in Berlin. This was the seedbed for pro-Nazi groups that emerged in Iran, in Egypt and, eventually, in Iraq as the Ba'ath Party."

"The Ba'ath Party? That's an odd name!" said Adam.

"True," said Bitar. "Ba'ath in Arabic means 'resurrection' or 'renaissance.' It was a bit of an oddball because its ideology was a blend of Arab nationalism, Pan-Arabism, Arab socialism, and anti-imperialism. Ultimately, its mission was to create a single Arab state under complete Arab control, but, just like the Nazis, in the form of a single-party state. Call it Arab national socialism, if you like."

"But...what was 'Pan-Arabism' exactly?" Adam felt once again on foreign ground.

Bitar sighed. Adam would clearly not have been one of his brighter students. "It means the political unification of all Arab countries in between North Africa and the Arabian Sea. But various efforts to make all this a reality failed."

"So, what about the other Arab states and what connected them to the Nazis?"

"Remember that nationalists have a lot in common, whether they are European, Arab, Asian or Latin American. In hindsight at least, it wasn't surprising after World War II to see countries like Egypt and Syria welcoming Nazi criminals. It's even more interesting that certain German Catholic bishops close to the Vatican helped many of these criminals to escape.

"The *Vatican* helped *Nazis* to escape?" said Adam, incredulous.

"Yes," replied Bitar, "both to the Arab world and to South America. But that's another story."

"I'll need to do some reading about that!" mumbled Adam.

Reinforced by the caffeine, Bitar resumed. "Anyway, back to Al-Husseini. He became the founder of the Arab League, an organization designed to unify Pan-Islamic unity in Egypt, Iraq, Jordan, Lebanon, and Saudi Arabia. He was then appointed leader of the Muslim Brotherhood and, later, the president of the World Islamic Congress whose goals include the complete annihilation of Jews everywhere. Fast-forward to 1967: he appoints Yasser Arafat to become his successor as leader of the Palestinian Arabs. Husseini dies from natural causes in 1974. A series of successors have since carried Husseini's flag. To some, he was the godfather of the 20th-century Islamists.

"Was Husseini the main influence in Arab thought?"

"No, not so," said Bitar. "There were several others. For example, there was a prolific Egyptian writer and educator in Islam called Sayyid Qtb. He spent time in Greeley,

Colorado and came to detest the American way of life as decadent and opposite to the teachings of Islam. He was a leading member of the Muslim Brotherhood in Egypt. It supported a return to the strict Muslim tradition as laid down in the Quran."

"So, he hated America, this guy Qtb?" said Adam.

"Correct," said Bitar. "However, he also took issue with the increasingly secular Egyptian government of Gemal Abdel Nasser, a former army officer who deposed Egypt's king in 1952. Qtb was later hanged in Egypt in 1966 for plotting to assassinate Nasser. Some would say his teaching was the 20th-century spiritual force behind the notion of *jihad* as practiced by Al Qaeda."

"I guess that brings us right up to date!" said Adam. "But I'm not sure I understand the split within Islam between Shiites and Sunnis since the death of Mohammed in, when was it, 632 CE?"

Bitar scratched his ear, thinking to himself, *This fellow Adam still has so much to learn!*

"Basically," said Bitar, "the Sunnis are Arab nationalists. The word 'Sunni' means followers of the *sunna*. That's a body of social and legal custom based on traditions of Mohammed's deeds, sayings and teachings handed down the generations. Shall I go on, Adam?" he asked.

Adam nodded once again.

"The Sunni," said Bitar, "prefer to have a capable strongman as the leader of their nation. Unlike the Shia, they don't care if that person is or is not descended from the Prophet Mohammed. Al-Husseini, for example, was a Sunni Muslim. The vast majority of the world's one and a half plus billion Muslims, maybe eighty-five percent, are Sunni. But nationalism alone is not good enough for the Shia: individual nationhood is less important than traditional Islamic rule over the global community of Muslims or *ummah*, under a single spiritual and temporal ruler, a caliph and a direct descendant of the Prophet Mohammed. So far so good, Adam?"

"Yeah, but if they are all Muslims, why don't the Shia and the Sunni all get along anyway?" Adam was still not sure he was on firm ground, and his face once again revealed to Bitar his puzzlement.

Bitar sighed and patiently tried to explain. "Look, while most Muslims today are Sunni, the Shia grew to resent them. This was especially true where the Shia dominated the Muslim population in countries like Iran and Iraq. This came to a revolutionary boiling point in majority Shia Iran in 1979 when the shah or 'king' was forced into exile. He was replaced by a theocratic government of religious leaders. They felt that the shah had gone too far to modernize and westernize what was then called Persia and that he had strayed away from Islamic tradition. As you know, that theocracy is still in charge of Iran to this day."

"OK, I think I get it now," said Adam.

"Fine," said Bitar, "but understand that the popular Shia revolutionary movement posed a threat to the rule of secular-minded Sunni strong men. That movement has since spread across what some call a geographic 'Shia crescent.' It's dominated by the Shia in Iran and Iraq, extends east to Azerbaijan, India and Pakistan and south into Shia minority populations in Kuwait, Saudi Arabia and Yemen. There are also Iranian Shia proxies fighting foreign wars of independence from Sunni rule. These include the Houthi in Yemen, and Hezbollah in Lebanon. So, you can see that this is a big issue within Islam."

Adam was about to reply when a sudden flash of lightening and rumble of thunder interrupted the conversation. Bitar, clearly exhausted after his lecture, asked if he could take his leave and if Adam could meet him at the same time and place the next day to complete his explanation. Adam's head was spinning with all that he had heard. He too was tired and willingly agreed.

The Darkest Side

When they met the next day, Adam had begun to digest the outline of the complicated history of crosscurrents that seemed to ebb and flow constantly throughout the Arab world. He was full of questions.

"Professor, what about all those groups we keep hearing about on the news, like Hamas, the PLO, Hezbollah, Al Qaeda, and ISIS?"

Bitar nodded. "It's confusing because of the differences and similarities between some of them, and it isn't a nice, tidy black-and-white picture. But the main things to grasp are, first, their shared hatred of Israel; next, their hatred of any foreign military forces operating in a Muslim country; and third, the secular and more pragmatic approach to governance by Muslim nationalists versus the more religious traditionalists. This last group includes the Wahhabis of Saudi Arabia, also called Salafis, who adhere to a strict and literal interpretation of the Quran."

"Professor," said Adam deferentially, "I need some help to tell one sect from the other."

"OK," said Bitar. "Here's a quick look at some of them. Take Hamas. It's is a nationalist, fundamentalist, Sunni-and-Palestinian-based resistance movement. The Arabic word *hamas* means 'courage,' 'zeal,' 'strength,' and 'bravery.' It was founded in the late 1980s and is now based in the Gaza Strip in southwestern Palestine. It provides legitimate social support to its people through a civilian wing called Dawah. It also deploys a military wing called the Qassam Brigades. Its sworn mission is to 'liberate' Palestine and destroy Israel."

"Great! Got it," said Adam.

"You might also like to know that Hamas is an offshoot of Egypt's Muslim Brotherhood, which originated in the late 1920s as a transnational Sunni charitable and political group. Hamas's Sunni leader today is Ismael Haniyeh—though I think a former long-term Israeli prisoner, now released, is its likely future leader, a man called Yahya Sinwar."

"Never heard of him," said Adam.

Bitar raised his eyebrows. "This guy Sinwar has quite a resume. He founded Hamas's secret police. He personally killed Palestinians who collaborated with Israel. Though jailed for two decades by the Israelis, he was freed in a prisoner swap in 2011. He went on to command the Qassam Brigades. He's supposedly first in line to succeed the octogenarian Mahmood Abbas as president of the Palestine Authority."

"Hmmm," mused Adam between mouthfuls of chili. "Now, what about the PLO?"

"That," said Bitar, "is also a Sunni group. It was founded in 1964 to 'liberate' Palestine from Israel through armed struggle and to restore the Palestinian homeland. Interestingly, the PLO's charter makes no mention of religion, even though its territory today, the Gaza Strip, is predominantly Sunni Muslim. It's a secular Islamic group whose majority faction is called Fatah, meaning 'victory.' Essentially, the PLO name has been replaced by Fatah."

"I vaguely remember something about that." Adam confessed his ignorance once more as Bitar resumed.

"Fatah," said the lecturer, "fought a civil war with Hamas in 2007 over a power struggle between them that had built up since the death in 2004 of Al-Husseini's successor, Yasser Arafat. Since then, they patched up their relations. Enough about Hamas, Adam?"

"Sure. What about Hezbollah?" asked the recent graduate.

"That's an all-Shia organization," said Bitar, "which serves as a foreign political and military proxy for the Iranian Shia leaders, or *mullahs*. Its name means 'the Party of God,' and it's based in Lebanon. It was founded in the mid-1980s, just a few years before Hamas, by a group of Lebanese Shia clerics. Its goal is to destroy Israel and to defend Lebanon and Syria from Sunni Islamists."

"And Al Qaeda?" Adam asked.

"That name," said Bitar, "means 'The Base.' It's a multi-national militant Sunni organization, founded in 1988 during the Soviet Russian invasion of Afghanistan. There are some sixty thousand active members today. It's allegedly supported financially by extremist Sunni factions in Saudi Arabia and Qatar. Al Qaeda's mission is to remove all foreign influence from Muslim countries and impose strict *sharia* law in place of all man-made law. Essentially, it wants to force a return to the strict 7th-century life of its top prophet, Mohammed. It regards liberal or moderate Muslims as heretics. And it hates American or other foreign intervention in the affairs of any Muslim country."

"Uh huh," said Adam. "And ISIS or ISIL?"

"Those initials," said Bitar, "mean, respectively, the Islamic State of Iraq and Syria and the Islamic State of Iraq and the Levant. Founded in 1999, this is a Salafi extremist militant group which broke away from Al Qaeda. It wants to recreate a worldwide Islamic state—or caliphate—in Iraq, Syria, and far beyond. Like Al Qaeda, it wants to impose strict *sharia* law. It's also a breakaway group from Al Qaeda because, unlike that group, it set out to grab land and govern it. It paid its way by selling Iraqi oil from captured oilfields, smuggling, taxing the people under its control, selling stolen artifacts, demanding ransoms from kidnappings, and extortion. Now, it essentially competes with Al Qaeda to lead the *jihad* for a world caliphate."

Adam wondered how *sharia* law compared to man-made law adopted in the West. Also, what did that term *jihad* really mean?

Bitar explained patiently how *sharia* theology governs both the spiritual and secular life of Muslims. Its origins, he explained, stemmed from the verbal legal tradition or, in Arabic, the *sunna* or daily practices, and the *hadith* or traditions attributed to the Prophet Mohammed. However, he noted that different Muslim countries and communities have their own interpretations of this tradition. These opinions are reflected in the opinions—or *fatwas*—of Islamic scholars or *imams*, because there is no one single authority, such as a pope, in Islam.

Adam admitted he was unclear about the meaning of the term *jihad*, and Bitar clarified it: "To many of us here in the West," he said, "we tend to think it means 'war.' That's true where Muslims are expected to 'struggle' to defend Islam from nonbelievers or foreign influence, using force as needed. This is typically how extreme Islamists might define it, like the groups we just mentioned. But more moderate Muslims think of *jihad* more as an inner personal struggle, to live out their faith and build a good society for their people."

Adam felt he had learned more in the past few days about Islam than in his entire lifetime. But this concentrated course in some essentials of Islam was still a lot to absorb.

It crossed his mind that Bitar had mentioned the Heilmann maps when they'd met in Paraguay, though the topic had not come up since. At least the 'professor' had no idea that they were now in Agnes's possession. Adam would keep it that way, at least for now.

As Adam and Bitar parted at last, it struck Adam that now was a good time to give Agnes a call with an update.

Something to Hide

Agnes was still at her aunt's house in Budapest when Adam telephoned. Her temporary stay of a few days was now entering weeks. Her aunt, a widow, had encouraged her to stay with her for as long as she wanted, especially after learning about what had happened to her own brother, Tibor Lantos.

Aunt Fanni was a warm-hearted fifty-something. A retired teacher and an avid reader, her short, graying hair and worried frown reminded Agnes of her uncle. The two women decided to visit Lantos as soon as the doctors allowed it.

He was sitting up in bed, with his head wrapped with bandages like a turban. They were relieved that he not only recognized them, but also smiled with joy at their visit.

"The nurses here are tough, but they mean well," he said. "You're my first family visitors. How are you?"

He explained that his wound would leave a scar on his temple, but that otherwise he might be free to leave the hospital within a week. The police had advised him not to return to his home in Szentendre, but to find other accommodation elsewhere until they had completed their inquiries. His sister rose to the occasion and asked him to move into her house. He readily accepted.

When Adam reached Agnes, her uncle had already begun to settle into his new quarters. She had started to resume her research work with him. Adam was glad to hear this, shared his family news with her, and then came to the point.

"Agnes, two things. You remember that former Middle Eastern professor of mine that you met on our trip? I just met with him here in New York. Tell Uncle Tibor he was right about him—but also tell him that he's not a bad guy after all. I can explain later. The other thing is—you know that package we brought back from South America? I've learned that some powerful people are after it. Do you understand what I'm saying?"

"Yes." Agnes knew he was right.

"That stuff is something that you need to hide. You can't leave it at your aunt's house. Where else is there?" asked Adam.

Agnes thought for a moment. "Well," she said, "I suppose I can open a new bank account here in Budapest where they have safe-deposit boxes."

"Great idea!" said Adam. "Then please, for your own safety, do that as soon as possible. Put the package there, at least for now. Please!"

The anxiety and urgency in Adam's voice made it clear to Agnes this was an urgent task.

Once their call ended, she retreated to her bedroom, retrieved the plastic bag containing the maps from her suitcase, and carefully placed them into her backpack. That afternoon, she took a taxi across the Danube to Buda.

The manager of the small branch of Magyarbank was only too happy to open a new account for her. He offered her a large safe-deposit box into which she promptly placed the wrapped contents of a worn-looking plastic bag.

Later that afternoon, Tibor called her mobile phone. A friend in his agency, the Hungarian Information Office, had just called him with a warning. There were reports of German BND people arriving in Budapest and making inquiries about a young woman who may know about some missing stolen documents. Other reports suggested that the intelligence services of several countries were also making inquiries and had feet on the ground in Hungary.

"I think you need to leave Budapest for a while to let things calm down. Why don't you visit Adam in New York? He'd love to see you. As you have been wonderful to me and helped save my life, the least I can do is buy you a round-trip airfare."

Agnes had never visited the United States, and here also was a chance to see Adam again. A plan began to form in her head.

Bad Apples

Halycon Club life was starting to wear on the Tinker family. It was one thing to spend a few days there, but several weeks was already plenty enough. Fred decided to check out their New York apartment and then think about flying back to Montego Island to check on their summer home.

He was going through the mail at his Eightieth Street four-bedroom penthouse apartment when his mobile phone rang. The display indicated a number in London, England.

"That you, Charlie?" asked Fred, surprised to hear a familiar voice.

"Yes, indeed it is!" Charlie sounded excited and upbeat. "How are you, Fred? Sorry I had to be abrupt on our last call, but things were heating up here. I'm still under the gun. Where are you now?"

"In New York," said Fred, wondering what was coming next.

"Good. I'll be there in two days. When can we meet?" Charlie asked. They set a date, time and place. Charlie suggested breakfast at the Mayfair Sovereign Hotel on Park. Fred agreed to book a table for two.

"Fred, do you still have that little gold bar I sent you? Please bring it when we meet."

Fred obliged and duly arrived at the hotel to find Charlie already seated in the restaurant. It was just after 8:00 a.m. There were a handful of other business breakfast meetings going on. Charlie had a corner table in an alcove for greater privacy. They spent a few minutes catching up on family life. Then Charlie shifted gears.

"Fred, I have to be brief." His face became serious. "I have other meetings scheduled in New York this morning. What I'm about to tell you must not leave this table. You and I go back over many years as business partners. Correct? Until now, my business and other activities have been kept separate. Those 'other activities' involve some sensitive work with certain people in the British government. One such activity involves the consortium in which you expressed interest as an investor. By the way, did you bring that gold bar with you, as I asked?"

"Yes, it's right here." Fred pulled the matchbox-sized ingot from his inside jacket pocket.

"Hand it to me, please. Remember that I cautioned you not to drop it or damage it?"

"Yes, I do. As you can see, I've looked after it carefully!"

Charlie inspected the object. It seemed undamaged. Then, to Fred's surprise, Charlie stood up, turned to face the wall behind the table, and deliberately dropped the item on the wooden floor.

It split into four uneven pieces.Fred's jaw dropped open. He was speechless.

Charlie turned and resumed his seat. A waiter hurriedly approached to ask if everything was all right. Charlie asked if the "broken pottery" could be swept up and removed. The waiter promptly obliged.

Charlie knew Fred would be stunned. "Fred," he said, "this was not a real gold ingot. It was a fake, designed to draw normal business investors like you into a consortium. The idea was to make this consortium look as legitimate as possible."

"Charlie, are you telling me I've been sold a bill of goods for some phony purpose?"

"I'm saying, Fred, that you and others like you were used as bait."

"Bait?" said Fred. His jaw dropped. "For what purpose?"

"To catch some bad apples before they become poisonous."

Fred remained incredulous. "Charlie, I just gotta say, I'm lost. What's this all about?"

Charlie's eyes narrowed as he stared hard at his longtime friend and associate. He asked Fred, "Have you seen press reports lately about hidden Nazi gold located in Europe and Latin America? I ask because I am aware of a conspiracy launched by a global network of Nazis to start up and try to win another World War. The conspirators need vast funds to do something like this. They know that there are billions hidden somewhere, but they don't know exactly where to look."

Fred interjected. "Wait a minute! Does this have something to do with my son, the one you met in Paraguay?"

"Fred, we just don't know for sure. But we do know that he and a young woman were there in Paraguay in a town called Nueva Germania, just a day or two before an elderly woman was found murdered there. The murder report came to the attention of the world press because the victim was the daughter of an infamous German Nazi, Klaus Heilmann, who allegedly died in Berlin in 1945. There are people who think the woman knew how to find most of the hidden loot. We really don't know who killed her. But the indications are that they're the same people behind the conspiracy I mentioned."

"Charlie, I will gladly ask my son Adam what he knows. But I must tell you something too." The mention of Nazis reminded him with a jolt about a guilty secret he had carried with him all his life. "When I was a child in Germany," he now told his friend, "I was very impressionable. When I heard Hitler speak, I so much wanted to join the Hitler Youth. But my father forbade it and got us out of Germany to Switzerland and from there to America. It was only after the war ended that I started to see what the German Nazis were all about. To this day, I feel so ashamed that I bought into their message of hate-filled glory as a kid. What I'm trying to say is, I'll do whatever I can to help you."

"That's in the past, old friend. Not to worry. We must now fight against it ever happening again. Find out what you can from Adam. Now, I really must leave to catch another meeting." He glanced at his wristwatch. "It's been wonderful to see you at last!" He stood up and hastily made his way out to the street.

Another Time Zone

When the airline tickets arrived, Agnes tore open the envelope, expecting to find a pair of round-trip tickets in economy class. She shrieked with joy on finding round-trip business class tickets instead. Her uncle had outdone himself, weak as he was.

The Polish airline LOT had just launched the only nonstop flight between Budapest and JFK. She could leave Budapest at noon and arrive in the United States at four in the afternoon of the same day. What could be better?

Her aunt took her to the airport two days later. As they parted ways, Agnes pressed a small, sealed envelope into her aunt's hands.

"If anyone calls you about me, especially a stranger, please say that I've gone to visit friends in the country, but I never told you where. Here's an envelope containing the key to my safe-deposit box. Please hold onto it for me?"

The flight took off on time.

Ten hours later, the jet touched down at JFK.

Agnes decided not to tell Adam she was coming, to surprise

him. She had booked a single room at a small hotel near the Budapest café on Second Avenue. She decided to take a tour bus, get to know the basics of getting around, and then give Adam a call.

Before her flight, she had mailed the second of her three Magyarbank safe-deposit box keys to Adam to let him know that the 'stuff' he had mentioned was safely stored. She had also had the foresight to send him photocopies of all the Heilman maps before locking the originals away at the bank. Fortunately, she had kept his family's home address on Montego Island.

She had threaded the eye of a third safe-deposit box key through a simple necklace which she wore as she walked through US Immigration and Customs Enforcement. Their agents were more interested in the purpose of her visit than in her personal accessories. She produced her return ticket and convinced the inquisitors that, yes, she would indeed return to Budapest within two weeks; and no, she was not here seeking to work illegally.

The hotel room on Second Avenue was adequate, though hardly worth a review on TripAdvisor. She booked a Big Bus Tour of Manhattan. Someone suggested she also take the riverboat tour around Manhattan Island. Within two days, she began to feel the vibe of being a New Yorker.

She then decided it was time to call Adam's mobile phone, thinking he would still be at the family house on Montego Island. When he told her he was in New York, she felt a sudden thrill. They arranged to meet at a small café near Central Park.

Hesitant and awkward at first when they met, they both giggled and then hugged. Adam put his arm protectively around her waist and led her to a table in the back of the café. Each updated the other. Then Adam popped a question.

"What now?" said Adam, almost teasing her.

"Did you get my package?" said Agnes.

"What package?" said Adam, in sudden alarm.

"Oh no! I sent it to your parents' house in Montego Island!" cried Agnes.

"But we've not been there for weeks!" Adam explained why they had relocated to New York and was about to explain why they had not returned to the family's Manhattan apartment when Agnes broke in indignantly. "Then can someone there forward it to you here?"

Adam remembered the caretaker. Perhaps he could send it on.

He placed a call and left a message.

Home Invasion

F red had started to go through the mail on an earlier, fleeting visit to the family's New York apartment. He had returned there to finish up the task after his meeting with Charlie. The housekeeper had been in while they were away and had piled up the usual wave of bills for his later review. She had dropped all circulars into the trash, as instructed. It looked like Fred could tell Jill that everything was in order.

He decided that day to book a round-trip flight to Montego Island, to check that all was well there too and to collect the mail. He would leave the next morning from White Plains and return that evening. There was no point in hanging around on the island, especially out of season.

A text message arrived on his mobile phone the morning of his arrival, just as he was hailing a cab at Montego Airport. It was his caretaker.

"Mr. Tinker, there's a problem at the house. If you're here, you had better come over as soon as you can."

There were two State Police cars in his driveway as the cab pulled up. Fred produced his driver license and verified his identification.

"What's going on, officer?"

"Sir, there's been a break-in. You won't be pleased at what you see inside. You need to take a look."

The shock hit him violently.

The whole ground floor was a mess. Lamps, chairs, tables, photographs, and more were all over the floor. Chests of drawers had been flung open, and their contents thrown everywhere. Expletives had been sprayed in red paint all over the walls and mirrors. It was as if the place were a madhouse.

"Sir, please let us know if you think anything of value was taken."

As best he could tell, there was little of value to justify this home invasion in the first place. It was a vacation home after all, not a jewelry store.

"Nothing that I can tell at the moment," said Fred, trying hard to keep his composure.

The caretaker emerged from behind the house. "Mr. Tinker, I don't know what to say. I've never seen anything like it!"

Fred stepped over piles of broken family photograph frames and started upstairs to inspect the bedrooms.

The mattresses had been slashed open, and bedsprings and padding were strewn about. Cupboards and drawers had been emptied out. Was this simple animal vandalism or were the people who did this looking for something? And if so, what? Fred descended the stairs and asked the caretaker for a report.

"I came in early this morning, sir, and found the front door open. That's when I saw the mess."

"Do you think anything went missing?" asked Fred, his mind trying frantically to inventory anything of value he could think of that might have been taken. But nothing came to mind.

"I got the mail, sir," said the caretaker. "Here it is. Someone had gone through it, but none of it was opened." He handed a pile of mail to Fred who stared at it blankly.

"When were you last here?" he asked.

"I came by late yesterday afternoon, sir, because your son Adam left a message asking me to collect a package someone had sent him from abroad and forward it to him in New York by overnight courier."

Fred absently made a mental note to ask Adam about the package. He thought nothing more of it as he stepped outside and watched the police put a piece of yellow 'crime scene—do not enter' tape across the front door.

There was nothing more to be done except for Fred to give instructions to his caretaker for a cleanup.

But that would have to wait while the detectives finished their work.

Package Deal

When the package from Montego Island arrived at the Halcyon Club, Adam made sure to pick it up promptly. There they were: photocopies of all the Heilman maps and a small envelope, marked *Magyar bank*, containing a single safe-deposit box key.

His father returned that evening and asked to speak with him privately.

"Adam, don't tell your mother or your sister, but our house in Montego Island was majorly vandalized sometime last night. The place is a complete mess. The police are investigating."

Adam felt his adrenalin shoot up followed by a sudden tension in his stomach.

"The detectives want to comb the house for clues. It looks like they took nothing of value, maybe nothing at all. It may just be vandals."

"Dad, that's really *awful*! What can I do to help?"

Fred's expression revealed his atypical vulnerability. "Look, Adam," he said, "don't discuss this with anyone—anyone at
192

all. The police need to do their work. I have some mail for you. By the way, our caretaker told us he forwarded a package to you last evening by courier. Did you get it?"

"Yes. Thanks, Dad. Just some paperwork from Hungary that I forgot to pack." It was beginning to get too easy to tell his father white lies.

Later that day, Adam hit on an idea.

First, he would make his own set of the map photocopies, in addition to the ones Agnes had sent him. He would then take the new photocopies and change the map coordinates on them, map by map. If at some point the map hunters caught up with him, he would give them the doctored copies and let them think they had found what they wanted. He would tell them, if asked, that someone burned the originals in Hungary before he had brought them to New York.

Finally, the untouched "original photocopies" which Agnes had sent to him would find their way to some small New York area savings bank's safe-deposit box, along the lines of exactly what Agnes had done in Budapest with the originals.

He found a suitable small savings bank in the telephone directory, presented himself there, opened a savings account, and requested a safe-deposit box. He then deposited the "originals" that Agnes had sent to him, added one of the two safe-deposit box keys to his keychain, and slipped the second one into his jacket pocket.

A Small Favor

Charlie called Fred shortly after the home invasion episode. He sounded anxious when Fred told him about what had happened at his Montego Island retreat. It seemed to confirm his worst fears.

"We don't have a lot of time, Fred," said Charlie. "I think there's a connection between the vandalization of your home and our exploration consortium. Let's meet for lunch. I can't discuss this on the phone."

They found a diner on Third Avenue. It was grimy and uninviting, but popular with assorted office staff in the area. The noise level served to muffle anyone or any device that might overhear their conversation.

"Fred, I have to tell you something. You're not going to like it. Remember I told you that you and some other legitimate businesspeople were being used as bait to attract and flush out some bad apples? Well, the whole consortium is a fake operation."

Fred was beside himself. *How on earth did I ever get suckered into this business?* he thought. Charlie could almost read his mind, but he pressed on anyway. "That consortium was created to lure some bad characters out of the woodwork and take them down. To make it seem credible, several legitimate businesspeople like yourself were invited to participate. You're the only one of them now who's being told about this."

"Why me?"

"Because you're a legitimate businessman with a clean record—or at least, I hope so!" Charlie's engaging humor was, if nothing else, disarming. "That's why!" he continued. "We also need a little favor from you. You can help by continuing the fiction that this consortium is a genuine new exploration company and that you are one of its genuine investors. We also need you to attend a meeting of 'prospective investors' here in New York in a few days' time. The idea is to flush out some bad people into the open and delude them into thinking they have it made—that is, by locating someone else's money, not theirs, to help them find the hidden treasure they need for their agenda. But there's a wrinkle."

"What's that?" said Fred, with an air of weary resignation

"They need certain maps to guide excavators to the site or sites where the loot is hidden. They have people in several intelligence agencies looking for those maps."

Fred interjected. "Might one of those people be called Jones, allegedly with the State Department?"

"Yes. Others include the two Germans you met at the Pullach office of the BND. But even in Britain, there are people in government service who sympathize with the hardcore Germans and Islamic extremists behind the idea of starting World War III. My job is to identify and watch as many of these folks as possible. When the time is right, and we have most in our sights, then we'll take them all down."

Charlie paused to let all this sink in. He could see that Fred was wavering.

"Fred, we really do need this favor from you. We want you to attend the first consortium meeting and appear to be the credible businessman you are. We will have others there to observe who else shows up in addition to those we already know about. Will you do it?"

Fred rubbed his chin. Did he really want to get deeper into this thing that had started to ruin his life? He reflected and then responded.

There was a long pause. "OK," he said, clearly with reluctance. "For you, I'll do it."

The First Seeker

B arely a day later, Adam was about to leave the club and meet Agnes some blocks away. The switchboard called his room.

"Mr. Tinker, sir. There's a Mr. Jones calling for you. He says he is with the State Department. Will you take the call?"

Adam's antenna told him to be on guard. He had never heard of Jones…or could this be the same Jones that his father had referred to some days ago? He made a quick decision.

"Please tell him that I'm out, and you don't know when to expect me back."

He felt the need to reach Agnes and warn her that their pursuers were starting to close in. He had not yet told her or anyone else about his plans and action with the maps.

At the club entrance, he hailed a cab. It stopped, and he got in. Just as he thought it would set off, the opposite rear door opened, and someone entered.

"Hey, this is my cab! If you want to share a cab, try somewhere else!" cried Adam indignantly.

The heavyset man beside him tapped the cab's divider window, and the cab set off.

"Mr. Tinker? Mr. Adam Tinker? You and I are going for a little ride."

Adam felt his heart begin to pound and sweat breaking out on his neck and forehead. Was this guy going to assault or kill him?

"I just need a few moments of your time, sir. My name is Jones. State Department security. I believe you have in your possession some documents that don't belong to you." It was not a question, but a statement.

"I don't know you or what you're talking about," quipped Adam, putting on a brave face—yet feeling sudden terror underneath and heavy sweat in his armpits. He tried to jump out as the cab slowed and turned a corner. The door was locked. The driver appeared unconcerned about what was going on in the back of his cab.

"Mr. Tinker, I don't think you realize you could be in a lot of trouble. There are people out there looking for stolen documents, and, if they find you, they won't be having a polite conversation with you like this. Do I make myself clear?"

The man turned to the driver.

"Drive this guy back to where you picked him up and drop him off. Meantime, Mr. Tinker, here's my card and my phone number. You'd better call me sooner than later. Otherwise, you may regret it."

Jones stopped the cab, got out, and melted away into the flow of pedestrians. The cabbie took Adam back to the Halcyon Club and dropped him at the entrance without a word.

He was shaken and still sweating profusely. He took the elevator to the upper floors, opened his bedroom door, and flopped in a daze onto his bed. After a few minutes of gazing blankly in silence at the ceiling, he slowly regained his composure. His mind began racing as he reached for the bedside phone. He then called the front desk.

"Hi," said Adam into the mouthpiece. "Can you remind me whether there is a second entrance to the club?"

"Yes, sir," said the doorman stationed at the front door. "There's a rear entrance which is open from dawn till midnight."

"Thanks," said Adam. "No more calls tonight, please. I'm turning in for this evening." He put down the phone, stood up, grabbed his wallet, and left the room. Making sure that the doorman did not see him, he slipped quietly to the back of the building and exited it through its rear door.

The Consortium

The Wall Street branch of the Bank Nineveh PLC was hard to find in the warren of streets that makes up the financial district. Situated in an alleyway off Water Street, it was almost a stone's throw from the East River but still hard to find, even for a seasoned New York cabbie.

It was also ideally suited to the kind of meeting in which Mr. Frederick Tinker, Chairman and CEO of the Tinker Hedge Funds, found himself one overcast morning.

Standing at the entrance on his arrival were two large blond-haired men, who looked as though they could be night club bouncers. Their menacing appearance and forced smiles were not reassuring. They inspected Fred's invitation card, then directed him to an elevator and asked him to take it to the second floor.

The smell of jasmine filled his nostrils as he exited the elevator into a hallway. There at the end of the hallway was a large, polished mahogany double door, adorned with two gleaming, round, and highly polished-gold handles. The doorway opened into a medium-sized boardroom. Several men were standing around, murmuring to one another.

They looked up at the newcomer.

Fred quickly surveyed the room, which was furnished with a plush, deep-beige carpet, two glittering chandeliers, and a pair of lion sculptures of Middle Eastern origin, which together imparted an artificial air of culture and graciousness to the space.

He recognized two faces instantly. They were the two he vividly recalled from his visit to Pullach. As one of then moved toward him, he felt his muscles tighten.

"Mr. Tinker! Ludwig Farben! We are so delighted you could join us today! You remember Dr. Thiel over here, my colleague from Berlin? Now, let me introduce you to some of the others here."

Patting Fred on the back, he guided him around the room. As he did so, more faces appeared at the door, and the room began to fill up.

"Here is Minister Lukman of Egypt. And here, First Counselor Ahmed bin Khouri of the Saudi Embassy." Fred struggled to remember all the names. But he noticed that many were either German or from the Middle East.

During his final round of handshakes, he saw a breathless Charlie Fortescue entering the boardroom. "Gentleman," gasped Charlie, "I must apologize for being so late. The traffic was the worst I've seen here in memory! Please, do be seated. We have a few items to discuss before lunch."

Seats were preassigned. Fred found a tent card with his name on it and the name of his company. Several chairs remained unoccupied.

As the last person present sat down, the branch manager introduced Charlie, who then opened the meeting. "Welcome, everyone, to the first meeting of the new Global Exploration Consortium, the GEC. I am Charles Fortescue, the consortium's managing partner. It is my distinct pleasure to welcome you all today to what promises to be a group of extraordinary people doing something quite unique. You have each received a prospectus outlining the scope of the GEC project. Unless there are questions, may I proceed to give you an updated report on the status of our plans?"

There were no questions. Charlie proceeded to outline the funding and personnel needs involved and to share a timeline. There were murmurs of approval.

"There's only one thing standing between us now and the successful execution of our investment plan. To realize the considerable value of our discoveries, we need precise directions of where to conduct our exploration. I am glad to say that we're very close to finding those directions, and, when we do, I shall be happy to share a summary of them with each of you."

A hand went up. The Egyptian minister wanted to know more details of how and where the directions would be found. Charlie smiled an empathic smile and acknowledged the question, almost as if he had expected it.

"Minister Lukman, yours is a perfectly valid question which indeed deserves an answer. The matter of locating the related plans is highly sensitive. The process of obtaining
202

them demands the utmost delicacy and the tightest security—for obvious reasons. But rest assured that my people are working on it at this very moment, and I expect to hear within forty-eight hours that their mission has been accomplished."

The answer seemed to satisfy the minister. There were assenting nods around the table.

The double doors opened once more, and all present turned to see who had arrived. Fred stifled a gasp. Standing in the doorway was the so-called State Department man named Field who had called on him in Montego Island. Beside him stood General Pugh, the same fellow who had invited Fred around for a friendly chat at a house on Montego Island.

A few moments later, more people arrived. Most were European. One introduced himself as the economic counselor at the Italian Embassy; and another as a French businessman. There were two Swiss pharmaceutical executives and an Austrian politician.

Fred's mind was frantically processing. *If Charlie invited all these people, why did he need me to be here?* The only possibility was that within this group were the suspects he was after but could not yet identify.

Charlie continued his opening remarks. "No need for concern if you just arrived. Everyone will have a secure zip drive to take with them after lunch, and on it will be all that you want to know at this early stage. Now, perhaps we can adjourn next door for lunch."

A meal of cold poached salmon with a dill sauce was served,

followed by a simple fresh fruit salad. Iced tea and water were also served. Predictably, given the nature of the bank and its host, no alcohol was offered.

Fred found himself explaining the basics of hedge fund operations to the Austrian politician seated beside him.

After a while, the man took a shine to Fred and leaned in toward him. "Mr. Tinker, I understand that your family came from Germany and that when you were a small boy, you dreamed about joining the Hitler Youth? Yes?"

The observation caught Fred off guard. Before he could respond, the man said, "Well, this project of ours will offer you another opportunity to turn that dream into reality! There is a whole global network of people like us who also share that dream. Some of them are in this room."

Fred said one word. "Oh?"

"Yes, Mr. Tinker. Do you observe that many countries from Europe and the Middle East are represented here today? Some are civil servants. Others are businessmen or simply individuals like me. Many of us are members."

"Members of the consortium?"

"No, members of the *Familienverband*, the Family Union. One big happy family of Germans and their friends in Europe and the Middle East who are preparing now for the final battle."

"Battle?" said Fred innocently.

"Yes!" continued the Austrian. "We and our old friends

204

from all over the Middle East are preparing to complete the führer's goal of creating a great world empire. Once we find the resources carefully hidden by our grandfathers and fathers, there will be nothing to stop us succeeding in that mission."

Fred nodded, as if in agreement. He then said, "That's very interesting to me. Who are the others here in this *Familienverband*?"

The Austrian pointed out six key players and reminded Fred of their names. Farben and Thiel, the two Arab officials, and the two Americans, Field and Pugh.

At last, Charlie rose and tapped his empty iced tea glass for silence.

"I would like to thank Nineveh Bank's branch manager, Amir bin Daoud, for his hospitality today, including this splendid lunch. We hope you have all had a chance to get to know some other members of the GEC. We look forward to updating you within the next few days about next steps. Our meeting is now adjourned. Thank you for coming."

Charlie had made a successful effort to avoid direct or indirect contact with Fred, as he had promised he would.

None Like It Hot

The back entrance of the Halcyon Club led into a dark and narrow alley off Forty-Fifth Street. As he reached Forty-Fifth and hailed a cab, Adam placed a call to Agnes to alert her to be at a bar near her hotel on the West Side. Something told him not to mention anything more over the phone. She immediately picked up the tension in his voice and knew he had something important to tell her.

She was waiting for him in a small booth at the back of the bar.

Adam quickly updated her on his encounter with the stranger in his cab. "They're getting closer," he said. "We need to do something."

"Who is 'they,' and what do you think we should do?" asked Agnes.

"That's just it." Adam was stumped. "I don't even know who 'they' are myself. The guy in the cab told me he was with State Department security. Maybe yes, maybe no. I just have a feeling he wasn't acting alone, and that he was pretending to be a legitimate US government official. Why else would he muscle his way into someone else's cab in broad daylight? And why did the cab driver say nothing and do nothing?"

Adam told her about the maps she had copied and sent him, how he had made a second set of copies and had then doctored their coordinates. She was impressed at his ingenuity. At least, if cornered by a hostile party, he could offer up these doctored maps to whoever came looking for them, and so throw them off course.

As Agnes was about to respond, she glanced out the side window toward her hotel a block away. Three police cars screeched to a halt at its entrance. Several men, some in plainclothes, jumped out and into the lobby. Agnes's room was on the third floor. Before she left to meet Adam at the bar, she distinctly remembered turning off all the lights. But a few minutes after the police team had entered the building, the lights went back on in her room.

"Adam, I don't like this. I need to get away from here. Why would the New York police be looking for me or for something in my possession?"

He had to come up with a plan, and fast.

An hour later, the couple were on their way to Agnes's new accommodation, at the Halcyon Club.

A Likely Story

Adam called his father's room early the next morning. "Dad, would you have breakfast with me in the dining room?"

Fred was surprised at this atypical invitation, and from someone not known to be an early riser. But he concurred. "Fine, boy. Be down there at 8:30 sharp."

They ate a hearty breakfast, and Fred gave an update on the repairs to the Montego Island house. Apparently, the cleanup and repairs were moving along nicely; but there was the little matter of whether the family should keep the house or relocate in the light of recent events.

"Sooner or later, I'm going to have to tell your mother about what happened there—and she won't be happy," said Fred with a long face, clearly dreading another outburst of hysteria from his spouse. While he vented, Adam waited patiently for the right moment to break his own news.

There was a moment's silence, then Adam jumped right in. "Dad, there's something you need to know. There's a woman staying here at the club."

"So what?" said Fred. "Plenty of women stay here, mostly on business."

"Yes, but I booked a room for her." As he spoke, he almost wished the words had never left his lips.

"You did *what*?" spouted Fred, thinking, *How many more shocks do I need to my system?*

"Dad, it's a long story," said the son. "But the time has come to fill you in. There's a lot I haven't told you."

An hour and half later, Adam had emptied his soul. All of it, that is, except the part about the doctored maps, which he somehow forgot to mention. But to his surprise, Fred smiled and thanked him.

"Adam, you may not know it, but you've helped me at last to pull a lot of pieces together. Until this morning, nothing made sense to me. I have to say I am mightily impressed at hearing what you've been through and what you've accomplished. You may not realize it, but you could be saving a lot of people a lot of trouble—and worse."

He shared his recent activities involving Charlie and the consortium. It was ironic that father and son had been unwittingly involved in the same game all along, and with some of the same players. For the first time Adam could remember in a long time, they had a good laugh.

"Dad, you need to meet Agnes. She's amazing. Good-looking too. But she's only here as a tourist and will have to return to Hungary in a few more days."

Adam called Agnes's room, woke her, and invited her down

for breakfast. The look of surprise on her face when she saw Fred beside Adam was cause for both father and son to have another good laugh.

To her relief, and Adam's too, Fred listened to her attentively and patiently. He offered without hesitation to cover her board and lodging at the club until her return to Budapest. Agnes beamed with happiness, which made her look even more attractive. She was already beginning to feel attached to the Tinker family. And Fred felt something positive about her that he couldn't yet articulate, except that she seemed to be very bright.

"Now that we are all on the same page and in the same book," he said, "we'd better reach out to my friend Charlie. He may be able to help us."

Adam knew better than to argue with Fred, who promptly stood up and left the dining room to make a phone call.

Agnes was still troubled by what had appeared to be a police raid on her rented hotel room the night before. Why so many police cars and police? Was she on a wanted list somewhere for some crime she didn't commit? Had someone set her up as a criminal? This was a loose end. She wouldn't let go of it till she had the answer.

A Revelation

"Charlie! You there?" shouted Fred into the telephone's mouthpiece. "OK. Let me tell you what's been going on." He paused to collect his thoughts. "Some guy called Jones tried to strong-arm my son yesterday and threatened him unless he turned in some stolen documents wanted by the State Department. This sounds like the same Jones who came to my house in Montego Island with another guy called Field, the one who showed up at the consortium meeting."

Charlie's voice came over, but on a poor connection. "Well, Fred," he said, "we now know that Field is definitely a member of the *Familienverband*. It sounds like Field and Jones may be partners. There are at least two other suspects. They were the two you met in Germany, namely Farben and Thiel. We also think that the 'official investors' from Egypt and Saudi Arabia are there to represent the most extreme anti-Zionist and anti-Semitic people in the entire Arab world."

Fred was clearly shaken. "I don't like it, Charlie. This latest incident with my boy happened in broad daylight, right outside my club. I think it's time to put this thing to rest, don't you?"

"What do you mean?" asked Charlie.

Fred shared his latest revelation. "I think I've found the maps you told the consortium you were looking for."

"But that was just a bluff!" exclaimed Charlie. "There *are* no maps. We were going to close the consortium up in a few days and either make arrests or have the bad guys deported."

"Charlie, take it from me," Fred retorted. "I know about these maps and who has them." He stopped himself just in time from revealing more over the phone. "I have photocopies of the originals."

Fred heard a click on the line and another male voice in the background. He thought he heard a door shut too, as if Charlie had asked another listener to leave the room. The tone of Charlie's voice went low as he said, "Fred, meet me at noon today at the Hilton Midtown, and show me what you have. Put them in an ordinary, large, brown paper carrier bag."

The Hilton lobby was busy with tourists flooding in and out like ants. Fred spotted Charlie standing in a corner, tapping text messages into his smartphone. They shook hands.

"Let's get some coffee and look these over," he said, pointing toward a small coffee shop off the main foyer. Once they had placed their orders and had found a table, Fred pulled out at random one of the photocopied maps and spread it out on the table.

Charlie recognized it instantly. It was of a 13th-century castle, Ksiaz Castle, he explained, in what was now the Lower Silesia area of Poland, close to the eastern border of the Czech Republic. It had been owned by the German Hochberg family since the early 1500s, until one of its owners had fled to England to become a British citizen at the onset of World War II. The Nazis then occupied the castle. That had been in 1941.

They had called it, in German, *Schloss Fürstenstein*. It had become the core of a huge Nazi underground network of deep tunnels known as Projekt Reise, or Project Giant, consisting of a vast complex of concrete-reinforced tunnels.

The Ksiaz map's headings read:

Projekt Reise—Streng geheim

Schloss Fürstenstein

Gehiemer Tunnel dritte Ebene

Charlie translated from the German.

Project Giant—Top Secret

Furstenstein Castle

Secret Third Level Tunnel

"We happen to know quite a lot about Ksiaz Castle already," said Charlie. "But what we didn't know till now...and this is remarkable....is that there is a *third* level of tunnels beneath the building. What's fascinating to learn is that, until now, only *two* levels of tunnels have been discovered."

They continued poring over at least twenty more maps. They were from a long list of countries, including some in Europe and others in South America. In all cases, there were arrow markings pointing out directions through the tunnels to the *Lagerflächen,* or "storage areas." Each map was marked with the same initials: EJV. In the margin of each map was printed a legend containing symbols and their meanings.

One of them read: **EJV: Eigentum von Juden und Vertriebenen.**

"What that means," said Charlie, "is 'Jewish and Displaced Persons Property.'" The look on his face showed that he was clearly impressed, even stunned, by this new revelation. "Well, Fred, you have really done yourself proud to find these. How on earth did you do it?"

"Charlie, it's a long and convoluted story, and I'll share it with you sometime." Fred scratched his ear for a moment, knowing full well that he was taking credit for someone else's discovery.

"I understand," said Charlie, taking another envious glance at the Ksiaz Castle map. "Let me make a copy of just one of these maps so I can use it as proof to show our 'investors.' Then I think you should put all these for safekeeping into a bank safe-deposit box, just for now."

As they parted, neither noticed the tall young man with blond hair observing them from across the lobby and casually following them into the street.

Problem Solved

Fred took a taxi straight back to the Halcyon Club after his meeting with Charlie Fortescue. He made a point of delivering all of the remaining maps to Adam's room in person and suggested that Adam put them in a safe-deposit box. But Adam's mind was racing so much that, once again, he forgot to tell his father that the copies he had given to him were the doctored copies.

Meanwhile, when Adam called up to Agnes's room to tell her more about his conversation with Bitar, she was still preoccupied about the police visit to her hotel the night before. She was clearly frightened.

"Adam, we need to make a plan. Something tells me that people are looking for us because they think we have those maps. But I have an idea."

They joined one another for a light snack in the club café. There was no one else present, but they still spoke in hushed tones. Adam's face told her he too was feeling stress, but for a different reason.

"Agnes," he told her, "I forgot to tell my father that I doctored the set of maps that he took to his meeting with this

Fortescue guy. Perhaps I should own up to this?"

To his surprise, Agnes gave him a crafty smile and said, "My instinct tells me that you should tell no one else just yet, not even your father, about the doctored copies. Let's see what happens and how your father's contact reacts to them. We can always explain later that we have the true copies."

Though Adam felt like he was in the doghouse for not coming clean with Fred, Agnes's next words were comforting. "Look, Adam. Here's what I think we need to do. First, I think we should find a very smart Hungarian lawyer here in New York who supports the idea of reparations for expropriated Hungarian Jews. He would need to understand how much and how little has been done for them to date. There may be such a lawyer like that that here in New York. Uncle Tibor might be able to recommend one."

"Now that's a cool idea," said Adam brightly. *This girl is as smart as a whip*, he thought.

"Then," she continued in a low and conspiratorial voice, "I suggest we show this lawyer just one—but only one—of the falsified maps of buried gold and other stolen property. He or she may then recommend specific Hungarian Jewish support organizations and even be our spokesperson."

Said Adam, "I like the idea. But what kinds of organization are out there, *Agnes*hhhh?"

She smiled at his pitiful effort to sound like a native Hungarian speaker, then shared with him some of her current research. "Well, for instance, there's something called the World Jewish Restoration Organization. It provides limited financial help to all Holocaust survivors and their families whose property was stolen by the Nazis and, in this case, by pro-Nazi Hungarians."

"But why them?" Adam asked.

She had a ready reply. "I found out that one of the WJRO's beneficiaries is a Hungarian foundation known by the acronym of MAZSOK. That means, in English, the 'Jewish Heritage of Hungary Foundation.' MAZSOK helps provide pensions to about seven thousand Hungarian Holocaust survivors. We can then see what they—or some organization like them—can do to find the hidden property, produce it, and then redistribute it to deserving parties."

"Hmm. Not a bad idea," murmured Adam. "If they do a good job, then we can see about giving them a second or third map. But if they mess up, then we can look for another support group and give that a try."

Agnes emailed Lantos for a referral to a capable New York lawyer to provide the guidance and support needed.

Her uncle had been anxiously waiting to hear from her and promptly replied. "Glad to hear from you, Agnes! I hope all is well. I'm feeling much better, and my sister is still putting up with me in her house. Now, about that lawyer. There's only one name I would suggest. It's György Balogh, or to Adam, "George" Balogh. He's the best man for this job."

Adam was curious. He asked Agnes why would Lantos, though still working for the Hungarian government, not insist on Agnes delivering all the maps to him for government use?

She rolled her eyes and secretly thought, *Why don't young Americans like Adam read the news to find out what's going on in the world?*

She had to spell out what, to her, was the obvious. "Adam, you just don't seem to understand what's going on in Hungary today. There's a political resurgence toward the extreme right. The present government's leadership was recently elected with less than one half of the votes counted."

"Really?" said Adam, as if this was the first time he had heard about current Hungarian politics.

"Yes, really!" said Agnes, sounding exasperated. "It's already well-known that today's Hungarian leaders say one thing to other foreign leaders, notably in the European Union, and then they say something quite different to Hungarian voters at home."

"Like what?" Adam said lamely.

"Here's what!" Agnes's tone clearly told Adam she was getting impatient with him. "For example, they tell the Israelis that they support Israel against Arab and Palestinian interests. Then they tell their domestic audience that a prominent, globally recognized Hungarian billionaire, who happens to be Jewish, is resisting the government's move to the center right—which they like to call 'illiberal democracy.' They also oppose lifting Hungary's major restrictions on waves of immigration resulting from wars in the Middle East. They promise the European Union they will comply with immigration quotas for all EU members, and then they clamp down on immigration completely. As a result, it looks like Hungary will now lose its voting rights in the EU."

She paused and stared at Adam to see if any of this was sinking in. Satisfied that he was beginning to grasp the political reality in her mother country, she ventured further. "Uncle Tibor does not share the nationalist notion of illiberal democracy for Hungary. I know his feelings. Based on the very limited reparations from the Hungarian government to its Jewish community to date, he would rather see us find a private way to put the maps to use to truly benefit that community."

"So," said Adam, "he's part of what some people here in the United States like to call the 'deep state,' but in Hungary? He's working from inside the government to counter its efforts?"

"You could say that," Agnes replied.

She then placed a call to the lawyer György Balogh to say she was calling at the recommendation of Tibor Lantos and wanted to make an appointment.

A Learned Friend

Agnes and Adam selected one of the doctored original map copies. It appeared to indicate loot specifically stolen from Hungary and hidden in Austria. Armed with the chosen map, they met at the lawyer's office.

György Balogh turned out to be younger than either of them had expected. His late father had started the firm after migrating to the United States from Hungary during the uprising against the Soviets in 1956. His son György was short and stocky, with slightly graying black hair and a neatly cut handlebar mustache. His energetic and warm manner suggested he worked hard to stay physically and mentally fit. He spoke quietly, in clipped sentences, as his eyes scanned the young couple as they told him their story.

"You two have clearly found some remarkable material," said the lawyer, rubbing his chin. "There will be many who'd like to get their hands on this map. We don't yet know what value it may represent, but I will hazard a guess that it'll probably be quite significant."

Balogh pulled a sheaf of papers from a folder and studied

them for a moment.

"Perhaps a little background might set the stage for some next steps," he said. "Let's see. In 1991, after the collapse of the Soviet bloc which then included Hungary, the Hungarian Parliament passed a law for partial restitution of private property. The compensation received was only up to ten percent of market value, for use only in Hungary to buy shares in privatized companies or land at state auctions. However, the law did not provide compensation for assets such as securities, insurance policies, bank accounts, or looted artwork."

He rustled his papers as he searched for more data. "Six years later, in 1997, another law created The Jewish Heritage of Hungary Public Endowment, or MAZSOK, just as you discovered, Ms. Lantos. This entity was granted funds to pay modest monthly pensions to a few thousand Hungarian Holocaust survivors. Then, a year later, a Hungarian government compensation program was introduced to pay a tiny amount for each parent or sibling killed during the Shoah."

Agnes piped up and commented that the compensation to Holocaust survivors in Hungary seemed minimal.

"I don't disagree," said Balogh. He then leaned across his desk and pulled up a green folder. After rifling through several papers as if to find his notes, he shared a brief history with his two new clients.

"Five years later, in 2003," he said, "after pressure from the Jewish world, this small payment of two hundred dollars was increased to about one thousand eight hundred dollars.

But it was payable only to claimants who had already applied for the first payment in 1998. Apparently, The World Jewish Restitution Organization, which, by the way, is based in Jerusalem, continued to press the government to expand the program and admit new claims from survivors who hadn't applied for compensation earlier. All in all, a dismal picture for compensation for, or restitution to, Holocaust survivors today, in 2018—a mere seventy-three years after the end of World War II."

"Well, Mr. Balogh," broke in Agnes, sounding impatient, "what do you suggest we do next, please?"

Balogh shuffled through his papers once again. "Here are some options to consider. You could offer this map to the Hungarian government. However, the current domestic political climate suggests that little would be done to find, produce, and distribute the property to its most deserving beneficiaries."

"I couldn't agree more," said Agnes emphatically, casting a glance at Adam.

Balogh nodded. "You seem well aware of the contradictions, Ms. Lantos."

This was only the second time for Adam that anyone had called her by her family name. He stifled a laugh just in time to avoid Agnes's indignant glance.

"Namely," Balogh continued, "that the Hungarian head of state visited Israel earlier this year and expressed zero tolerance for anti-Semitic statements in Hungary—and in another breath, expressed admiration for the self-confessed anti-Semitic and pro-Hitler wartime leadership of Hungary that helped send almost half a million Jews to their deaths. Bottom line—the current Hungarian government is probably an unsuitable recipient for this map."

He extracted another document from the pile littering his desk. "Thirteen years ago, in 2005, a United States District Court in Florida preliminarily approved the Hungarian gold-train settlement. It was alleged that the United States mishandled personal property taken, seized, confiscated, or stolen by the pro-Nazi Hungarian government from Hungarian Jews. This allegation arose because the US Army took custody of it at the end of World War II and then improperly disposed of some of it. Essentially, the US military helped themselves to some of the stolen items."

"What was the nature of that settlement, Mr. Balogh?" asked Adam.

"Under that settlement," replied counsel, "the US government was supposed to pay about twenty-one million dollars to fund social service programs benefiting Jewish Hungarian victims of Nazi persecution. But, to this day, my research shows that no such settlement payment has ever been made. In other words, the US government does not seem to favor even partial restitution to the Hungarian Jewish community."

"So, what *else* can be done?" Agnes's question conveyed her growing sense of frustration. *Maybe going to a Hungarian lawyer here in New York was not such a good idea after all,* she thought. Her eyes said the same thing as she glanced once again over at Adam.

"Another option is to create a foundation," mumbled Balogh, stroking one end of his handlebar mustache. "Let's assume that the stolen property can be located from this map. There may be a way to retrieve it privately. You could expect that the government of the country where a hoard like this is found will want to intervene to regulate the retrieval process, and at a price. But if you could finance the search and retrieval process with private funds, that could be a useful bargaining tool with the government in question. However, there's always the risk of someone in government trying to exploit something like this for their own benefit."

Adam broke in. "My father told me he plans to invest in an exploration company offering a very high rate of return for a fairly small investment. Perhaps I could run this idea by him to see if he's interested or knows of others who might be?"

It was Agnes who interjected again, ignoring Adam's suggestion. "Maybe you're right about not taking this to any government. But why not put out a feeler first, to see whether that assumption is true? It seems to me that we can't just dismiss this option, especially if it turns out that no one in the private sector is interested."

Balogh again rubbed his chin in thought. "There are people I know in the US government. I could ask them a hypothetical question along the lines you suggest, on a 'no-names basis.' I could also try to find out the current status of the 2005 settlement, in case I missed something. Otherwise, and apart from these options, others may be either to store the map in a safe place or else to destroy it and be done with it. However, there's one final option which I think might help. Let me outline it for you."

Foul Play

The morning papers were late again at the Halcyon Club. Fred's morning was incomplete without them. He would stubbornly refuse to read news off a digital device or even listen to the television or radio. Instead, he would cling to traditional newspapers and print magazines for all his nonbusiness news updates. The one concession he made was to read digital business news, if only in grudging recognition of its immediacy and something that he knew was never going to go away.

This explained how he missed a shocking news item that was almost eclipsed by news of yet another bombastic outburst from the White House with all its unfortunate implications.

He had decided to forward all the family mail to the club, at least until this whole matter had blown over and normal life could be resumed. While he skimmed through the inevitable pile of unopened envelopes from assorted contractors, the club's doorman approached him apologetically in the lounge with a belated copy of the day's *Wall Street Journal*.

Fred's eyes scanned the news summary column on the left front page. He stopped and caught his breath.

Noted British financier found dead in Hudson River. Foul play suspected.

Brief details followed of a body found floating by some children playing near the Brooklyn Bridge, on the Brooklyn side of the river. The police would not release the name of the victim pending notification of next of kin, but simply stated that a British passport was found on the body. It appeared to have a fatal head wound.

There was something disturbing about this report that compelled Fred to seek Adam's help with a search on his handheld.

"Sure, Dad. Here's an update. 'The man's passport was identified as that of…'" Adam's voice trailed off. "Oh no!" he cried. "The passport was in the name of Charles Fortescue! He was apparently shot in the head by an unknown assailant." He continued to read the latest update from his handheld. "'Initial ballistics reports suggest that the weapon used had a built-in sound suppressor of the type used by an unspecified European country's military.' But it doesn't say which country, Dad."

Fred felt sick to his stomach. Was it possible that Charlie's death had something to do with their meeting, literally the day before? They had met in a public space, but as far as Fred could remember, neither he nor Charlie had told anyone else about their rendezvous. Unless, of course, they had been followed by someone.

Fred also wondered if he should call the police, but then dismissed the idea because they might think he was a suspect. There had been no exchange of business cards or

227

phone numbers at the consortium meeting, and so, even if he had wanted to call someone who had been there, he had no way to do so.

While this confused thinking rippled through Fred's mind, Adam spoke. "Dad, this has to be shocking news for all of us. But it looks like we need to act before anything else goes wrong. I have an idea."

He told Fred about the meeting with György Balogh. He then admitted at last that he had falsified the maps that he had photocopied—and inadvertently given the falsified set to his father for him to show to Charlie. But then it dawned on them both that this oversight on Adam's part might have been a blessing, especially if Charlie's assassin had stolen the one doctored map that Charlie had taken with him.

If the killer's motive had been to find and steal maps, then he would be going on a wild-goose chase, only to discover a dead end after a costly and time-consuming effort—not to mention murdering a man for nothing. This would buy Fred and Adam time to find a home for the copies of the original unretouched maps, failing which, they could simply destroy them.

The only remaining question would then be what to do with the originals sitting in a safe-deposit box in an obscure Budapest bank; and with the genuine photocopies tucked away in a small local bank deposit box in the Hudson Valley.

Adam now asked Fred to recall the names of consortium members who he thought might be suspect.

"There were Americans and Europeans. They included the

guy called Field, supposedly from State Department security; a retired US Army general named Pugh, who paid a call on us on Montego Island; and two Germans, named Farben and Thiel. Two others were officials from the Middle East—an Egyptian minister named Luckman, and a counselor from the Saudi Embassy." He could not remember exactly the last one's name.

Adam scratched his head and thought for a moment. "What if we could persuade our lawyer Balogh to reach out to at least one of them to indicate he may be able to offer an 'authentic exploration' document of interest to them? Balogh could hint that this was a copy of the original, that some falsified versions had erroneously been passed to the late Charles Fortescue, but the latter had expressed a wish to share the correct map copies with consortium members only hours before his murder? This could attract the attention of one or more consortium members who might want to preempt the other investors and obtain an accurate map."

Fred's response was skeptical. "That's fine, as far as it goes. But you would then need to prove that the map or maps would help to locate buried Nazi loot to be used by criminals to finance a third World War. And even if you could do so, would someone using stolen property for that purpose actually be committing a criminal offense for which they could be prosecuted?"

"Well, Dad, it was your original idea to invest in an exploration project that could yield a handsome return, wasn't it? Here is an idea that our lawyer Balogh proposed."

He outlined Balogh's idea. "Under United States law, hate

speech, as such, is protected and is permissible under the First Amendment. However, under a United States legal doctrine known as *imminent lawless action*, freedom of speech is not protected by the First Amendment if the speaker intends to incite a violation of the law that is both imminent and likely. This means we would need to prove such an intent."

Fred signaled his agreement so far.

"Here's how Balogh thinks it could be done," said Adam. "Let's assume that any one or more of the six suspects takes the bait of a single 'genuine' map offered to him by Balogh. We'll just call that suspect *him* or *the signatory*. Balogh would then explain to the signatory that, in exchange for giving access to the 'true' map, the receiving party would need to sign a legally binding contract. The contract would include several key terms." He paused to collect his thoughts.

"First, the signatory would also have to declare the names and addresses of all parties to the process, whether they were investors, exploration contractors, or final beneficiaries." He paused to let his opening point sink in.

"Second, the signatory would be required to make a detailed written declaration of how he intends to use the map to find the stolen property; that is, explain the detailed processes he would use to extract it from its hiding place, and then provide details of how he would dispose of the property, and for what purposes, once it was retrieved."

As Adam spoke, he failed to observe that Fred was watching him closely.

"These various written declarations would all be subject to Balogh's approval as preconditions to him handing over the map, on behalf of his 'undisclosed clients.'"

Adam added, "It also assumes that we would grant Balogh power of attorney to represent us, his clients. All these preconditions would be presented by Balogh to the suspect as burdensome, but necessary for receiving the accurate map. But that's not all."

"Thirdly," he explained, "the signatory would be legally required to have independent certification, in stages, once he had located the property, salvaged it, and was ready to put the proceeds to their intended use, as documented in his declaration." Another pause.

"Fourthly, the signatory would need to accept a legal obligation to pay Balogh and his client not only their legal and other costs, but also a substantial penalty amount if it were to emerge, at any time, that the signatory's certified use of any of the proceeds proved to be false."

"OK," said Fred, nodding.

"Furthermore" continued Adam, "if a court of law were to find the signatory guilty of a material misrepresentation, then the legal costs of any such claim incurred by Balogh's client would be for the signatory's account. And finally," said Adam, "all financial proceeds and tangible property from the salvage operations would need to be inventoried and certified by an independent firm of accountants, to be selected solely by Balogh."

Adam went on to explain that the accountants would

document all the salvaged items in detail. The items discovered would meanwhile be secured in an undisclosed location of Balogh's sole choice until certifiably ready to be monetized and disbursed under his sole authority. "I think," said Adam, "Balogh called this an 'escrow arrangement.'"

Fred nodded again.

"The whole underlying idea, Dad, is that the signatory would then have to make a choice."

He explained that, in theory, a signatory might choose to state in writing, and honor his true intent about the intended use of the proceeds. In this case, that would be to use the proceeds to help start World War III and to annihilate world Jewry. This would include intent to harm American Jews as US citizens. It was just conceivable that an American citizen might do this, thinking falsely that he was protected under the First Amendment.

Balogh had indeed pointed out that, assuming the signatory was an American citizen like Field or Jones or Pugh, he might try to shelter his stated intent under the First Amendment and say he was exercising his right to free speech.

"However," said Adam, "as I said just now, there's this legal doctrine called the *imminent lawless action test*. It established that advocacy of force or criminal activity does not receive First Amendment protections if the advocacy is directed to inciting or producing imminent lawless action, and it is likely to incite or produce such action. In this case, the intended action would, by definition, include harming Jewish Americans."

232

Balogh had stated the obvious: that, realistically, owning up to his true intent would be an unlikely choice for the signatory to make. Instead, he would probably choose to lie, in writing, about that intent—and thereby commit fraud. This could give rise to several claims by Balogh's client. These might include fraudulent misrepresentation or even racketeering under laws designed to combat organized crime in the USA.

Fred interjected. "I think he means RICO, which I recall stands for the Racketeer Influenced and Corrupt Organizations Act." He reminded Adam about a brush he once had with the Mafia in New York years ago. Some gangsters had attempted to shake down the Tinker Hedge Funds without success and had ended up going to jail for twenty years.

"But here in New York," said Adam, "we would need to prove fraud, of course."

Balogh had also suggested making a secret recording of all his conversations with the signatory about his intent. "By the way, Dad," Adam pointed out, "Balogh pointed out to us that, under the legal concept of one-party consent, it would be legal within the state of New York, anyway, to make such a recording, provided it wasn't used to commit an illegal act and was for our own use. It might stand up as evidence in a New York court. That would not necessarily be true in other states. Anyway, what Balogh suggested was to create a transcript of his recordings in hard copy, and then try to present it as evidence in court."

The lawyer had also pointed out that further proof would

help to establish the true intent of the proposed beneficiaries of the map. This would mean research for any written evidence linking the signatory and his associates to hate speech, here in the United States or abroad. "Hate speech is banned in much of Europe, but not in the United States," Balogh had noted.

"So," said Adam, "it seems fair to assume that samples of hate speech related to any of these suspects may be discoverable and help the case for prosecution. The idea here is to entrap both the American extremists and their Arab and German friends."

Adam studied his father's face as he absorbed and processed the feedback.

"Dad, I know this all sounds like a complicated long shot."

Fred nodded silently in agreement.

"But short of destroying all the copies and the originals, we can't see how else to resolve this, or how best to handle these priceless maps," said Adam.

Fred said not a word for what seemed like an eternity. Here was his only son, struggling to find a full-time career and yet talking as if he were a trained young lawyer, or at least a law student. The father was quietly impressed—but did not want to show it, in case it went to the boy's head.

At last, Fred responded. "Well, it may be worth a try. It'll take time and resources—people and money, that is—to pull this off. There are no guarantees it'll work. But if it does, then you would still need to figure out how best to dispose of the maps."

Adam agreed. He was feeling more and more of a connection to his father.

"Believe me, Dad, the combined value of these maps could be such a huge sum that there would be many interested parties anxious to get their hands on them. Agnes and I have talked about this, and here's what we think. Assume that we can trap some or all these criminals as proposed. We could then go public. We can tell the world at a press conference who these criminals are and what they're about. If we don't expose all of them, at least those who escape will have to go to ground for a while."

Fred shifted uneasily in his chair as Adam prattled on without noticing the nature of his father's movement—for Fred now felt pulled in different directions. Despite the boy's commendable efforts to grasp the legal basics, his judgment about what to do next seemed immature, idealistic, and impractical in the real world.

"Son," said Fred, "this is a big, risky, and possibly a very dangerous undertaking. You'll likely need more than just one single lawyer to handle this matter. I think you're maybe going to have to put together a crack team of lawyers and researchers, at the very least. Frankly, I have my doubts about your approach. But for now, I'll support you as much as I can!"

Adam thought, *I think I won my old man over at last.*

But it would take what happened next to convert Fred to join the cause.

Mr. Pimlico

It happened out of the blue, and without warning.

Fred was reading his daily digest of the financial press a day later when a call came in from the club's front desk. "A Mr. Harold Pimlico left his card for you early this morning, sir, and asked if he could meet you here at the club on an urgent personal matter."

Fred raised his eyebrows. He had never heard of anyone by that name. What could a total stranger want with him, and what could an 'urgent personal matter' be? He duly retrieved the visitor's card. It bore the name of Harold A. Pimlico, Director, and a company called Merchant Voyages LLP. There were two numbers on the card. One had a 212 area code, suggesting a New York telephone number and office. The other was a London number, judging by the 011 44 1 prefix.

When he called the New York number, a familiar woman's voice answered, with an accent which sounded like one he had heard some time ago on another London call. "Mr. Tinker, sir," said the anonymous female voice, "I have a message for you from Mr. Pimlico. Could he meet you today at your New York club for lunch? It's rather urgent."

Fred's antenna was up. "Who is this Mr. Pimlico, and why does he want to meet with me?"

"I can't say, sir, except that he was a friend of the late Mr. Fortescue, and that it is very urgent," said the voice.

Fred hesitated for a moment. "Very well, then. I'll change my plans and arrange for lunch here at the Halcyon Club at noon."

Shortly before noon, a man calling himself Pimlico arrived. Fred came down from his room to meet him and show him to the club's café. There was something vaguely familiar about his guest, but Fred couldn't put his finger on it. The man appeared to have a good head of salt-and-pepper, dark-brown, graying hair, along with a mustache and round wire-rimmed glasses with thick lenses.

"Mr. Tinker, I am good friend of the late Charles Fortescue. We were colleagues who worked together for many years. Terrible to lose him! But let me come straight to the point. I am aware that you and your son have located certain documents in which several other groups have a very strong interest indeed. So strong, in fact, that there's reason to believe that your life and those of your family may well be in danger. I am here today to offer you some help and some reassurance."

Before Fred could respond, the visitor looked quickly around the café and seemed relieved that no one else was yet present for lunch.

"Would you excuse me for a moment, Mr. Tinker, and point me to the gentleman's restroom?"

Five minutes later, the visitor rejoined the table. Fred had not seen him approach from behind, and when he looked up, he gasped and turned white as if seeing a ghost.

"Charlie? Charlie Fortescue? But...but it was in the paper! It said you were dead! Shot by someone..." His voice wavered in shock.

A smiling Charlie Fortescue sat down beside his host. "Fred, I had to do this. First of all, to get in here unnoticed, and second, to make sure that not even you could see through my disguise."

"But—" stammered Fred.

"Yes, yes, I know!" said Charlie with a mischievous laugh. "It all seems very theatrical, even comical, doesn't it? But let me try to explain. Did you ever hear the wartime story of 'The Man Who Never Was?'"

"No," mumbled Fred, still clearly in shock.

Charlie settled into his chair, then launched into a tale. "During World War II, a corpse was found floating in the ocean near the west coast of Spain. It was dressed in the uniform of a British military officer. Attached to the corpse's wrist by a chain was a briefcase containing Allied invasion plans. But he was not, in fact, a military officer, nor were his plans authentic. Sure enough, the Spanish picked up the corpse and gave the briefcase to the Nazis in Madrid. They bought the ruse and passed the contents of the briefcase to

Berlin. It threw the Germans off track completely on where they thought Allied landing points would be on the coast of France."

"That's some story!" gasped Fred, his head still spinning.

"Yes, it is," said Charlie. "My death too was staged. Thanks to a cooperative medical school, I found a cadaver and faked it to look like me—with the addition of a bullet to the head."

But...but why?" Fred felt bewildered and almost speechless.

"Because," said his friend, "things have taken a very dangerous turn, and there is at least one employee of mine who I now know is working for the very people I'm trying to find and neutralize."

Fred was now clearly out of his depth. "Charlie, you have me completely confused."

"Fred, you already know about the consortium, right? As I told you before, that too was a ruse—to attract the interest of certain extremists. Now that I am Mr. Pimlico, and Charles Fortescue is supposedly dead, someone must pick up from where he left off as the consortium's managing director. The logical person to play that role, now that Fortescue's conveniently out of the way, is my assistant, Dick Harvey."

"Didn't I talk him on the phone, at your London office? I even went to his London club for dinner."

"Yes, but what you don't know is that he's the son of a prominent right-wing member of Parliament. His father not only happens to have been knighted but is also an active member of an underground Nazi party in Britain. We have tangible written evidence to prove that Harvey is of the same mind-set as his father and also is working for the other side. We are sure that Harvey is the extremists' inside man. If he thinks you have the maps, he'll stop at nothing to get them from you. I had to warn you."

"Good grief! I don't know what to say!" Fred felt a sudden chill run up his spine.

He barely heard Charlie's next reassuring words. "Fred, there's no need for concern. Just follow my instructions, and this whole affair should be over sooner than you might think."

Some Kind of Traitor

Adam told his father that he had instructed the lawyer Balogh to draw up a draft contract, and to offer it "on behalf of his clients" to all interested members of the consortium, at Balogh's suggestion, to see who might take the bait. After all, it would look odd if only one party—or even all six known suspect parties—received preferential treatment.

Fred had raised his eyebrows but said nothing, knowing full well that he, not Adam, would foot the lawyer's bill.

Meanwhile, and just as Charlie Fortescue had predicted, Dick Harvey had quickly and smartly assumed the role of the consortium's managing director. He had called Balogh within hours of receiving the lawyer's letter offering to sign an agreement of understanding containing certain rigorous terms in exchange for a single "authentic" map.

"Mr. Balogh, as the consortium's new managing director, my duty is to keep the executive committee fully informed. Please forward to me the draft contract for our consideration."

"It would be my pleasure, sir," said Balogh into the

telephone. He felt a spark of satisfaction, now that someone had nibbled at the bait.

The lawyer had carefully noted the Harvey's New York address and phone number. He had also obtained from Harvey the names and contact points of other members of the consortium's executive committee.

"We have two members from the Federal Republic of Germany, two from the United States, and one each from Egypt and Saudi Arabia," Harvey had said with misguided pride, thinking that this international mix would make an impression on Balogh and perhaps his clients too. It certainly did, though not exactly as Harvey had intended.

The next consortium meeting was set to occur in one week. Harvey promised to do his best to move the proposed contract along rapidly to a signing.

While this was in process, Fred had acquired an elegant and slightly worn dark-tan leather attaché case, complete with a pair of combination locks. It was one of those small, almost square-shaped attaché cases that seem so compact that they can barely hold more than a pad of paper and a pen.

It had been a gift from Charlie, who had told him, "This is no ordinary attaché case, Fred. It contains hidden video cameras and ultra-sensitive audio recording features concealed in the frame. Be sure to take it to the consortium's next meeting, place it on the table in front of you, and point the hinges toward the center of the room. It's critical that we capture the fullest possible audio and video evidence of the proceedings and what each participant has to say."

The next consortium meeting took place in a private room of a small but exclusive Upper East Side hotel. Once again, Fred found himself sitting at an oval boardroom table. The Egyptian counselor sat to his left, and the American named Field to his right. Fred carefully placed the attaché case on the table in front of him so that the hinged side faced squarely into the room.

The proceedings began. "Gentlemen, I'm Richard Harvey, and it's my honor to open this second meeting of the Global Exploration Consortium. However, I would first like to request a moment's silence for my predecessor as the managing director of the consortium, the late Mr. Charles Fortescue, whose recent tragic demise was a great shock to us all. He was also a long-standing former colleague of mine."

The group obliged with a short moment of silence.

"As some of you know," continued Harvey, "Mr. Fortescue and I had been working closely together on this project for some time. However, I am happy to report that his unfortunate passing will have no adverse impact whatsoever on the operation or management of this project."

Harvey reached for a sheaf of papers and held them up.

"At our first consortium meeting, Mr. Fortescue promised to produce some long-hidden maps indicating the locations of certain concealed property. He had indeed intended to produce photocopies for this very meeting today. Steps have now been taken to obtain what we hope may be the first of several authentic maps."

He paused to let the points sink in, while reaching for a stack of blue folders.

"An undisclosed party has made us an offer of a single map. We are currently negotiating the purchase with that party's legal advisor. He has prepared a document for each consortium member to review which outlines the terms and conditions for the release of that map to us. You're each invited to read and review the document in this folder."

Harvey handed them out, one by one. A period of several minutes followed as the participants skimmed the document. Fred noticed that neither of his immediate neighbors bothered to open their copy. Evidently, they had already seen it.

Some hands went up, and questions followed.

"My impression is that these terms are highly restrictive." It was the French businessman whose accent gave him away. It struck Fred that the man's question was legitimate enough to suggest that he, like Fred himself, was another regular businessman who Charlie must have beguiled to lend the consortium an aura of respectability.

Harvey smiled and quickly responded. "Sir, your point is well taken. However, some members of our group here feel that the potential gains from our exploration efforts will far outweigh the costs and risks presented by the document."

Another voice piped up. It was Field. "Mr. Harvey, those of us on the executive committee are confident that we can sign this document. We feel that, practically speaking, certain written commitments and requirements may—or may not—

be honored in practice. The uncertainties involved in the kind of exploration that we plan to undertake are such that we cannot know at this stage what can and cannot be honored. It's the strong recommendation of the executive committee that we proceed as soon as possible to signing this document."

Harvey nodded, and then appeared to scribble Field's comment as a footnote for the minutes of the meeting. He then lifted his head and reassumed a businesslike manner. "Gentlemen," said Harvey, "we have until noon tomorrow to read and decide whether to sign or not sign. Simply put, those of us who choose not to proceed will no longer be able to vote in this consortium going forward, but instead, at their option, will become silent investment partners."

It was the moment for Fred to ask some questions, carefully framed in advance for him by Fortescue. The responses could be recorded by the concealed microphone in Fred's attaché case. The hidden fish-eye video lens would identify the speakers.

Fred cleared his throat and raised his hand. "If I understand clearly what Mr. Harvey and Mr. Field have just proposed, members of this consortium are being asked to make and honor specific written commitments about how the hidden property is to be found, retrieved, and then used. There also seems to be a question about whether any such commitments can be honored. Could Mr. Field please explain what he feels should be stated as the use of the property in question?"

Field looked up sharply at Fred. He hesitated for a moment,

glanced over at Harvey, then directed a stony look at the questioner beside him. "Each investor will receive a portion of the proceeds from whatever is discovered in the exploration process. Remaining funds, if any, will be used at the discretion of the executive committee." The man's cold tone indicated he had no desire to explain himself further.

This reply did not appear to satisfy Fred. "What then does the executive committee plan to do with any remaining funds from the discovery?"

A momentary silence filled the room. Field then tried feebly to hedge. "As I stated, that will be up to the executive committee."

Fred tried another tack. "I suspect that all potential investors here today would agree with me that there should be complete transparency in advance about the full use of any such recovered property, if only as a matter of due diligence. I assume we're all of a mind, right?"

A murmur arose from around the table. Fred noticed that Field's face twitched, and that Harvey had fixed an icy glare on him.

This time, it was the Egyptian named Luckman who spoke. "That will not be necessary."

Fred was still not satisfied. "Oh, but I think it's not only necessary, but also a condition of my own investment, at least."

"Mr. Tinker, most of the property in question will likely be used for charitable causes," said the Egyptian. What had been his friendly and warm greeting to Fred before the meeting had now turned decidedly chilly.

"Such as?" said Fred, coolly.

"Well," chimed in Field "for example, we would direct it to support a number of social causes for distressed families in the Middle East. That's why among our members here today are representatives from Egypt and Saudi Arabia."

Another momentary silence filled the room as Fred the inquisitor stroked his chin. It was a sign that he appeared to be judging Field, Luckman, and Harvey.

"Can you assure us as investors—and in writing—of the end uses of any proceeds other than those used to pay investors? I feel strongly that this is a key precondition of any such investment by this group. Would everyone agree?"

All but the six suspects murmured their approval of Fred's suggestion.

It was the turn of a reluctant Harvey to speak once again. "I have here a confidential list of all possible beneficiaries. They include, as my colleague from Egypt indicated, several charities providing support to distressed civilians in the Gaza Strip and to several veterans' associations." He waved the list in the air. "This list is available for anyone to inspect after this meeting. But for security reasons, we cannot allow it to leave this room."

Here was the opening that Fred and Charlie had been hoping for. No one had noticed that Fred appeared to be wearing a hearing aid. It was, in fact, a special miniature radio receiver. Fred heard Charlie's voice speaking softly into his ear.

"Try to point the camera to whoever it is that hands you that list," said Charlie's low voice. "Then follow my directions to move the attaché case so that the camera captures an image of the list and everything on it."

As Harvey reached over to hand out a document, Fred leaned forward to grasp it and then placed his elbows on top of the closed attaché case as if to read it. Prompted by Charlie's direction, he nudged the attaché case to focus the hidden camera on the document's text in his outstretched hands.

It was all there. There were twenty names listed of German and Arab organizations that, though dressed up to look like charities, were in fact major neo-Nazi groups, based mainly in the United States, Britain, France, Germany, and in two Arab countries, Egypt and Syria. Few of the individual names were recognizable to Fred as his eyes scanned the list, but he suspected that the executive committee of the consortium would be highly unlikely to reveal them to any third party.

Prompted by Charlie once again, he asked another question. "Mr. Harvey, are we to understand that the consortium — that is, its executive committee — intends to share this list with the lawyer who represents the anonymous map donor?"

Harvey cleared his throat and swallowed. "Mr. Tinker, that's a good question. But as my colleague Mr. Field just explained, there are so many uncertainties and unknowns in the proposed exploration process that it would be difficult to make a cast-iron commitment of any kind relating to precisely who would be the non-investor beneficiaries."

Fred persisted. "Then, Mr. Harvey, perhaps you could tell us at least the gist of what you intend to tell the lawyer as to the likely use of the proceeds? And, to answer my earlier question, can you also tell us exactly what language you propose to use with that lawyer?"

"Very well," began Harvey reluctantly, thinking, *Why the hell did Fortescue ever invite this guy into the consortium in the first place?* "We shall tell him that any funds remaining after distributions are made to the investors in this consortium will be dedicated to support several international agencies and veterans' organizations in their charity work."

"Fair enough," said Fred reassuringly. "Will you also show us, the investors, a draft of this document before presenting it to the lawyer in question?"

"That's for the executive committee to decide, according to our bylaws."

"I see. OK, then," said Fred in mock sincerity. "Thank you. And one more thing. How do you propose to locate the property in question once a suitable site has been identified?"

Harvey turned to the German, Ludwig Farben, as if for help. It was forthcoming.

"Mr. Tinker," said the BND man, "we plan to use a special new underground radar technology. It's from a German company, Midas Electronics, that we know well. It can produce a full color, 3-D analysis of what lies below, as much as one forty-five meters, that is, one hundred and fifty feet underground. Built-in sensors can find metal, water, or cavities at that depth. It can see through containers buried underground and show what's inside them. So, for example, let's assume some valuable property is hidden under a building, or, let us say, even in a train concealed in a tunnel. It can indicate the contents. I've seen this done successfully with my own eyes."

As he spoke, he glanced at his BND colleague, Dr. Thiel, who nodded. It occurred to Fred that these two Germans might have more than a passing interest in Midas Electronics.

Charlie Fortescue could check that one out, he thought.

Prompted once again by Charlie's quiet but assuring voice in his ear, Fred delivered another probing question. "One last thing, please." He thought he noticed Harvey bracing himself. "How do you propose to allocate the proceeds of whatever property you discover to the veterans' associations?"

Fred saw Harvey wince as he shot a glance at the two Germans. This time, it was Herr Doktor Thiel who spoke. "My dear Mr. Tinker, you need not be concerned about such details once you receive your share of the proceeds as agreed under the terms of this consortium. But I can assure you, the remaining funds will be put to good use for a number of worthwhile charities."

The steely glint in Thiel's eyes told Fred that enough was enough. Charlie's voice picked this up too, as if he were present in person. "Ease up, Fred. Time to back off. We got some of what we wanted."

Fred smiled and thanked Harvey, Farben, and Thiel for their helpful explanations, then stood. He casually picked up the attaché case with his left hand and extended his right hand to invite a handshake from Harvey and the Germans. He noticed Harvey's sweaty palm, as well as the cold, iron grip in the handshakes of Farben and Thiel. He turned to leave. As he did so, he thought he noticed Farben nod at one of the two tall, blond men at the door.

His instinct warned him not to return directly to the Halcyon Club. Instead, he told his driver to drop him off at the Fifty-Seventh Street entrance to the Bergdorf Goodman department store in Midtown.

He alighted nimbly and slipped quickly into the entrance, only to emerge moments later at the Fifty-Sixth Street entrance, where he removed his coat, put it over his arm, and melted away into the Fifth Avenue crowds, just as Charlie had directed him to do.

A Debriefing

Charlie was anxious to retrieve the attaché case, and to get Fred's first-hand impressions. But he also had some other things to share with his new agent.

They met at a deli on the East Side, where the noise level of the patrons was almost loud enough to drown out their conversation.

"Fred," said Charlie through the hubbub of voices, "I think you already know your son Adam was working in Hungary with a professor from Columbia?"

"Sure, I do," said Fred.

"Did you know that the professor in question was shot and injured by an unknown assailant, in his home?"

"Yes, I read something about that."

"Well, let's say that we—that is, our organization—has a worldwide network of contacts. One of them happens to be a police detective in Budapest by the unlikely name of Kiss. Did Adam ever mention that name to you?"

"Nope," Fred replied, wondering what was coming next.

"I thought not," said Charlie knowingly. "Detective Kiss was assigned to find the professor's assailant. He did so by studying the bullet that grazed the professor's head before it lodged into his fireplace. The bullet came from a special type of pistol called a Maxim 9 which has a built-in sound suppressor. He also learned that the main users of such equipment are in the military—and in this case, the German military. Only certain people are trained to use this weapon. They are superb marksmen who can hit a bullseye at one thousand feet. In this case, Kiss thinks the shooter intended just to graze the professor, not kill him. Kiss concluded that this was a warning shot by someone concerned that the professor was getting too close to a discovery."

Asked Fred, "What discovery?"

"Maps leading to multiple locations of hidden Nazi loot, mostly in Europe and in Latin America. That probably means the maps you have in your possession."

"Charlie, you know, I'm worried about getting deeper and deeper into this thing and about my family."

"Yes, I understand. Believe me, I do." Charlie's tone of urgency did not escape Fred's notice. "But," Charlie continued, "we're getting very close indeed to nailing some really bad characters here, and you still have a critical role to play."

Charlie somehow knew to play to Fred's outsize ego. He stopped speaking and watched Fred's face for a response.

"Look here, Charlie," said Fred, "I went into this consortium of yours believing it to be a good investment. Then I learn the thing is just a front to nail some bad guys. I know nothing about police work, and I really don't want to remain involved any longer than absolutely necessary."

"I agree, Fred." Charlie sensed that, despite his protests, Fred was hooked. "And I really don't want you or your family involved any longer than, as you say, absolutely necessary. But you should know that we're now in the closing stages of shutting down something really big and really bad."

"And that is...?" inquired Charlie's agent.

"We're about to close down an attempt to launch a Fourth Reich." Charlie couldn't have been clearer.

"Good grief!" cried Fred.

"Yes, indeed," said the spy. "Failure is not an option for us because there are too many governments involved and potentially thousands, maybe millions, of lives at stake."

"Charlie, should I still assume that folks like Farben and Thiel are among the key people involved?"

"Most definitely," stated Charlie emphatically. "And others like Harvey provide a helping hand and a link to the Arab piece of the game, as represented by the Egyptian and Saudi parties in the consortium."

Fred thought for a moment. "Well, now that you have the audio and video from the consortium meeting, what happens next?"

"Fred, remember when you and I met recently in the lobby

of the Hilton Midtown? I had one of our people posted there to keep an eye on us. She spotted a tall, blond young man who seemed to be taking an unusual interest in the two of us. Here, this is a photograph she took of the man. Recognize him?"

"Why, yes, of course. He was one of the two guys at the door when we entered the last consortium meeting. I remember that Farben nodded to him as I left the meeting. And, yes, now I remember: he was the one who greeted me when I visited the BND office near Munich!"

"Yes. And would you like to know more? He's employed as a sniper and marksman by the German Special Forces—the Kommando Spezialkräfte, or KSK. We think he may have been the shooter who fired at Adam's professor over in Hungary. This fellow gets around, doesn't he?"

"Wait a moment! Didn't you say he used a special type of pistol, a Maxim 9?"

"Yes. I did." Charlie's face went grim. "And my death was faked using a similar weapon. The purpose was to confuse the other side because, as best we know, the KSK don't yet have another shooter with this kind of new weapon. The idea is to make the bad guys think that another group from within the German military may also be after the maps and the hidden loot."

"So, this is what you do for a living, Charlie?"

"Been doing it for years," said Charlie, "and in all sorts of theaters. But this is a big one. I really need your help to put these people away before they cause major trouble."

Fred sighed with resignation. "Just tell me what more you want me to do," he said.

Close Quarters

A message awaited Fred on his return to the Halcyon Club. It was from his assistant at the Tinker Hedge Funds office. She had received several urgent calls from a Mr. Farben inquiring as to Fred's whereabouts and how to reach him. Could he please call this number to arrange an important personal meeting as soon as possible?

Charlie had once more provided special equipment for the occasion, this time in the form of a pair of horn-rimmed reading glasses. This was no ordinary eyewear. The bridge contained a tiny camera and audio receiver, both of which were invisible to the naked eye.

Farben arrived at Fred's office precisely as scheduled. He was alone. He wore a green topcoat and a dark loden-green Tyrolean-style wool hat with a narrow brim, tapered at the crown and decorated with a single brown brush with bright feathers on one side.

"I like your hat," said Fred, affecting friendliness as he ushered the visitor into his private meeting room.

Farben nodded. "Yes, it's a tradition where I come from. I am originally Austrian, you see. Though now, of course, I am a naturalized German citizen. The brush is made from the beard of a chamois goat. I shot it myself."

They sat down at the small teak conference table.

"Mr. Tinker, let me not waste your time and come straight to the point. What I wish to tell you is extremely sensitive. I'm doing this because I know from your record long ago that you were sympathetic to a certain cause. There is much urgency to complete the formation and funding of the exploration needed to produce the property discussed at our recent consortium meetings. I have reason to believe that you may know more about the maps related to the property than you have shared with anyone else involved in this project. Am I right, please?"

"Herr Farben," said Fred with his best poker face, "my interest in this project is based entirely on its merits as an investment opportunity. If you are referring to the questions that I asked at the last consortium meeting, then please understand that they're all part of my customary due diligence process. I invest neither my personal funds nor those of my clients until I have a complete view of a project from start to finish. It's critical for me to understand the use of all investment proceeds, if only to satisfy myself and my clients that their involvement is financially and legally legitimate."

"Oh, no doubt," said Farben, shifting uneasily in his chair. "And what about the moral aspects of your investments, Mr. Tinker? Do you take these too into consideration?"

"I'm not sure what you mean. But if any investment is likely to cause harm to our investors, my firm, or me personally,
258

then I need to assess that risk."

"Precisely. Now, when you were a boy in Germany, we understand you had an interest in joining the Hitler Youth. Is that correct?"

"Yes. But my father forbade it," Fred said in a matter-of-fact tone.

Farben studied Fred's face, then said, "We know that too."

Fred felt increasingly uncomfortable at the mention of *we*. "Who, might I ask, are the '*we*' to whom you refer?"

Again, Fred found his visitor's penetrating ice-blue eyes gazing at him intently. "We are what you might call a band of brothers. We are very private people. We don't need the press to follow our efforts. You will probably not find us on Google. But if you try, you may find a group called the *Familienverband*. It is a perfectly normal international association of German and Austrian families who share a common purpose."

"And that purpose is…?" asked Fred innocently,

"To answer that question," said Farben, "you would have to become a member. You see, it is a very private association."

"Are you suggesting that I might become a member?" asked Fred. "I mean, why would someone like me want to join it anyway?"

Farben looked up with a piercing stare. "You have German ancestry, yes? You once had an interest in joining the Hitler Youth, yes?"

"I can't deny either point. Does that qualify me to become a member?"

"Not exactly. You see, the *Familienverband* requires a series of interviews of each candidate, to make sure that its goals and those of the applicant are one and the same. You would need to have several interviews with our selection committee. But there is no point in discussing this further unless you can shed some light on the location of certain *maps*. Do I make myself clear?"

"Quite clear. And as to maps, not least of hidden treasures, I don't think I'm the person to ask. The last time I even looked at maps was, well, just a week or so ago with the late Charles Fortescue. He was asking me about some trip that he and his family planned to take across the United States and wanted some suggestions."

"Mr. Tinker." The German's voice conveyed growing irritation and impatience. "Please understand that there are some very powerful people who need the maps I'm talking about, and they need them soon. I can assure you that anyone else who possesses those maps may be putting themselves at grave risk. If you should come across someone like that, please, do be sure to let me know immediately."

Fred clearly felt the threatening tone as Farben stood up, bowed, and left the room with, "Have a nice day, Mr. Tinker."

Day of Reckoning

Charlie, once again disguised as Mr. Pimlico, duly reappeared at the Halcyon Club late on the same afternoon as Fred's meeting with Farben. The British spy had warned Fred to expect him to reappear in his disguise as Pimlico, knowing that, by now, the club was probably being watched.

"Fred," said Charlie excitedly as they shook hands, "you did really well to help us build a case against Farben and his cronies. We're not quite there yet, but we are getting closer by the day as these people start to show themselves."

They found a quiet corner in the club's café and ordered some coffee.

"I have some news for you," said Charlie. "We have friends at the FBI who don't like extremists of any color any more that we do. They've been working on a program with the Internal Revenue Service—yes, your very own IRS, God bless them—to audit certain United States banks where far-right American groups like to keep their money.

"What does that have to do with the consortium people, Charlie?" asked Fred.

"Well," said Fortescue, "on the pretext of conducting selected tax audits, they have discovered that some alt-right groups here in the United States are not only taking money from German and Arab extremist groups but are also using it to stockpile weapons. Further indications are that these same groups are preparing for a future uprising."

"Well, well, well!" said Fred. He sounded skeptical. "So now you've got me involved with a bunch of treasonous right-wing American revolutionaries too!"

"You could say that," Charlie murmured. "But what I find so interesting is seeing the crosscurrents at work."

"What do you mean?"

"You read the papers, Fred, and you see stories about an extreme right-wing resurgence these days in Germany. For example, look at the crowds of skinheads and others displaying Nazi salutes a few months ago in Chemnitz, that industrial town in eastern Germany close to the Czech border. All it took was an anti-immigrant story, probably true, that an Iraqi and a Syrian had stabbed a native German to death. Then, all hell broke loose, and the local police were overwhelmed." He paused.

"Ironically, at the same time, the neo-Nazis in Germany have also found common cause with Islam and certain Arabs to unite against Israel and the Jews. It's the same old story from the 1940s all over again, except that the Germans are now also grappling with the stress of absorbing large numbers of Arab immigrant refugees arriving in Germany from Syria and Iraq."

"It is weird, now that you mention it," Fred agreed.

"Anyway," said Charlie, "we are now fast approaching a point where some members of our consortium are going to be taken out of circulation. My friends at the FBI are working with the Attorney General of New York's office to indict some of our consortium friends and hopefully put them away for a long, long time."

He noticed that Fred's attention had wandered. As if to confirm it, Fred said, "Charlie, am I at liberty to bring my son Adam into the loop here? Because I think he knows even more about some things related to this matter than I do. After all, it was he and his girlfriend Agnes who found not just the maps, but also the lawyer who is fronting for us on those maps."

Fortescue thought for a moment. "Yes, I hear you. But the less he knows at this point the better. I don't need to get him more involved and put even more responsibility on your shoulders."

They quickly debriefed on the latest consortium meeting. Then Fred shared his encounter that afternoon with Farben. This time, Charlie retained his disguise as Mr. Harold Pimlico. When he later exited the club through its front door, he looked to all the world like an ordinary, bespectacled, older member of the club.

Shortly afterwards, Fred called up to Adam's room and left a message that they needed to talk in private at the club for dinner. It was the father's turn to brief his son.

"Adam, you now know that both of us are involved in this

business with some unsavory people, and that Charlie Fortescue is on our side."

"Yes, Dad, I do. I guess he's part of the Brits' MI6?" Adam sounded more than a little naïve.

"I couldn't say for sure, son, and I haven't asked. But that seems to be a fair assumption. However, he's not working alone. I learned from him that steps are in hand to indict certain undesirable people. But he asked me not to tell you anything more than that, if only because he does not want you to come to any harm—and nor do I!"

"That's interesting," said Adam, thinking of the cat-and-mouse games that he and Agnes were already playing. He asked, "How will these undesirable people be indicted, and what charges will be brought against them that will stick and put them away?"

"I'm not a lawyer, so I can't answer that," said Fred.

"OK. But we have a lawyer, Balogh, who can—maybe?"

They agreed that Adam should meet with Balogh somewhere discreet rather than at his law office. It was already clear from Adam's encounter with the man who called himself Jones that some questionable characters knew he was living at the Halcyon Club and were watching all of its comings and goings. It would be too obvious to leave the club openly to visit Balogh at his office.

Two days later, Balogh and Adam met at a café in Central Park.

"Mr. Balogh," said Adam, "I couldn't tell you over the

phone why I needed to meet with you, so here goes." Adam looked around, and, as far as he could tell, there was no one else close by who could overhear the conversation. "What can you tell me from a legal standpoint about what an indictment might look like for someone caught conspiring to commit acts of terrorism, expressing hatred, or just plain treason? And, for that matter, how do those three things differ?"

"That's an interesting group of questions, Mr. Tinker." Balogh tugged at each end of his thick, black mustache. "It can be tricky because there are both federal and state laws involved. I think we should focus on federal law, at least for now. Let's start with terrorism. There's a US Code of Federal Regulations that defines that word. If I recall correctly, it is something like 'terrorism is the premeditated, politically motivated violence perpetrated against noncombatant targets by subnational groups or clandestine agents.' There would therefore need to be a political or ideological agenda behind such an attack."

"And hatred?" asked Adam.

"A hate crime reflects some element of bias, typically because of a victim's race, religion or sexual orientation which results in loss of trust, dignity or, worst case, loss of the victim's life. In other words, it's where a victim is targeted because of his or her personal characteristics, and there's a clear intent to commit crime against that person by the perpetrator."

"Hmm," said Adam. "Those definitions seem to show a clear distinction between terrorism and hatred."

The lawyer pulled out a file from his briefcase. "If you want to be more precise," he said, "you might use the FBI's definition of a hate crime which is, 'a criminal offense against a person or property motivated in whole or in part by an offender's bias against a race, religion, disability, sexual orientation, ethnicity, gender, or gender identity.' But keep in mind that, under United States law, hate itself is not a crime, and that the FBI is required to respect freedom of speech among other liberties."

"But then, what about treason?"

"Again, I'm pretty sure that's defined in another code. It's along the lines of 'any United States citizen who takes up arms against the United States or supports its enemies is treasonous.' Wait a second! Here it is. 'Whoever, owing allegiance to the United States, levies war against them or adheres to their enemies, giving them aid and comfort within the United States or elsewhere, is guilty of treason and shall suffer death, or shall be imprisoned not less than five years and fined under this title but not less than ten thousand dollars; and shall be incapable of holding any office under the United States.'"

Adam tried to digest the language for a moment. He was enjoying playing lawyer. "Well, that suggests to me," he said, "that any noncitizen with a hostile political agenda toward the United States and who supports and abets violence against people or property in the United States could be indicted for terrorism. It also suggests that any US citizen who does that could be indicted for a hate crime, and possibly for treason too."

"You may be right," agreed Balogh. "That would have to be addressed in a court of law. But if you're right, and those indicted are found guilty, they could be put away for life with little or no possibility of parole."

A Shopping Trip Gone Wrong

Both Jill and Eve Tinker felt more and more restive at being cooped up at the Halcyon Club. It had now been almost three weeks since they had abandoned their summer home on Montego Island. Somehow, Fred and Adam had so far managed to conceal from both women, at least for now, the nature and extent of the appalling vandalism at their island summer home. Fred had also vigorously discouraged them from stopping in at their New York apartment, while assuring Jill that the housekeeper was still coming in regularly to keep the place up.

Meanwhile, it was anyone's guess about the current state of the Montego Bay house. Fred had still told Jill nothing about that. All he could do for now was to cross his fingers and hope that their caretaker and his team would do their best to clear up the mess made by the intruders.

And so, it was on a bright, sunny day with a gentle fall breeze when mother and daughter finally decided to break away, set out on a shopping expedition, and enjoy lunch together. Neither one bothered to tell Fred or Adam where they were going; and it never occurred to the men to ask.

Jill had dressed up for the occasion. Eve had tried to look presentable too, despite the gold ring still stubbornly lodged in her nostril. They felt excited and eager to go hunting. Standing at the curbside by the club, they were chattering and laughing when Jill spotted a Yellow Cab approaching. She hailed it, and they got in.

"Bloomingdales, please sir, on Fifty-Ninth."

"No problem, ma'am."

The two women were still chatting when Eve noticed they were now in the East Village.

"Wait a minute, we said Fifty-Ninth Street. Why are you driving south instead of north? We're in the East Village!"

"There's a big meeting at the UN, ma'am, and the traffic's all messed up. I'm trying to take the FDR drive along the Hudson to avoid the Midtown roadblocks. Bear with me."

This seemed to satisfy Eve, until she noticed minutes later that they were still heading south and were now on the Lower East Side. While she was still wondering about the route, the driver came to a sudden halt in a quiet side street where there was no one about. Eve looked out the window and sensed they were somewhere in the financial district. Jill glanced through the window at what looked like the entrance to a private bank.

A brass plate on the door read "Bank Nineveh PLC."

She was still taking this in when the front door of the bank opened and two large young men with blond hair and piercing blue eyes stepped out onto the sidewalk beside the cab. Eve rolled down her window.

"Mrs. Tinker and Ms. Tinker? Please come with us," one of them said in accented English.

Jill was stunned into silence.

Eve shot a glare at the two men. "We're not coming with you or anyone else! Mother, get out of this cab on my side. We're leaving!"

Jill and Eve attempted to exit. But they found both passenger doors locked.

"Driver, open these doors immediately!" Jill demanded.

The driver said nothing. He just sat still.

"Oh my God!" shrieked Eve in a sudden panic.

"We're being kidnapped!" Jill screamed in terror.

Before they could react further, the cabbie unlocked the cab doors and the two men from the bank reached inside, one on each side of the cab, and hauled the women out. They kicked and screamed. No one else was around to witness the kidnappers forcibly drag mother and daughter into the premises of the Bank Nineveh PLC.

While they were still screaming and kicking wildly, the two brutes hustled them into an elevator, where they were taken to a second floor and ushered into an elaborately decorated boardroom. Laid out on the table were some highball glasses, a large jug of orange juice, and a plateful of pastries and cookies. As the two women were absorbing their surroundings, three other men entered and signaled to the two security men to leave.

"Mrs. Tinker, and Miss Tinker," said a stranger, a man with a pronounced German accent. "We must apologize for the unexpected nature of our meeting with you today. I do hope our security people did you no harm. Please, do help yourselves to some orange juice and something to eat."

A hidden side of Jill Tinker suddenly burst out in an explosion of rage. "Who the hell are you people, and what is this all about? I will not be manhandled like this! And don't you people even dare to touch my daughter!"

"Very spirited, Mrs. Tinker. We certainly mean no harm to either you or your daughter. We just need some cooperation from both of you—and from your husband."

"What has this—this *abduction*—got to do with my husband?" demanded Jill.

"Dear Mrs. Tinker, this is just a business matter. I'm sure it can be resolved very soon, and then you can be on your way to whatever destination you wish." The accented English carried an undertone of extreme menace.

"Who are you people?" yelled Eve. "Are you going to hold us here, kill us, and dismember us—like, like those people in the Saudi Consulate in Turkey?"

"Come, come, Ms. Tinker, we would not even dream of such a thing," the man said with an icy smile. "All we need is for your husband to cooperate with us on a small request, and then this unfortunate matter will be closed."

"I don't understand what you're talking about!" cried Jill. "I want us both to leave—right now!"

"We quite understand, my ladies. But let me tell you that our meeting today never happened, and anyone here you think of identifying at some future time will deny it ever happened. After all," he said, turning to his two male companions, "we bankers are not in the business of kidnapping ladies, are we now?"

That cold, steely smile barely hid an implied threat. Jill went suddenly silent.

"Be assured, Mrs. Tinker," said the stranger, "that as soon as we reach your husband, we're certain he will cooperate—and then you will both soon be on your way. Please, be seated and relax. If you need anything, just come to the door, and one of our people will be only too glad to help."

"I want to speak to my husband—now!" said Jill, struggling to regain her composure.

"You will do so, just as soon as we have finished speaking to him. Please wait. This should not take long." The three men the left the room. Jill noticed that two of the three said nothing but just observed. Both looked like they were from somewhere in the Middle East.

Jill waited for a few seconds and went to the door. It was unlocked. She opened it and was about to step out, when one of the security guards blocked her path.

"I want to use the bathroom."

The man gestured to an adjoining restroom.

"Your handbag, please. It will be returned to you when you leave."

She complied. The goon reached into her pocketbook, even though he had already removed her mobile phone.

Calling Fred would have to wait.

A Delicate Decision

F red was caught off guard when his office assistant put through a call from "Mr. Farben, sir." It was late that morning, and it had never occurred to Fred that Farben would call so soon after their meeting the day before.

"Mr. Tinker, may I assume you have considered my request and have come to a decision?" Fred instantly caught the sinister tone in the German's words.

"I'm addressing what you discussed with me, but I'm not sure I can be of any help to you." Fred was stalling for time.

"Mr. Tinker," said the menacing voice, "please understand that I'm a very practical man. Your cooperation means a lot to me. Will you cooperate or not?"

"I don't know what you mean." Fred's efforts to stonewall were not working.

"Then let me tell you something to help you," said the voice. "Your wife and daughter are sitting in a room not far from me. I've assured them that they'll soon be on their way to wherever they are going. That assumes, of course, that you'll cooperate on the matter we discussed yesterday. I'd be most concerned that nothing happens to them, like an unfortunate accident. Do you understand what I'm saying?"

"Jesus!" cried Fred. "What is this? Are you holding my wife and daughter hostage?"

"At this point, Mr. Tinker, they're simply our guests. I'd like to keep it that way. Wouldn't you agree?"

"Where are you? Where are they?" Fred demanded feebly. He had never expected anything like this to happen.

"Deliver to us what we've asked for, and then they will be free to be reunited with you. Otherwise, we cannot guarantee their safety."

"You bastard, Farben! How dare you involve my family in this business matter!"

"I'm a patient man, Mr. Tinker, but I'm also human, and so there are limits to my patience. You have five hours to deliver what I asked for. After that, I cannot assure you what may happen next."

There was a click on the phone and the line went dead.

Fred sat back in his chair, completely stunned. He felt a sudden sour taste in his mouth, swiftly followed by a terrible, overwhelming tension and sense of guilt and helplessness. *What have I gotten myself into? What have I done? What can I do?*

His first thought was to call Charlie. Surely, he could help. Fred reached for his mobile phone and scanned the list of recent incoming calls. He found what seemed like a familiar number. He dialed out. Busy. He dialed again. Still busy.

Then he called Adam. "Adam, we need to talk in private as soon as possible." He told his son nothing about Farben's threats.

They met shortly afterward in Fred's bedroom back at the club. Adam pointed out to his father, at last, that the maps Fred had shown to Charlie Fortescue had been falsified by Adam, as a ruse to throw others off course. But what if they copied a few more falsified maps and gave them to Balogh to offer the consortium?

"Adam, you don't need to know why I'm suggesting this, but all I can tell you is I urgently need to have copies of some of those phony maps, for business reasons."

"OK, Dad. No problem." Adam sensed from his father's tone that something serious was going on, but this did not seem the right moment to ask questions.

Within the hour, Adam duly returned from a local copying service and handed a large manila envelope to his father. He had made sure to exit and reenter by the club's back door.

"I copied all twenty of the falsified maps. There are five in this envelope."

"Great job, son! I now need some privacy please to make a call."

When Fred called Farben's number, it was not Farben, but Thiel who answered.

Fred came straight to the point. He had in his possession not just one but several maps that Farben had requested; and would hand them over at the same time as his wife and daughter were reunited with him.

Thiel told him to step outside the club in one hour and look for a certain Yellow Cab. The driver would be waiting nearby. The cab would be easily identifiable. Its trunk lid would be open. Fred was to get in the back seat, and then the driver would bring him to his wife and daughter. But he must first show the driver that he had documents on him.

As instructed, Fred appeared at the club's entrance. He quickly spotted a nearby cab with its trunk open. He approached the driver and waved a large, heavy envelope in the air. The driver nodded and silently pointed a thumb to the back seat.

They set off in what Fred thought was a southerly direction. After some ten minutes, the cab suddenly swerved into a one-way side street. As it turned, a black van followed and pulled up behind the cab. Two large, blue-eyed, blond-haired men got out and quickly ran forward to the cab, flung the passenger door open, and pulled Fred from the back seat. He thought he recognized them. But before he could say a word, they had blindfolded him and bundled him into the back of the black van. It then reversed to the corner, tires screeching, waited momentarily for an opening in the traffic, swung into the road, and sped off.

About fifteen minutes later, the van stopped, and Fred heard the ignition turn off. The van's sliding door was opened. Two pairs of burly arms grabbed him and frog-marched the stumbling businessman up some steps and into a building.

Fred caught a familiar jasmine scent in the air—like the one he remembered from the building where the first consortium meeting had been held. He also remembered a squeaking noise as the elevator door closed. The burly arms gripped him firmly on either side. He was still blindfolded, and remained so till the elevator reached a higher floor.

Fred heard the elevator door open. Someone removed the blindfold. He found himself blinking and staring at two men. Farben and Thiel were standing there to greet him.

"Mr. Tinker, what a pleasure to see you again," said Farben. "We assume you had a pleasant journey to this place? Oh, and please let me have your mobile phone, just for a little while. We can turn it off for you, for your privacy—and it will be returned to you as soon as we finish our verification."

"Farben, I have here what you want. Now where are my wife and daughter?"

"All in good time, Mr. Tinker. But first, we need to see the maps. Please, make yourself comfortable in this conference room. This should not take long."

An hour passed. The conference room door remained unlocked, but one of the goons stood guard outside. He brought in a jug of water and a glass on a silver tray and placed it beside Fred.

At last, Farben reappeared, this time accompanied by his associate Thiel.

"Well, Mr. Tinker, you have done the consortium a great favor, and we thank you. You can be assured that, by now, your wife and daughter are safely back where they started. In fact, why not give them a call yourself?"

He handed back to Fred the mobile phone that had been confiscated on his arrival.

"Jill! Are you there? Are you both all right?" Fred's voice was choking and panicked. Another bigger wave of guilt washed over him.

"Oh, Fred, we're fine—but these terrible people grabbed Eve and me and held us hostage somewhere in Lower Manhattan! They just returned us to the club! *What is going on?*"

"Jill, it's a long story! But, right now, I just need to know you are both OK" Fred stammered.

"Yes, yes! But where are you? And should I call the police?"

"I'm just finishing a...business meeting. I should be back within an hour or so, and we can talk then. No need to call the police."

Jill sensed that this was not a good time for Fred to explain anything more.

"OK, OK," she said lamely. "See you soon." She hung up. *Surely*, she thought, *Fred can explain to me what exactly is going on.*

Farben nodded to the blond-haired goon who had ushered Fred from the room and into the elevator. As they left the building and frog-marched Fred into an adjacent side street, Fred thought he recognized the same cabbie who had driven him here a few hours earlier. He was bundled into the back seat. One of the goons slammed the door shut. The cabbie promptly locked it, then turned on the ignition and drove off.

Some forty minutes and several traffic jams later, the cab pulled up at the front entrance of the Halcyon Club. Only then were the cab doors unlocked.

Fred promptly exited, without offering the driver a tip.

A Close Call

Fred stepped into the Halcyon Club lobby and, still shaken, promptly placed a call to Charlie. Minutes later, the distressed husband found himself struggling to contain his hysterical wife and daughter.

"We *must* call the police!" insisted Jill.

"Jill, no, not yet!" begged Fred. "Not till I sort a few things out. And I'm not sure we can offer the police any evidence for what happened today. I'm not even sure they would have grounds to arrest anyone."

"But these men are thugs and criminals, Dad..." Eve spoke, barely able to contain her fury.

"Yes, they are." Fred was almost at his wits' end. "But I have an idea how to deal with them. So just leave this with me, at least for now. Please!"

Charlie had promised Fred he would get to the club within twenty minutes. After Fred had taken an awkward leave of his wife and daughter and pressed them to go upstairs to their rooms, he went downstairs and entered the lobby. As he did so, 'Mr. Pimlico' entered the building. Seeing Fred, he put an index finger to his lips and silently pointed to a quiet corner of the reading room. The place was empty.

As they sat down, he said, "Fred, I know this was a very close call today." Charlie tried to sound apologetic.

"Charlie," muttered Fred, "if only I had known what I was getting into, not to mention the involvement of my wife and daughter, I would never have gone along with your plan. But I have only myself to blame for this mess."

"Fred, you're quite right. But let me assure you that we had that Bank Nineveh bugged so well that you could have heard a mouse cross their carpets. Also, my team was right there in a van nearby, ready to break in at a moment's notice if Farben and his buddies started to act in any way violently. Thanks to you and your family keeping your cool and going with the flow, it never came to that—and so, we did not have to blow our cover just yet."

"Well, that's the last time I play cloak-and-dagger, for you or anyone else!"

"You did very well, and I owe you for it. I'll never ask you to put yourself or your family in that position again."

Surveillance

Unbeknown to the Tinker family, Charlie had made sure that a large team of agents from Britain's MI6 and the CIA were jointly watching every movement of the six main suspects leading the consortium.

Both agencies had a good read on the Germans and Americans involved. But both were sadly lacking when it came to the Egyptian and Saudi elements.

Charlie knew that the consortium's executive committee member from Egypt, named Minister Luckman, was acting in an unofficial capacity as a member of the Egyptian Ministry of Foreign Affairs. He also knew that the Egyptian government had been quietly watching several of its ministry officials and had shared their concerns with Charlie's agency.

There were strong indications that Luckman was an active member of Ansar Al Islam. This violent group consisted of Egyptian Sunni army officers who had secretly turned against their own government, and who had a clandestine affiliation with Al Qaeda. It had turned on both Egyptian Coptic Christians and on members of any moderate form of

Islam. Their natural allies were the hardline Wahhabi Saudi clerics.

Charlie also knew that the consortium's Saudi representative, First Counselor Ahmed bin Khouri of the Saudi Embassy in Washington, had only recently been posted there. He had been seconded from the Ministry of the Interior's Division of Internal Security in Riyadh, though little else was known about him.

But there was someone else intimately familiar with many of the individuals supporting the extremist Wahhabi camp. Professor Yussef Bitar, the same lecturer from Columbia University who had been run down by a car in Buenos Aires, was intimately familiar with members of a wide range of extremist Islamic groups. As a young student, he had flirted with the Egyptian Muslim Brotherhood, but had later renounced the group on learning in depth about its violent record since its founding in 1928.

After he had met with Bitar in New York and learned so much from him, Adam decided to share with his former professor some of what had been going on with the consortium and its quest to find hidden Nazi loot. They met discreetly at a diner, coincidentally on the same afternoon of the abduction of Adam's mother and sister.

As soon as Bitar heard the name Luckman, he caught Adam by surprise.

"Luckman? Oh, I knew of him ages ago."

As Bitar spoke, it sounded to Adam as though Luckman was yesterday's news to him.

"He was always a loyal member of the Muslim Brotherhood, talking about the need to bring back the caliph to rule over a world united by Islam and controlled by *sharia* law. It would not surprise me if he has an interest in grabbing billions of dollars of hidden loot to support any and all violent uprisings against Western secular influences and against secular Muslims. People like him call such Muslims *takfiris,* or apostates, who deserve to be killed."

Adam wanted to hear more. "Tell me something about the Muslim Brotherhood and whether or not it's important to us here in the United States."

"Well," said the lecturer, "the Brotherhood's old guard still follows the guidance of its founder, Hassan Al Banna. That is, to build up an Islamic world community, or *ummah,* and do it gradually, with a nonviolent approach of preaching *sharia* in schools and social organizations. But over the years, certain younger pro-*sharia* Muslims wanted quicker results. Remember I told you about an Islamic writer called Sayed Qtb, writing back in the 1950s and 1960s? His writings encouraged violent struggle—that is, violent *jihad*. I told you he was executed for his involvement in an attempted assassination of a secular Egyptian President, Gamal Abdul Nasser. I also told you that Qtb was probably the inspiration behind groups like Al Qaeda and ISIS that we know today."

Bitar looked up and scouted the dimly lit West Side diner to make sure he still had an audience of one. "Want to know something? In 2001, the largest Muslim charitable organization in the United States, the Holy Land Foundation, was raided by the United States authorities and designated as a terrorist organization for its financial support of Hamas. It claimed only to be supporting education and social services for needy Palestinians. Then, in 2008, the Holy Land Foundation was prosecuted for raising twelve million dollars from the United States and giving it to Hamas, a violent sister element of the Brotherhood that I already told you about. All revolutions need money, and so I'm not surprised that Luckman and his friends are after big money."

Adam interjected. "That's interesting. Because that information could help nail these guys. I'd like to run that by our lawyer and see what he thinks."

Later that evening, Fred broke the news to Adam about the kidnapping and how he had exchanged five doctored maps to free Jill and Eve. Adam couldn't believe his ears.

Two days later, Adam sat with the lawyer in a small hotel conference room a few miles from György Balogh's law office.

"Mr. Balogh," asked Adam, "I need to know if we have solid grounds on which to prosecute the two Arab leaders of the consortium for treason."

"Treason, eh?" mused Balogh. "Well then, let's start with a redefinition of what that means under US law. Here's a legal quote: 'Treason against the United States shall consist only in levying war against them—the States, that is—or in adhering to their enemies, giving them aid and comfort. No person shall be convicted of treason unless on the testimony of two witnesses to the same overt act, or on confession in open court.'"

"So?" queried Adam.

"Under American law," continued Balogh as he sifted through papers on his desk, "the definition of the term *enemies* is 'a nation or organization with which the United States is in a declared or open war.' Therefore, and as an example, despite the many issues we may have with the Russians, we have not declared war on them. So, they are not enemies as such. However, let's say there's a North Korean present in the United States, intent on using force to overthrow the US government. Well, he could be prosecuted for treason because the Korean War was never formally concluded. Certain nonstate parties such as Al Qaeda and ISIS might also be considered as treasonous enemies."

Balogh paused to let his points sink in. He took a deep breath before continuing. "Now, treason law also recognizes two kinds of allegiance to the United States. Citizens of the United States owe permanent allegiance, wherever they are in the world. But in addition, noncitizens who are in the United States and receive protection from them owe a duty of temporary allegiance, based on a Supreme Court ruling of 1872. This is because, while in the States as noncitizens, they are governed by American treason law. They can't escape prosecution for treason just by asserting foreign citizenship."

"I didn't know that. Does this mean that Luckman and bin Khouri could both be charged with treason?"

"Well, there would have to be two witnesses to the fact they were engaged in an act of war against the United States, or their confession in open court. Do we have such witnesses, to your knowledge?"

Adam rubbed his chin. "I'm not sure. At least, not yet."

"Then let's find them." Balogh outlined a plan of action.

Time for a Sting

Fred, Adam, and Charlie huddled in a corner of the Halcyon Club's reading room. It was mid-morning. The space was empty and likely to remain so thanks to the pouring rain outside.

Adam reported his findings from Balogh, including a plan to entrap the two Arabs and the two Germans so that they could successfully be arrested, tried for treason, and jailed. It took only minutes before Charlie brought up another idea.

His contacts in the FBI would use an undercover agent to approach the consortium's six suspects with a proposal for an armed uprising in the United States. Its agent would represent himself as a white supremacist eager to subvert and overturn the US government. He would offer his services, in exchange for a large amount of money that would be used to buy weapons and equipment and to buy media time to promote anti-US government agitation. This would include funds for dissemination of false news on social media, street demonstrations, and cash to pay thugs to destroy property and cause unrest around the country.

If the FBI could gather tangible evidence of a conspiracy by the four foreign nationals to subvert the US government, they could build a case to prosecute them for treason.

"Mind you," said Adam, "according to our lawyer, there have been relatively few successful prosecutions for treason." Adam pointed out what Balogh had told him. "The last person convicted of treason was a Japanese-American sentenced to death in 1952 for torturing American prisoners during World War II. Even then, the defendant, Tomoya Kawakita, received a commutation to life imprisonment."

"Did Balogh mention the Rosenbergs?" asked Fred.

"Yes, in fact, he did," said Adam. "He pointed out that the Rosenbergs, who handed over US nuclear secrets to the Soviet Union, were executed—not for treason, but for espionage. Balogh had also told him that charges of treason were rare, and that in the entire history of the United States, there had been only thirty cases. People like Aaron Burr had been acquitted of treason after trying to secede from the Union in 1807, for lack of proof and witness statements. During the 20th century, there were successful treason convictions for three broadcasters."

"For broadcasters?" asked Fred. He felt puzzled.

"Yes," replied Adam. Balogh had told him about Axis Sally, also known as Mildred Gellars, who had broadcast anti-American propaganda from Germany in World War II. Her treason conviction resulted in a twelve-year jail sentence. There was also Iva Ikuko Toguri D'Aquino, known as 'Tokyo Rose,' who had made anti-American broadcasts from Japan during the war. And then there was the poet Ezra Pound. The last two had also gone to prison for twelve years.

Charlie interjected, indicating his concern about catching and prosecuting the Saudi member of the consortium. "There's the ticklish matter of US and Arab relations. The Saudis have shown the world they will not hesitate to murder critics of their government. Yet the United States keeps on buying their and selling them advanced weapons, because it remains anxious not to let them get into bed with the Russians. Therefore, we can't count on any domestic administration to support our sting unless we can prove in advance a deliberate attempt to overturn the US government. The Saudi and the Egyptian governments get along with each other and so, if we are perceived as taking down their nationals—however disreputable they may be—that could be a problem. But not one we can't overcome."

Based on Balogh's advice, Adam pointed out the need to prove a clear connection between Luckman and the Saudi on one hand and violent Islamist preachers and terrorists on the other. He recalled Balogh's point about the unlawful use of force and violence against persons or property, or against the civilian US population, or any segment thereof in furtherance of political or social objectives. There would therefore need to be clear proof of a political or ideological agenda behind such an attack.

Charlie observed that, since the Muslim Brotherhood briefly came to power in Egypt in 2012, hundreds of storefront mosques, or *zawiyas*, had sprung up. There were now more than one hundred thousand mosques throughout the country. Many mosque *imams* preached extremist views and demanded the imposition of Islamic law, or *sharia*. The current Egyptian government had suppressed the elected Brotherhood government and clamped down on many thousands of such preachers. This was particularly so during the month of fasting, or *Ramadan*, when the government made it illegal to preach intolerance of moderate Muslim religious groups like the Sufis, as well as Christians.

"You know," said Charlie, "the present Egyptian government has tried to get across a moderate view of Islam to curb Islamic violence, especially toward Coptic Christians. But there is huge counterpressure, not only from extreme preachers but also from religious edicts, or *fatwas*, coming from long-established centers for Islamic study like Cairo's Al Azhar University."

Adam asked if there was a way to prove a link between the Muslim Brotherhood and Luckman, and between extremist Saudi preachers and Al Khouri. Charlie simply replied that, yes, there was a way—but declined to go into detail.

Charlie knew that British Intelligence had inside sources which could help to stitch together a provable link and then document it. There were enough corrupt parties within the Egyptian and Saudi extreme religious establishment that, if all else failed, certain players could be blackmailed into cooperating.

It was well-known to various governments that monies collected nominally for the benefit of Muslim charities had found their way into the pockets of certain extremist preachers and organizations. The British were constantly intercepting telephone, text, and email traffic about minute details of 'charitable' donations that were quietly being siphoned off to the bank accounts of certain highly visible Egyptian and Saudi clerics.

It was now time to get down to details and stop the suspects in their tracks.

Taking the Bait

Charlie's team kept a close watch on Minister Luckman's rented New York apartment. It was in a nondescript high-rise on the West Side. The landlord had readily agreed to provide access to the building for unspecified 'national security purposes,' in exchange for a handsome tax-free cash deposit to his personal bank account.

Luckman was a creature of habit whose comings and goings were predictable. During one of his outings to a nearby Lebanese restaurant for dinner, Charlie's bugging team quietly broke into Luckman's apartment and rapidly wired the place to capture every possible sound and view. It added to their satisfaction that they caught Luckman there on video several times with assorted ladies with whom he spent the night. This could come in handy when the time came to break the news to him and, subject to his future cooperation, to his wife and family.

Meanwhile, the sting operation began with an FBI agent posing as a white extremist. He had reached out to an exiled Egyptian extremist cleric based in Doha, Qatar, about an 'idea he might find interesting'. The agent and the cleric had met in person and talked about ways to stir up trouble against the government of the United States.

Ibrahim Al Muharib was the host of an Al Jazeera TV show with millions of viewers. He had been carefully selected by Britain's MI6 as the unwitting messenger to the Muslim Brotherhood about starting an insurrection in the western United States. Given his influence among Sunni extremists and a history of past associations with assorted murders, Al Muharib was a wanted man by Interpol. He had been sentenced to death in absentia in Egypt, sanctioned by several Arab countries and banned from entering the US and the UK.

In other words, he was the perfect messenger boy to the Brotherhood in which Minister Luckman was a key figure.

Charlie had prepared his team to look for every possible message from the Brotherhood to Luckman that could serve as future evidence of a plot to subvert the US government. They intercepted each incoming email and text message for scrutiny. They opened every piece of mail or any package in his mailbox, photographed it, and then put it back into Luckman's apartment mailbox. They followed his every movement and watched for any interaction that could be observed and photographed with any third party.

As he walked the streets or took the subway, they would closely observe any brief exchanges of items or words, known as 'brush passes', where exchanges were quickly and discreetly made with a passerby. When he ate out, watchful eyes would record and photograph any encounters with others, or messages passed to him discreetly.

Several days passed after the 'white supremacist' had approached Al Muharib in Qatar. There was no sign of any message from the Brotherhood to Luckman.

A similar watch was put on Al Khouri, the young attaché at the Saudi Embassy.

But still no sign that the Brotherhood had taken the bait.

Charlie was about to recast his plans when he learned that Al Muharib had done something unusual. He had flown under an assumed name to Geneva, Switzerland. He also learned that a close associate of the German named Farben had left abruptly for Geneva from the BND office near Munich. It was a guess, but perhaps this signaled a meeting in Geneva between Farben's underling and Al Muharib.

The Geneva station of MI6 promptly sprang into action. It took little time to identify the elderly Arab gentleman coming through Customs at Geneva Airport. By arrangement with MI6's Swiss counterparts, the elderly passenger on the flight manifest—a 'Mr. Ali Hamad'—was allowed through Immigration and Customs without delay.

A chauffeur-driven Mercedes awaited him and whisked him directly to the Grand Hotel Kempinski overlooking the lake.

The underling from the BND's Munich was already sitting waiting in the lobby as 'Mr. Hamad' entered the foyer. Thanks to a helpful housekeeper who was duly rewarded, a man dressed as an engineer had already entered the cleric's suite, ostensibly to inspect the plumbing. When he left some thirty minutes before Hamad's arrival, the entire suite had been bugged and several tiny, discreet video cameras had been activated.

Charlie's watchers followed every move as the young underling from Munich took the elevator to the sixth floor. The transcript of the conversations between the German and Mr. Hamad were in Charlie's hands barely an hour after a brief, twenty-minute meeting had taken place in the Arab's suite.

Al Muharib sealed his fate with the words, "Tell your supervisor to signal your man in New York. It is time to light the fire that will consume the United States and its diabolical government, and all its allies."

The Arab was giving the green light to proceed to insurrection in the United States—and not giving it to Luckman, after all, but instead to their German co-conspirators. How clever of the Arab to light the fuse through the Germans so that they, and not the Arabs, would get the blame if caught.

The watchers now switched their attention closely to Farben and to all his communications and all his movements.

Farben's lifelong career in the BND had made him exceptionally cautious with secret communications, methods and operations. Even Charlie's engineers could not directly access the interior of the New York condominium that Farben had rented from a German businessman. Instead, Charlie's team paid Farben's next-door neighbor a large financial inducement to take an all-expenses-paid vacation and to sublet his space to an important government employee for a month or so.

The employee was one of Charlie's technical experts. He drilled a small hole through the adjoining wall to Farben's condo, then inserted a super-sensitive needle microphone through the tiny opening just above the floorboards. The tip of the needle also contained a miniature multi-directional video camera that could be manually swiveled in any direction.

The results were initially poor. Farben liked to parade around naked in this space and muttered often inaudibly to himself. Incoming phone calls were intercepted through a splitter in the building's basement which another member of Charlie's team had setup late one night. Farben and his callers took great care to make their conversations sound as harmless as possible.

Two days passed, but the listeners and watchers captured nothing incriminating. Then, at last, there was a break.

A call came in that was traced to the BND office near Munich. "Our friend said it's now the time," said the voice of a younger man, speaking in German. The voice matched the voice of the German who had met with Al Muharib in Geneva. The caller then mentioned the name of another friend who would contact Farben. The friend in question was an American, a white supremacist, and someone who had "reached out to our friend in Doha, Qatar."

He would identify himself as 'Brad Mueller', a family friend, when he called.

The call from Mueller came in a day later. He and Farben agreed to meet in a remote part of upstate New York where Mueller would "share news of the family."

A Walk in the Woods

Two nondescript men booked separate rooms at the Loose Goose Inn, a scruffy and run-down motel on the outskirts of Berlin, a small town in northern New York state. To all the world, neither man knew the other — that is, until they met at a predesignated hillside parking lot buried in the heart of black bear country.

The FBI plant's real name was Mitchell Dixon, aka Brad Mueller. He had been a white supremacist in his early youth but had become sickened by the leadership and its devotion to hatred of just about anyone else, including "the Jews, the US government (which is run by Jews), Israel, and all people of color."

Mitch was also a hunter in his own right. He preferred bird hunting in the South over anywhere else. But it was he who had chosen the small town of Berlin, New York, to meet with Farben in person.

Mitch was pretty sure his target would not forget the town's name.

They each looked around at the parking lot before making contact. There were only a few other hunters gearing up for the day. Before Mitch and Farben set off, Mitch, in his guise as Brad, gave Farben a few tips.

"The early black bear hunting season here in New York runs from mid-September to mid-October. We hunters are legally permitted to use a bow, crossbow, muzzleloader, handgun, shotgun, or, where allowed, a rifle. In this area, called the Northern Zone, it's illegal to carry a rifle larger than .22 rimfire or a shotgun loaded with slug, ball, or buckshot afield if accompanied by a dog, except when coyote hunting."

"OK," said Farben. It had been a while since he had gone hunting, in the Austrian Alps.

"But," said Brad, "we don't want to attract attention, do we? So, I suggest we use a crossbow instead. Here, I have a spare one for you to use. Oh, and by the way, you don't have to wear an all-fluorescent outfit here to conform with the law. A bright orange baseball cap is strongly recommended—just in case another hunter takes you for a bear or a deer!" He tossed an orange baseball cap toward Farben.

"I might also suggest you take off those jeans of yours," said Brad. "It's OK to wear 'em for dinner in Berlin, maybe. But if we spot deer, they will spot you first because they see shortwave blue colors about twenty times better than we ever do!"

He handed Farben a pair of camouflage pants. The German disappeared behind his rented car and discreetly changed pants. While he did so, Mitch made sure that the transmitter in his hunter's cap was firmly in place and that the two-way microphone was tucked firmly behind his left ear, under a

300

crop of salt-and-pepper hair. He tapped the microphone twice, then heard three clicks one second apart that confirmed that the FBI team was tracking him and his quarry.

The two hunters set off on foot and made small talk for the first thirty minutes, treading softly through the fallen leaves and speaking in lowered voices. They asked one another about family and background. Mitch wove a story about running away from home and family as a teenager and joining up with the National Nordic Alliance in Seattle.

"The NNA gave me a sense of belonging which I have to this day, and a mission to rid the United States of its diabolical federal government and all its inhuman impurities in this great country of ours. I mean the blacks, browns, yellows, and Jews."

It did not take long for the two men to forge a connection.

It was then that Farben tested the waters. "I understand you met with a certain person in Qatar recently?" he said casually.

"Why, yes. I surely did. I heard this guy Al Muharib was Mr. Unpopular with Uncle Sam, among others. He seemed like my kind of guy."

"Really? Why did you want to meet him?" asked Farben, probing gently. Brad didn't fail to notice this nibble at the bait. Nor did the other listeners.

Somewhere in the distance, a hunter's gunshot shattered the silence.

"Well," said Brad, "I was on a business trip out that way. The NNA asked me to look this guy up to see if he could help us."

"What sort of help do you mean?" asked the German.

"I mean help to raise some big money so we could start to make real trouble for Uncle Sam right here in his backyard."

The wind suddenly sprang up as if to carry off his words. Farben clutched at his borrowed baseball cap as it almost took flight. "Why would you want to do that?" he asked his fellow hunter.

"Do I have to tell you why?" The FBI plant gave the questioner a toothy grin. Mitch recited almost word for word the same spiel he had given to Al Muharib.

But Farben was still suspicious. "What makes you think that someone like me would be interested in doing something to harm or even overthrow the US government?" he asked cautiously.

A squirrel rushed across their path and scurried up a huge pine tree.

"Aw! C'mon, Mr. Farben! Let's not play games here! You and I—and maybe some folks in the Arab world—have some common interests. You may not care about white supremacy over people of color in this country, but you sure as hell do care about getting rid of the Jews. Right? And they run the US government. Right? So, do we have a common interest or not? Level with me!"

"How do I know you are not playing games with me, Mr.

302

Miller? You go to Qatar 'on business,' and you reach out to the host of an Al Jazeera television show who happens to be a radical Islamist preacher who you say passed you on to me. I don't even know this person."

It irked Mitch that Farben was so close to biting the baited hook and yet was still far from making any admission of his interest in joining forces against the United States government with a known American white supremacist.

"OK. OK. I hear ya. So, just forget about this conversation, right? It never took place. Now, let's go find a bear or two to shoot. By the way, I go by Brad. Mind if I call you Ludwig?"

The next two hours passed slowly as the hunter and the hunted moved softly, one after the other, through the early fall brush in search of prey. The wind had died down, and a slight chill breeze now wafted through the trees, warning of more severe winter weather to come. At last, Mitch stopped and signaled silence to Farben, for he had spotted a movement in the undergrowth some three hundred yards ahead.

Mitch crouched, then moved slowly to a hollow beneath a huge fallen fir. He beckoned Farben to follow him and began the process of cocking his crossbow. It had a heavy draw weight of some one hundred and seventy-five pounds. A younger man might have been able to pull the bowstring back to the loading position just with his own body strength alone, but Mitch knew, at age forty, he could no longer do that. He had decided instead to invest in a cocking rope.

He faced his crossbow to the ground, slipping the ball of his boot into the foot claw centered at the crossbow's midpoint.

The foot claw was shaped like a horseman's stirrup. It served to stabilize the crossbow while the hunter pulled up the bowstring till it was taut. After hooking the cocking rope clamps onto the bowstring on either side of the shaft, Mitch tugged to make sure he had even tension on each side, and then heaved the cocking rope's handles evenly toward him until a click told him the taut bowstring was now engaged. Thanks to his use of the cocking rope, the stress of creating the cocking tension was cut in half.

He put the safety switch to safe and loaded a bolt.

Peeping slowly over the crest of the hollow, his eyes searched the forest ahead for the spot where he had seen a movement minutes ago. But he saw nothing. The eerie silent stillness of the forest and its endless envelope of trees seemed to have swallowed up anything that moved. He lowered his head and put his gloved hand to his lips, signaling to Farben to remain silent.

They waited, ears straining for the slightest sound. Mitch peeped once more over the top of the hollow, this time with his loaded crossbow at the ready. He thought he saw a shadow flit between the trees and catch the sunlight some seventy yards ahead. Straining forward, he heard a soft rustle of dead leaves on the forest floor coming from the direction of the fleeting shape. He leaned his head forward till his right eye almost touched the telescope lens on his weapon. As he adjusted the sights, he now saw a rapid movement, as if the creature ahead was breaking cover.

This might be his only kill of the day. He took aim, then fired.

The bolt was a heavier hunter's bolt which, in hunter-speak, weighed more than four hundred grain. It flew at close to three hundred feet per second and hit its mark.

Then, the unexpected happened.

There was a scream of agony—not of an animal, but a strangely human sound. Farben thought he heard a curse in German. It sounded like "*Scheisse!*"

Mitch stood up, shocked. Had he hit a human, not a bear or a deer? But there was no hint of bright orange hat or clothing on the figure. A tall shadowy silhouette rose up to its full height from the undergrowth ahead. It then began to stagger off at a trot, and away from where the two hunters stood, dumbfounded.

That struck Mitch as odd. Why would someone wounded by a crossbow bolt run off and not stop still or try to stagger forward for help?

Farben's mind was somewhere else. He was pretty sure that the man Mitch had just shot was his underling Gunther, his personal bodyguard, security chief, and occasional assassin.

"What shall we do?" said Farben, sounding unconvincing.

The tone in Farben's voice seemed strangely odd, strangely calm. It was as if he had expected something like this to happen all along. Mitch was now highly alert. Things had taken an unexpected turn. Yet Farben seemed strangely unconcerned about a wounded man who simply ran off without asking for help.

"We gotta report this to the state police," said the FBI plant.

"It's part of the regulations and requirements for getting a hunting license." He pretended to dial an emergency number on his cell phone.

"This is Brad Mueller. I'm reporting a hunting accident. I just shot someone, thinking they were either a bear or a deer. Thing is, my crossbow bolt hit a man, and, to my surprise, he just ran off. Yeah, officer. He ran off, I tell you!"

He gave the approximate coordinates of latitude and longitude. He spelled out his name again and gave his address as the Loose Goose Inn.

Hopefully, the FBI team would now be on the lookout for a wounded male likely to be heading out of the woods to a car and toward the nearest hospital or local pharmacy. North Adams Regional Hospital was fifteen miles or about a thirty-minute drive away. Mitch hoped that the covering team would have eyes on every possible source of medical help within a wide radius.

"I think we should go back and get a drink," he said. "The cops will probably be there at the Inn waiting for us, to get a statement."

Farben seemed to agree. They retraced their steps.

As predicted, there were two men in state police uniform waiting to take a statement. Only Mitch knew they were two local cops working in concert with his own FBI team.

When they had left, Farben checked his smartphone for an email or text message. He wondered if Gunther, if he was indeed the wounded man, was observing strict silent protocol, just as his special military training had required.

The Closer

Mitch—that is, 'Brad'—and Farben found a local diner nearby. They ordered cold beers and beef chili. The weather outside was turning more and more wintry. The warmth of the diner offered relief from the gnawing outdoor cold. The generous plateful of hot turkey chili helped too.

The FBI agent decided he would wait to see if Farben would revive the topic that had brought them together in the first place. Mitch speculated out loud, but in a low voice, about the man he had accidentally shot that day. Why would he would have run off rather than seek help? Farben too seemed puzzled. Gradually, their talk turned to family and comparisons between life in America versus Germany.

"You know," said the German, "the right is rising in Germany today. The economy is getting weaker. People are getting angrier. They want immigration to stop. They want to see the millions of Turks, Syrians, Iraqis, and other refugees deported back to their countries of origin."

"Yeah, well," said Brad, nodding, "we got something like that brewing over here. The jerks in Washington that were put there by the voters have sold 'em out! All the politicians do is bicker with one another. That's ticking off the whole country right now."

He took a big mouthful of chili. Swallowing hard, he said to Farben, "Let me tell you something. There's a small machine shop in Kentucky that didn't even make firearms in 2008. Today, it makes more rifles than Smith & Wesson. And the big seller? Why, it's an assault-style rifle. Other folks out there are making rifles with larger .308 caliber rounds. One of the other hottest sellers these days in the Sub-2000 rifle, because it folds up small enough to squeeze into a backpack. It's real discreet, but handy."

"That's...interesting," Farben responded. "But I understand that the big banks are so worried about the mass shootings here with assault-style rifles that they are tightening their lending to rifle makers?"

"Yup, but no big deal," said Brad, "because there's plenty of community banks, credit unions, and metal cutting machine shops out there to provide the capital needed to make more guns. Guns are real popular here today. Y'know, there's this Crusader rifle made in Florida with a safety catch marked 'Full Libturd' that takes aim at political liberals! Ain't that something? And, there's a special edition pink assault-style rifle for breast cancer awareness! Kinda wild, right?" He laughed as if he had just cracked a hilarious joke.

"So," Farben countered, as he stealthily moved the conversation forward. "There's plenty of guns and some funds to make them. Do you think there's enough money for what you talked about earlier today?"

"You mean a full-scale revolution here? Why do you ask?" Brad prayed that the electronics in his cap and behind his ear were performing as planned.

"Because," said Farben, "I'm aware of a business opportunity that could raise billions of dollars that could support something like that."

"Tell me more." Brad seemed almost disinterested as he gulped down a large spoonful of chili.

Farben's expression changed to a hard stare. It seemed to him to be the right moment to make his pitch. "I belong to a consortium of some very wealthy people. They are investors in a project that could produce billions of dollars within one year or less. The project is about to be launched. We just need time and initial capital to get results. And when we do, there's a whole infrastructure awaiting orders to launch a new movement."

"What movement?" Brad bit into a large kaiser roll, looking almost bored.

"Brad," said the foreigner, "there are thousands of people in my country who are children of those whose fathers and mothers fought for the Third Reich. They are hungry for revenge for what the so-called Allies did to their families and their country. They are ready to fight for a Fourth Reich where the German people and their friends around the world will install a new world order. Those who hurt us before will pay the price. So, simple to say, your proposal to help with a massive armed insurrection in the United States is of interest to us. We have many friends here in America who are also ready to rise up and support a new Reich and

310

to continue the work of its predecessor."

"Then, Ludwig, you and your friends are preparing to hurt America today and overthrow its entire system, right?"

"Exactly."

Mitch prayed that the microphone at his ear had captured every single word, to the letter. "Well, now that we're talking," he said, "tell me more."

"I can introduce you to some people here in New York state. They happen to be Arabs—Islamists, actually. They have been working closely with us to develop a special program for current and past members of the US prison population— specifically, for prisoners who have converted to Islam. The idea is to help these people organize and prepare for revolution here."

"What kind of special program?" Brad made his question sound routine. He watched Farben pause before he spoke.

"Oh," said Farben, "various skills like weapons training, unarmed combat, and, of course, instruction in the Quran. They take their recruits to remote forests on the East and West Coasts where simple training camps can be set up and removed quickly to avoid detection."

"You say these folks are working with you?" Brad said through a mouthful of chili.

"We are natural allies. After all, just like you who are white supremacists, both we and the Islamists have a shared mission—to destroy the corrupt and chaotic democracies in the West and to bring order to the world."

"Are you saying that we white people are natural allies…with *Islam*?"

"For now, yes. You both want to overthrow the US government. There will come a time when you and they will have to decide who takes the lead here. The Islamists want a world ruler, a caliph, to take over and replace apostate, Western, man-made law with what they call God's law, the *sharia*. You and your friends may or may not be able to live with that, in which case…"

"OK. I hear ya. So, yeah, I'd sure like to meet these folks."

The IED Foundation

The chosen venue was the Waterman Motel. Shabby and run down, it sat on a small, wooded promontory on the northern side of Lake George. It could be accessed only by water or from a winding two-mile-long driveway from the main road.

The Islamic Education Development Foundation had held its annual conference there for the past five years. A good relationship had developed between the hotel staff and the foundation's leaders. The annual meeting was an important source of revenue without which the hotel could barely keep its doors open in the summer. In turn, the foundation depended on attracting a growing group of Muslims and prospective converts from other religions.

However, unlike the hotel, the foundation was never at a loss for funds. It was subsidized by at least one wealthy patron, the government of Saudi Arabia.

The IED, as it was known, had asked for a special meeting of its executive committee to be held there in the late fall. The stated purposes were to plan for the following year's conference, and to welcome an unnamed, distinguished special guest.

Farben and Brad arrived at the hotel late on a Friday afternoon, in time to attend the first session and to welcome members of the executive committee. At first, the meeting seemed innocent enough. There were soft drinks and some Middle Eastern delicacies to enjoy. To Mitch's silent dismay, not a drop of alcohol was to be seen. Glancing through the window, he noticed the room was close to the rear of the motel and a small loading dock.

As Brad looked around, he noticed about forty males of various ages dressed in white robes and headdresses. One of them made a beeline toward Farben with both hands outstretched in greeting, smiling through his beard.

"Brother Ludwig, we are honored to have you join us! How was your trip here?"

The two made brief small talk. Farben introduced his friend to Mitch. "Meet First Counselor Ahmed bin Khouri of the Saudi Embassy. He is an investor with us in a consortium that will serve our common interests. Counselor bin Khouri, meet Mr. Brad Miller. He too shares our common goals."

They shook hands. But just as Mitch was preparing himself to be scrutinized in person by the Saudi, a singer's voice rang out from a side door. The Saudi leaned in to the two visitors and began whispering to them about what was happening.

"This is the call to prayer, what we call the *Adhan*. In English, this word means "to listen," so it alerts everyone that it's time to pray." Al Khouri then handed Brad and Farben a translation from the Arabic.

Allahu Akbar
God is Great
(repeated four times)
Ashhadu an la ilaha illa Allah
I bear witness that there is no god except the One God.
(repeated two times)

Ashadu anna Mohammedan Rasool Allah
I bear witness that Mohammed is the messenger of God.
(repeated two times)

Hayya 'ala-s-Salah
Hurry to the prayer
(repeated two times)

Hayya 'ala-l-Falah
Hurry to success (Rise up for Salvation)
(repeated two times)

Allahu Akbar
God is Great
(repeated two times)

La ilaha illa Allah
There is no god except the One God

"You will now hear another call, this time for everyone to line up to pray. This is called the *iqama*."

The *imam* for the occasion moved to the front of the group. He turned to face east and away from the blazing sunset.

"This is the fourth of five daily prayer times. It's called the *Maghrib,* and is our way to remember God as the sun sets. Now, the *imam* will face east toward Mecca. Why? Because there, in the center of the Grand Mosque, is a sacred building. It's called the *Kaaba*—meaning, in English, 'The Cube'—and we Muslims believe it's *al-beyt Allah,* the original House of God, and so the very first mosque."

As Mitch was listening intently to Al Khouri's whispered words, a sudden movement outside the window caught his eye. A large tractor trailer had just pulled up at the nearby rear loading dock. Despite the fading daylight, Mitch thought he saw a large Coca-Cola logo on the side of the vehicle. Perhaps it was just a late-afternoon delivery.

He was about to turn his attention back to the room when he noticed several men emerge from the rear of the trailer, followed by a stooped figure. It moved slowly between them in the fading light toward the hotel's rear door. The silhouette in flowing robes suggested that of an elderly man. Something about the man struck Brad as familiar.

Moments later, the *imam* finished his prayer and became silent. A side door opened. Two men in black tracksuits burst in and quickly surveyed the assembled group. Their eyes stopped scanning the moment they saw Brad, standing out like a sore thumb in his suit and tie. As they began to move aggressively toward him, the Saudi Al Khouri stepped forward, raised a hand, and shouted some words in Arabic. The two black-clad males stopped in their tracks seconds before reaching Brad. His heart leaped into his throat. The men backed off and retreated to their point of entry. There was a pause. The room became hushed.

A voice from within the group spoke. *"Asdiqayiy, wasal dayfuna almashraf!"*

Al Khouri translated. "This means, 'our honored guest has arrived.'"

Preceded and followed by a pair of well-built young men, an older man of perhaps seventy or more entered the room.

Brad recognized him immediately.

It was unmistakably Al Muharib, the man he had reached out to and had then met in Qatar.

As if on command, the assembled group sat in unison on the floor, legs crossed, and turned its collective attention and gaze to the newcomer—all except one man, who stepped forward and, to Mitch's surprise, spoke in English.

"Our revered brother, Ibrahim Al Muharib, has just made a dangerous journey to be with us tonight. He comes to us through Canada, thanks to one of our drivers who works for the Coca-Cola Company."

A peal of laughter rose from the squatters. "He has a special message for all of us tonight." The speaker turned to the honored guest, bowed to him, then rejoined the others.

Al Muharib too spoke in English. "My brothers in Islam," he began, "I am honored to be with you tonight, and I will speak to you in English. Thanks to your help, I was able to cross the Canadian border hidden behind crates of one of the few Western beverages that we Muslims actually like to drink!"

More laughter. The old man's face suddenly turned serious and dark. "But make no mistake. We are in a war with the West and its corrupt, ungodly society. You are all soldiers in that war. Each of you can and must make a difference, at whatever personal cost. It is your religious duty to do everything you can to subvert and eventually to destroy all those who oppose ours, the one true religion. This includes any government that opposes us, as well as perverted homosexuals, apostate Muslims, and all Jews. Remember, we have the right in the Quran to defend ourselves. This means that under *sharia* law, if you fight and die for Islam or if you kill a *kafir*, a disbeliever in Islam, you will be assured of a place in paradise, forever."

A murmur of approval rose up from the audience. The speaker raised his hands for silence and continued.

"I am here to tell you that the day is soon coming when we and our allies—including our Muslim-American friends and others around the world who hate the satanic United States of today—will rise up and overthrow the US government and its ridiculous and wretched man-made Constitution. Our goal is to join with our allies and lead that uprising. For there is only one God, and it is Allah, and his word is the Quran. His will is that the world will be one world, led by a single caliph who is a direct descendant of the Prophet, may his name be praised, and who will govern under God's law only, as embodied in the Holy Quran, under *sharia* law."

More murmurs of approval followed, then total silence as all eyes were riveted on Al Muharib.

"My brothers in Islam, I have taken a great personal risk to be with you tonight. As you may know, I am banned from legally entering the United States, Britain, France, and Tunisia because their governments say I am a violence-inciting Islamist. Also, the governments of Bahrain, Saudi Arabia, Egypt, and the United Arab Emirates have designated me as a terrorist. If I am a terrorist, then I am a proud one who is a dedicated soldier for Allah. I call on each of you for your support in our struggle here in America to fight for the Caliphate, here in the so-called New World!"

The speaker rose, turned, and was about to leave the room when he caught sight of a familiar face. He gave a crinkly smile as he said, "Mr. Miller, what a pleasure to see you again, and here with our brothers! I see you have at last met my good friend, Herr Ludwig Farben! This is wonderful. May the peace of Allah be upon you both!" He smiled again and then abruptly turned and slowly left the hall, trailed by his bodyguards. A loud applause accompanied his exit.

Brad was puzzled. Apart from the abrupt arrival and departure of the honored guest, he could not help wondering why Al Khouri, as First Counselor to the Saudi Embassy, would share the same space as a self-confessed terrorist banned from legal entry into Saudi Arabia? Perhaps there was not just one, but two countries within that country's geography? Yet no one else present seemed to notice or care.

Before he could ponder further, Al Khouri took Brad's arm and directed him toward a trio of older men who were presumably leaders on the IED executive committee.

As Al Khouri steered Brad across the room, the FBI man

noticed the tractor trailer pulling away from the dock and disappearing into the early evening gloom, destination unknown.

He could not resist voicing an observation for his hidden microphone to catch. "Funny," he said, "for a guy like Al Muharib to arrive in a Coca-Cola trailer from Canada."

The listeners, he thought, might be interested to spot the trailer and its other destinations throughout the United States as it made its rounds, presumably before returning over the Canadian border.

Grand Alliance

There was someone else that Al Khouri wanted to introduce to Mitch. He headed toward a rotund, bespectacled man wearing a white, rounded skullcap, or *taquiyah,* under a white headdress called a *kefiyah.*

"Minister Luckman, let me introduce you to Mr. Brad Miller. He's a friend of our brother and partner, Herr Farben. He is also well-known in white supremacist circles here in the US. He can help us."

Mitch had been primed to expect the contact. "Glad to meet you, sir! I think we have a lot to talk about together." Luckman nodded. Al Khouri intervened once again. "There will be time to talk more after the final prayer tonight."

A dinner followed of simple fried lake fish, rice, and steamed vegetables, followed by a sweet pudding that no one could identify. The evening ended with *Isha,* a final and fifth prayer of the day before everyone retired for the night. Al Khouri pointed out to Mitch how Muslims once again take time to remember God's presence, guidance, mercy, and forgiveness at each day's end.

A small group remained behind, once all the others had left.

Brad found himself surrounded by Al Khouri, Farben, Luckman, and two others in white robes who, mysteriously, were not introduced.

It was Al Khouri who got the ball rolling.

"My brothers, our meeting today is important. It brings together a natural alliance of Islam with our European and American nationalist friends. We are all together in our cause of righteousness!" He opened his arms as if inviting an embrace. The group murmured its assent, except for Brad, who felt a sudden shiver in his back as he struggled to keep a straight face.

"We all share a common goal," intoned Al Khouri, almost as if in prayer. "I hardly need to state what it is. Tonight, we have another important guest with us, Mr. Brad Miller, who can help us with an American link to our plan. We all know that Europe and America are moving to the political right, because at last there is recognition that so-called democracy has failed in the West."

He paused and scanned to the group for its collective engagement. He seemed to have everyone's attention.

It was then that the Egyptian Luckman spoke. "Thank you, brother Al Khouri." The man's voice was low, but its intensity was to Brad's ears one of a fanatic. "Let me be quite clear," said Luckman. "The Arab world is closer than ever before to restoring its most desirable and just leadership — namely, the caliphate, which the West so cruelly destroyed early in the 20th century."

Heads nodded in unison, except for Brad's. His eyes — and

hidden microphone—were focused on the speaker.

Al Khouri spoke up again. "What our brother Luckman says is true. We now have secret armies that are prepared to overthrow the secular and Western-leaning despots and tyrants who oppress our Muslim brothers and sisters across the entire *ummah*—our beloved world community of Muslims—whether in Egypt, Jordan, Syria, Indonesia, the Philippines, or beyond. The time is now to coordinate our efforts and overthrow these regimes as well as those in the West which conspire to destroy us."

Luckman interjected once again. "Yes, brother Al Khouri, and we have infiltrated most of these criminal regimes. For example, Herr Farben is a senior leader in the German Federal Intelligence Service, the BND. He has a small but highly trained group of five hundred men under his command, including grandsons of former senior German SS officers. He has already successfully subverted the government of the Federal Republic of Germany by passing around all sorts of false reports disguised as intelligence that serve to undermine the credibility of its government. Thanks to the pending retirement of the current German Chancellor, we now have an opportunity to thwart the efforts of her successor."

He glanced over at Mitch, aka Brad.

"We also have here a potential friend here in the USA to link us to several white supremacist groups whose confidence and visibility are growing by the day—and with the tacit approval of a new kind of administration."

For an instant, Brad sensed the doubt expressed by Luckman

behind the words "potential friend." It sounded as if the Egyptian, for one, was not yet thoroughly convinced where Brad's true loyalties lay. But the FBI man's face revealed nothing but rapt attention to the speaker.

"Our good friends from the Arab world are right." It was now the German, Farben, speaking. "England is in turmoil, as the country wrestles with the matter of staying in the much-despised European Union or exiting it. Our disinformation program there is being helped by our other friends in Russia. It is being spearheaded by one of our best people, a man called Dick Harvey, who works for us from within the British Secret Service. He has helped us recruit a secret army of hundreds of well-trained soldiers, including many currently in the armed services. They share his views and ours that a nationalist government must take over and install a disciplined new order. Our Muslim brothers in Britain are working closely with him."

He did not elaborate further about England, but the extent of the plot now became clearly apparent. Once again, it was Luckman who spoke. "In France, Italy, Belgium, and Holland, we have Muslim immigrants who have successfully infiltrated the forces of Western law and order and government. They await orders to impose *sharia* law. In Eastern and Southeastern Europe, our Muslim cadres are already secretly armed and ready to revolt in Bosnia Herzegovina, Slovenia, Croatia, Bulgaria, and Turkey."

He paused for a moment and eyed the group, then had one final point to make. "As you may know, it only takes a small group of dedicated people to take over a corrupt state. That is our goal. And our brother who was here tonight, Sheikh

Al Muharib, a descendant of the Prophet himself, may his name be praised, is poised to make history and to become the new caliph of the world *ummah*."

A discussion then followed. It tackled some basic logistics, timetables, and details of weaponry.

Mitch swallowed his shock and kept a straight face as Minister Luckman continued his report to the group. "My brothers, we have a simple plan to blackmail the West. It has the full support of the Russian president. Thanks to his intervention, we shall soon have access to battlefield nuclear weapons and an arsenal of missile-deliverable toxins. When the time comes, our people are ripe to rise up, one after the other!"

Luckman drew a deep breath, pausing once again to let the gravity of his words sink in.

"They will target key towns with large populations. They will overpower and take over key command and control facilities as well as key media—television and radio stations. They will launch a massive program of social media to scare entire populations of *kafirs* into submission, whether Muslim, Christian, Jewish, Buddhist—we don't care. Any opposition will be met without mercy. The caliphate will rise again, God willing, and will rule."

Tip of the Iceberg

A nother group was meeting concurrently, at a secure location in Washington, D.C.

Its members included specialists from the governments of the United States, Britain, France, Germany, and, curiously perhaps, Indonesia and Russia. Each country's team received hastily edited live transcripts of the EID conversations at Lake George.

The lead representative of Indonesia's state intelligence agency, the Badan Intelijen Negara, or BIN, was making his presentation to the group. "The Muslim population of Indonesia totals some two-hundred-and-twenty-five million," he declared. "This makes it the largest Muslim community in the world. It's predominantly Sunni. As members of the group, you may know that the BIN has coordinated all national intelligence since the 2002 nightclub bombing in Bali. This resulted in more than two hundred fatalities who were mostly Australian, Indonesian, and British tourists."

He looked around the meeting room and saw the somber expressions of all present. He then opened a large, green, manila folder, handed to him by one of his aides, before continuing. "Regardless of the near omnipresence of Islam in Indonesia, such an event was insupportable by our government. Our economy depends on tourism, and it's a critical source of foreign exchange for our banking system. Tourism ranks fourth among our exports of goods and services. We simply cannot afford the loss of foreign investment and tourism. As a result, we are here today to reaffirm our very strong ties with Western intelligence services, in a collective effort to work with them to overcome the worldwide threat of terrorism, including Islamic terrorism."

As he sat down, the Russian delegate rose to his feet. "Members of the task force," he said, "my instructions from the highest levels in Moscow are to share with you in extreme confidence the Russian position on the matter in question. We have our own problems within the Federation with an assortment of Islamic and nationalist insurrections. Behind these terrorist groups are not simply our own citizens; there are many foreigners too. They come from Saudi Arabia, Indonesia, and all over Europe and North Africa. We therefore have a shared economic and political interest to support the containment of terrorist causes and forces around the world. That is why we are here today."

The Russian delegate predictably omitted any reference to the Russian authorities' own efforts to destabilize Western governments.

Each of the national teams led by the task force now made its own assessment of the Lake George transcripts, in order to tie them in with related intelligence. A clear threat began to emerge to the group of a world on the brink of a massive catastrophe.

Joint chiefs of military staff from the six-nation task force reported back to their governments for instructions; and then in turn reported their government's positions to the task force's international security committee.

It took little time to confirm the nature and extent of the threat and to form a consensus that it was in everyone's interest to neutralize it immediately.

Meanwhile, the FBI had been tracking Al Muharib's movements around the United States for days. Its trackers could now clearly pinpoint the location of all his key allies. The US authorities allowed him to escape through Canada where several rotating teams followed his every movement back to Qatar. Another special team awaited instructions there to pounce on him, confiscate probable incriminating evidence in his home, and bring him back to the United States, this time for prosecution and likely life imprisonment.

Simply put, it came down to cutting off the head of the snake.

The FBI put a round-the-clock watch on Al Muharib's extremist Islamist lieutenants in the United States, based on his various visits. Cast-iron evidence would be critical to achieve a successful prosecution that would put as many conspirators as possible away all for a long time.

The Washington task force now decided unanimously to permit American and British Intelligence to direct the elimination of the plot's leadership.

Mopping Up

The American and British security people argued among themselves about whether to make their cleanup public at the appropriate time or to go about the process with stealth and silence so that nothing leaked to the press.

Either way, mopping up the various cells would send an unmistakable signal to the Islamist and related extremist communities and their friends that their plans were thwarted, and that their foes would fight back with a vengeance.

Charlie Fortescue briefed the UK's Foreign Secretary, in person. He strongly advised that a stealthy, silent approach would sow more fear among the extremists than the loud, public relations announcements preferred by the State Department and its Secretary of State.

As can happen in such cases where time is of the essence, a compromise was reached. The plan was as follows.

Al Muharib would be captured, brought back to America, tried in a US court, and if found guilty, put out of circulation. The British would simultaneously eliminate and neutralize the European leadership of the proposed insurrection. Charlie and his opposite numbers at the CIA and FBI coordinated a plan to quietly dispatch Farben, Thiel, Luckman, Al Khouri, and the extremists' British mole, Dick Harvey, so that no one in the press would put two and two together and link their disappearances.

At 7:00 a.m. one Sunday morning, six bearded members of the Special Operations Division of the CIA appeared at the Caribou Café, located off Omar Al Mukhtah Street, in Qatar. All were dressed casually as tourists. They sauntered in one by one or in pairs, looking to all the world like typical foreign visitors. The café was chosen as the staging point to confirm that all six were present.

Their arrival in Qatar was unofficial, thanks to a Los Angeles class attack submarine. Its shallow-water mini submarine on board had discreetly infiltrated the men in pairs to land on a beach beside the Doha Hilton, early in the morning darkness.

An unmarked gray minivan was parked on nearby Shamia Street. The driver waited tensely for each of the six men to appear, one at a time, and clamber quietly into the back. An American chief petty officer was there to greet them and supply necessary equipment and ordnance.

At 7:25 a.m., the van set off toward Wadi Al Humra Street. It turned off and drove to the end of a cul-de-sac where it did a three-point turn and then parked. At the end of the cul-de-sac lay a white house, almost hidden from view by a thirty-foot high, whitewashed, stone wall adorned with bright-red bougainvillea. A small, wooden door with a lattice-shaped, iron speakeasy was the only point of access.

The surveillance team had previously spotted a regular early morning deliveryman bearing fruits and fresh fish daily from the local market. A member of the special operations team crossed the deliveryman's palm with large dollar bills, and, in exchange, a heavily bearded member of the special operations team took his place.

At 7:45 a.m., the replacement deliveryman rang the bell. A face appeared at the grille, and the door opened. Moments later, the entire special operations team moved in. They overpowered the guard with chloroform quickly and silently. Within ten minutes, the team neutralized the remaining armed guards. A disheveled and sleepy Al Muharib was roused from his bed and subdued with an injection. The team then carried his limp, unconscious body carefully out of the house and heaved his inert body into the van.

By 8:20 a.m., the van had reached the huge Al Udeid Air Base, twenty miles southwest of the Qatari capital. Here, a private Gulfstream V jet with four heavily armed US Marshalls aboard awaited a special package for onward transmission to Andrews Air Force base.

The snake was now firmly in US hands.

It remained for prosecutors to prove in court without a doubt that Al Muharib was indeed guilty of fomenting a revolution to overthrow the US government.

The British, meanwhile, were on a parallel schedule which took a decidedly different and more discreet form. They used the latest technology to deal with Herr Ludwig Farben of the Federal Republic of Germany's BND and the Egyptian official named Luckman.

Since there was nothing to be gained by embarrassing a friendly European or even an Arab ally, the British decided to eliminate both Farben and Luckman without reference to either's government.

The Americans had already developed micro-air vehicles, or MAVs. These were tiny, insect-like spy drones used for reconnaissance and surveillance missions. But the British had created their own lethal versions of these tiny drones, with the difference that scientists at its Defence Science and Technology Laboratory near Salisbury, known simply as the "dstl", had armed its flying insects with a deadly poison. This was a compound whose main element was gelsemine, a highly toxic and typically fatal substance known to induce almost instant paralysis and for which no antidote was known.

Ludwig Farben, a confirmed bachelor, had returned to Germany promptly, soon after he had kidnapped the Tinkers, obtained what he thought were accurate maps of hidden Nazi loot, and had attended the Lake George meeting of Islamic Education Development Foundation. As he approached the front door of his home near Pullach on the evening of his arrival, he felt a sharp pinprick on his neck. During his last few seconds of consciousness, it struck him as odd that a mosquito or a bee would even be around the neighborhood at that late hour.

Seconds later, he felt nausea, then acute muscle spasms, and then a terrible diarrhea. Before he could even reach a bathroom, he collapsed, completely paralyzed.

His inert, dead body was found late the next afternoon.

A job-well-done text message found its way soon afterwards to Charlie from his man in Pullach.

Had Farben realized what had poisoned him, he might otherwise have washed his neck promptly to save the damaged skin on his neck. He could also have applied some strychnine that might have countered the otherwise lethal dose. But it was not to be.

Charlie later learned that the British scientists had used some curious research by the author of the Sherlock Holmes series, Sir Arthur Conan Doyle. The famous crime writer had experimented on himself with doses of up to 200 units, or minims, of gelsemine. These induced a severe frontal lobe headache, diarrhea, and heavy depression. He wisely dared not apply a higher dose.

The British scientists used 700 units for their mosquito, just to be sure that the job would be done.

When the news of Farben's untimely death reached Dr. Thiel and the junior BND assassin, closet Nazi and blond, blue-eyed Gunther, both men conveniently and separately committed suicide.

The German government was left wondering why some of its most prominent spies would all mysteriously die within days of one another.

Simultaneously, some twenty miles northeast of the town of

Alexandria in Egypt, Minister Luckman lay on the beach with his wife at Abu Qir. He too had left New York in a hurry—after the Tinker kidnapping and the meeting at Lake George.

He had been planning a late afternoon trip with his wife around the ruins of the nearby ancient town of Canopus. Though not a strong swimmer, he decided he would take a dip in the ocean and swam slowly out a few hundred feet..

He was about to turn back to the shore when something brushed past him in the water. Moments later, what looked like a shark's fin rose above the water. He panicked and began to paddle furiously back toward the shore.

He had paid scant attention to the fisherman in a nearby white felucca, a traditional Egyptian wooden sailing boat. The man was fiddling with something in the hull of the boat. It might have been fishing gear—but it was something else. As he worked the controls on his special transmitter, his highly trained shark seized Luckman's torso in its jaws, dragged him far out to sea, and then snapped his spine into two pieces.

The remains of the Minister turned up along the beach the next morning.

Charlie received another text message, which read simply, "Man out of luck." He now owed a debt to his opposite number in the Mossad.

The State Department quietly addressed the fate of Counselor Al Khouri of the Saudi Embassy. He was given two days to leave the United States due to "activities incompatible with his diplomatic status". Upon his arrival in Riyadh, he was promptly arrested and jailed. A closed court found him guilty of treason. It used its judicial sentencing discretion, known as *tazir*, to sentence him to death.

One morning a month later, Al Khouri appeared in a white robe under guard in Deera Square, a public space also known both as Justice Square and, more informally, as Chop Chop Square. He knelt before his executioner whose sword, or *sultan*, swiftly severed his head from his body. The beheaded body was crucified and publicly displayed for three days before ritual burial by his shamed, shunned and grieving family.

Back in the United States, three Americans — Jones, Field and former General Pugh — were all arrested, charged with treason, found guilty and jailed for life without parole.

London's Hyde Park was the venue for Dick Harvey's demise. He was found dead one early misty morning, hanging from a sycamore tree. His body lay in full view of homes owned by several wealthy Islamist Arab sympathizers on London's Park Lane.

A British government press release indicated that he had worked on the Middle East desk of the Foreign Office. The official cause of death was depression, as referenced in a suicide note found on the corpse.

Reading between the lines, the message to certain questionable Americans, Europeans, and Arabs from Qatar and Saudi Arabia was clear.

Mess with us, and you can expect the same thing in return!

All That Glitters Is Not Gold

The remaining question for Adam and Agnes was how best to a handle the genuine Heilmann maps. They alone knew where the originals were safely locked away. They also knew that, once they revealed their location and access to the true maps to almost any third party, their control over these documents would be lost forever.

Based on Charlie's advice that any threat to them was now minimal, and with Fred's blessing, they decided to return to Budapest where Professor Lantos would be happy to see them. Between the three of them, they could then form a view on what to do next.

But somehow there had been a leak.

There were already rumors that assorted international organizations and foundations were gearing up to get what they saw as their share of the spoils. Callers claiming to represent The World Jewish Restoration Organization topped the list of groups that began to approach the Tinker family with aggressive phone calls and emails. A race seemed to be on to see who could be first in the queue to help themselves to the looted possessions of entire long-dead families.

It was a beautiful, warm, sunny day when Adam and Agnes landed in Budapest. To their delight, Lantos was there to greet them at Arrivals. Except for a small scar on his temple, he looked in good health and was happy to see them.

"We should celebrate!" he cried. "I've booked dinner for us tonight at Gundels. Adam, you are in for a treat! There's all sorts of Hungarian meats, fish, and game specialties there, like Örség goat cheese, Hungarian Mangalitza, quail, and goose liver from Orosháza."

"What's Mangalitza?" asked Adam, smiling. "Sounds like something mangled!"

"No! No! The name means 'a hog with a lot of lard,' cried Lantos, as he smiled at the pun. "It's our very own Hungarian version of Kobe beef, but actually, it's pork. In fact, you will see from photos that the Mangalitza pig looks more like a sheep with a thick, wooly coat. These are crossbreeds of the European wild boar and the Serbian breed. Really delicious!"

That evening, the three of them sampled a tasting menu accompanied by a flight of fruity, Hungarian wines. A final touch was the restaurant's pancake with its special secret recipe, a rich delight filled with ground walnuts, raisins, and rum filling, served flambéed in a dark-chocolate sauce made with egg yolks, heavy cream, and cocoa.

As they sipped tiny cups of strong Hungarian coffee, the conversation turned at last to the fate of the Heilmann maps.

Lantos put forward his ideas. "One option," he said, "is to destroy some or all of them. However, this would likely infuriate anyone with a legitimate claim, even though few individuals or families or organizations today could prove ownership."

"There's something to that," chimed in Agnes, sipping her coffee.

"Another approach," said Lantos, "would be to help create an international body or maybe a special foundation to own and control the maps. It might fund and even oversee the excavation and disposal of whatever lost property can be found. But deciding who would be entitled to get what and how would probably result in years of bickering and negotiation."

Agnes chimed in again. "I think that's right, about the bickering. Don't you, Adam?" He nodded in agreement.

"But here's a good question." It was Adam's turn to speak. "What would the original owners of the stolen property have wanted if their looted possessions could not have been returned to them after all? Perhaps they would have wanted to create a special museum to showcase unclaimed objects and to remind people that such massive theft, not to mention mass murder, should never happen again?"

He wondered who else could help to decide the fate of the maps, for he saw no obvious solution.

Lantos then raised another point. "The original maps now rest in a safe-deposit box in a small bank here in Budapest. If the present Hungarian government knew about that, it would certainly want to get its hands on them. Now, I am supposed to be working for the government here, and, normally, I would be inclined to turn them in."

"What are you saying exactly, Uncle?" asked Agnes.

"I'm saying that the present so-called illiberal democratic government has gone out of its way to encourage anti-Semitism here. On Adam's point, I don't think the original Jewish property owners would agree to giving access to the maps to the current Hungarian government regime."

He took a sip of coffee and all three sat in a thoughtful silence.

"There's another thing too," said Lantos. "The Heilman maps indicate that much of the loot is hidden in Austria and Germany. That means that the Austrian and German governments would insist on licensing and controlling all excavation activity. They would also want to control what happens to anything that is found. That process would involve armies of lawyers and arguments for years to come about who gets what and why."

The three fell silent again at all the unappealing options before them. Then, at last, Agnes broke the silence. "What if we simply made them disappear? Then there would be no such argument."

"Are you suggesting we destroy them?" asked Lantos.

"Not necessarily. But perhaps we can find someone or somewhere to serve as their secret custodian. Maybe that custodian can release a single map, to see how the Germans and others would handle things?"

"Who might be such a secret custodian? Who could we trust

to do that?" Adam wondered. He thought for a moment and then came up with a new and different idea. "Weren't there six death camps where Jews and other 'undesirables' were systematically murdered?"

Lantos replied, "Yes, that's right. Six. They were Auschwitz-Birkenau, Belzec, Chelmno, Majdanek, Sobibor, and Treblinka. All these sites today are in Poland."

Adam rubbed his chin. "What if we were to take the original maps and hide them individually at each death camp site? This way, we can symbolically return the stolen property to its rightful owners. And if someone later stumbles upon one of them, then let them worry about how to deal with whatever government parties get involved."

They decided to sleep on the idea.

Ten days later, the trio found themselves in Poland where they visited all six concentration camp sites.

It was an emotionally wrenching trip. Treading in the footsteps of so many murdered men, women and children made it an acutely painful set of visits indeed, but they consummated their decision.

To this day, no one else knows where each of the maps is buried.

A Fitting Epilogue

They were married six months later. Adam's family was delighted at his choice of a wife. Agnes was not only stunning to look at, but clearly possessed a smart head on her shoulders.

"At last," said Adam to his new wife just after the wedding ceremony ended, "we can now truly say we're newlyweds, for real!"

This brought a knowing smile to Agnes lips which Adam was all too eager to kiss.

There was only one sour note on their wedding day. Both of Agnes's parents refused to attend or even to send a wedding gift. It was Tibor Lantos who took Agnes's father's place and walked her down the aisle. Fully recovered, Lantos and his sister had made a special visit from Budapest just for the occasion.

Fred and Jill insisted that the couple be married at their newly cleaned up and renovated house on Montego Island. They ferried in one hundred and twenty guests by charter plane and arranged to put them all up overnight.

Among the guests were Charles Fortescue and Professor Yussef Bitar. Charlie asked Adam discreetly what had become of the original and accurate maps.

Adam had his answer ready. "Well, as none of them were our property, we felt obliged to dispose of them. This did not seem to be the best moment to pass them to the Hungarian government, even if some of the loot may have included major artworks from the National Museum of Hungary. Instead, there are some...private collectors...who are acting as custodians. They have assumed all responsibility to protect the maps at all costs. We are still working out the details with them."

Charlie knew he had to report back to someone in London about the fate of the maps. He also recognized that no single country could lay claim to any of them, including Hungary, without facing a massive legal challenge from other sovereign states, private organizations, families, and individuals. He was aware, as were the British and American governments, that it might be best to let the delicate diplomatic fate of the maps quietly disappear—at least until such time, if any, that the matter might need to be resurrected.

Unlike Charlie, Yussef Bitar had seen neither the real nor the doctored maps. He remained unaware that Adam and Agnes had found and hidden them.

When at last the bride and groom emerged from their wedding dinner and said their goodbyes to the guests, Fred took his son aside for a final word. "Son, if it hadn't been for you two, we might have found ourselves one day singing new lyrics to our Presidential Anthem, like 'Heil to the Caliph!'" It was one of Fred's few attempts at humor.

Yet there was something in those words that haunted Adam. He felt something was missing, something was incomplete about their recent efforts.

The young couple spent an affectionate, loving and tender wedding night at a nearby inn. But both of them also sensed a feeling that, at first, neither one could identify or articulate.

It was during the following morning that they began to see the light.

"You know, Adam," said Agnes, "we may have just helped make the lives—even saved the lives—of countless people by finding those wretched maps and then hiding them away again. I mean, not only millions of innocent Jews living in perpetual fear of their lives among non-Jews. What about all those who might have had to go to war, leave their families, and go off to fight another attempt to create a Fourth Reich? Just think about that for a moment!"

Agnes grew silent, and her wistful gaze told Adam to listen quietly to her. She asked him, "Do you remember who we really have to thank for finding those maps in the first place? Those two little kids in Paraguay, two little grandchildren of an awful Nazi. Remember how I told you about little Anna and her brother Hugo? First, they lost their parents, then their grandmother who, like their own parents, was also murdered! I feel we need to do something about them."

"Like what?" replied Adam lamely.

Almost as soon as the words left Adam's mouth, he felt the stupidity of his question. Agnes was right: two innocent little kids had led them to the maps in the first place. Who would look after those children and raise them now?

Before he could utter another word, Agnes was already surfing the web to find out about orphaned children in Paraguay. "What if we could adopt them?" she asked.

The generous thought quickly evaporated as her research drilled deeper. "Oh no! There's a thing called The Hague Convention. The good news is that Paraguay, the United States, and even Hungary are parties to this convention which governs the handling of adoptions. But the bad news is that it only recognizes intercountry adoption when a suitable family has not been found in a child's country of origin. And then, on top of that, you need US government permission from the Department of Homeland Security to bring a non-US child adoptee into this country."

"Well, that settles that!" The relief in Adam's voice was evident.

But Agnes refused to give up her research and continued to dig deeper. "Not so fast, honey!" Adam chuckled out loud at her attempt to sound like an American.

"Yes," she continued, "under Paraguayan law, intercountry adoptions are not allowed. Preference is given to citizens and legal permanent residents of the same country—and prospective parents must reside there. Well, obviously we don't qualify. But there is someone who might!"

Adam looked at her blankly.

She asked, "Adam, do you remember the woman who sat next to you at that club dinner in Buenos Aires and who later invited us to her home?"

"Why, sure. It was Isolde?"

"Yes, Isolde Rauff. Why don't we call her and see what she has to say about adopting two kids from Nueva Germania?"

"Sounds crazy to me, but—" mumbled Adam.

"Let's do it! What can we lose?" cried his new wife.

They placed a call. The line crackled and then went dead. They tried again. This time, the line was clear.

A familiar smoker's voice answered. "How wonderful to hear from you two again! Did you take our advice and go to Nueva Germania?"

The conversation must have taken more than an hour as both sisters took turns to talk into their telephone. "We really should get a telephone with a speaker on it," said Isolde, "so we can both hear at the same time!"

The sisters agreed to place a call to someone who knew someone at the Paraguayan embassy in Buenos Aires.

It was then that something nothing short of miraculous happened.

Argentina itself is not a member of The Hague Convention. It so happened that a group of human traffickers from Paraguay had just been caught at the border by the Argentinian police. The traffickers had tried to import kidnapped Paraguayan women and children, hidden under vegetables in a truck, to sell them into prostitution in Buenos Aires.

When notified and told that the police did not know what to do with the women and children, the Paraguayan Ambassador in Buenos Aires started the process for their repatriation. He happened a call at that time from a friend asking about the possible adoption by two Argentine sisters of two Paraguayan children named Anna and Hugo. It was a stroke of pure luck that these two children were among the group just rescued from the traffickers.

Agnes and Adam later learned that it was clearly more convenient and less costly for both the Paraguayan and Argentinian governments to provide temporary homes with the interested adoptive parents—namely Isolde Rauff and her sister.

To this day, Adam and Agnes are Uncle Adam and Auntie Agnes to the boy and the girl.

Perhaps one day, Anna and Hugo will learn how they were the unwitting keys to stopping World War III, the potential resurrection of a Fourth Reich, and the rebirth of a caliphate.